001352406

The Girl in the Face of the Clock

Also by Charles Mathes

# The Girl in the Face of the Clock

Charles Mathes

Thomas Dunne Books \ St. Martin's Minotaur  New York

THOMAS DUNNE BOOKS.
An imprint of St. Martin's Press.

THE GIRL IN THE FACE OF THE CLOCK. Copyright © 2001 by Charles Mathes.
All rights reserved. Printed in the United States of America. No part
of this book may be used or reproduced in any manner whatsoever without
written permission except in the case of brief quotations embodied in
critical articles or reviews. For information, address St. Martin's Press,
175 Fifth Avenue, New York, N.Y. 10010.

www.minotaurbooks.com

Title page illustration by Arlene Graston

ISBN 0-312-26895-5

First Edition: April 2001

10  9  8  7  6  5  4  3  2  1

For Arlene,
without whom nothing
would be possible.
Or fun.

# Acknowledgments

I am grateful to many people who helped me with this book, several of whom I met on the Internet through the wonderful DOROTHYL Mystery Literature E-conference: Carole Shmurak introduced me to her brother, Dr. Leslie Bernstein, who confirmed medical details; Barbara Franchi and Susanna Yager kept me straight about London; Ellen Sather provided support during dark hours and squirrelly encouragement. Thank you all, and special thanks to Tessa Reddish Jones, who went far beyond the call of duty (on foot and by tube) on my behalf.

Special thanks are also due to Ruth Cavin, my editor; to Meredith Bernstein, my agent; to SMP's great design and production staff; and to Feroze Mohammed and Heather Locken at Worldwide Library for supporting me in paperback.

Thanks, too, to Bonnie Selfe, archival person at a world-famous store in New York City which I'd give credit, but I don't want to issue any "spoilers" this early in the book.

Everything I know about stage combat I learned twenty-five

years ago from B. H. Barry. That I remember so much proves what a great teacher and fight director he is.

Though I work for a New York City art dealer, I am happy to say that I have never met an art dealer in this city or elsewhere who bears any resemblance to the dealer who appears in this book. Anyone wishing to know how I feel about Jane Kahan, whose gallery I have the privilege of directing, need only look at what I came up with when I needed a name for a heroine.

Finally I want to thank my wife, Arlene Graston, who goes over every word of my books before anyone else reads them. It is risky for a man to write about women, and I wouldn't have even attempted to without her guidance. However convincing my young women are I owe to Arlene; anything that does not ring true is probably one of those places where I stupidly refused to take her advice.

The Girl in the Face of the Clock

ececececececececececececececececece One

The basement room was a long, narrow space, mirrored on both sides. The floor was white oak, shellacked to a high gloss. The high ceiling was soundproofed, lest the tortured sounds that emanated from here worry anyone above.

Jane Sailor leaned back against the wooden bar that ran the length of the room at waist height and tried not to notice the reflections of endless Jane Sailors stretching off into infinity in front of her. Each of them had the same flat chest, the same pale blue eyes, and the same white hat as she did.

"All right," she ordered in a cold voice without a trace of mercy. "Let's do it again."

R. J. Hickey nodded happily. He was not much taller than Jane's five feet six, a scrawny man in his mid-thirties who favored the Gas Station Attendant look—bluejeans with a pack of Camels twisted into the sleeve of his T-shirt. He squared his shoulders, shook his greasy black hair in some kind of primitive pump-jockey ritual, then slapped Marcia Lee across her perfect face.

The sharp smack of flesh hitting flesh echoed off the cinder-block walls. As Marcia reeled from the blow, R.J. caught her with a vicious backhand. The lovely little blonde staggered backwards, but R.J. wouldn't let her get away. He grabbed her by the arm and hurled her down with such force that Marcia literally flipped over and landed on her back at his feet. R.J. reached down and grabbed a hank of flaxen curls in his fist. Marcia's hands clamped defensively around his wrist, but to no avail. Though she tried to scramble away from him, it was a losing battle. R.J. dragged her by the hair across the hardwood floor as far as the narrow dimensions of the room would allow—about fifteen feet.

"Good," said Jane when it was over.

"I hate this," muttered Marcia, not getting up from where she had skidded to rest. "I hate working without the mats. He keeps knocking my head on the floor."

"Did not!" exclaimed R.J.

"Did, too!"

"The reason you're knocking your head, Marcia," said Jane, pushing herself off the barre on which a thousand dancers had steadied themselves over the years, "is that you're afraid to let yourself roll all the way. The fleshy parts of your arm and your back will absorb the impact if you just let yourself roll. Remember: the floor is your friend. You can't be afraid of it. The floor is your friend. Now, let's do it for real. Full out."

"O-kay!" said R.J., rubbing his hands together in what looked like glee.

"Tech is at six," said Marcia with a whine and a pout. "I need to go home and take a bath. I'm going to be black and blue."

"Last time, I promise," said Jane. "I want to see you and your friend the floor get that roll perfect. You'll thank me Thursday night. You'll steal the show."

Marcia massaged her head with her fingers but didn't move. Jane's own poor scalp itched something terrible, but she suppressed the urge to take off the stupid white hat that was plastered on her head and scratch. She felt funny-looking enough beside this beautiful actress without displaying the bleached disaster that was presently serving as her hair.

"All right, all right," said Marcia, struggling to her feet and walking back across the narrow room to where she had been before. "But you be careful, R.J. I'm a woman. I'm delicate."

" 'She walks in beauty, like the night,' " said R.J. with a sigh, placing his hand over his heart. " 'Of cloudless climes and starry skies . . .' "

"Oh, please," said Marcia with a look of long suffering.

" ' . . . And all that's best of dark and bright/Meet in her aspect and her eyes.' "

Marcia studied her flawless reflections in the mirrors of the dance studio they were rehearsing in and didn't argue. She was still for an extended moment, then placed her hands on her hips, fixed R.J. in the dark and bright aspect of her eyes, and spoke in a low, ugly voice with a hint of a southern accent.

"You're a liar, Billy Tutridge. You're a liar and a fool. You're not half the man your brother was. As far as I'm concerned, you're not a man at all."

"Shut up," screamed R.J. happily. "Shut up, you harpy!"

Then he slapped her in the exact way they had been practicing for the last half hour. His hand never actually came closer than a foot from Marcia's face, but to the audience, who would be seated behind him, it would look like a direct hit.

Marcia spun to one side for the seventh time this morning, her hand appearing to come up uselessly to fend off the blow. In reality, as her hand passed her face it met her other hand, producing a sharp smack of flesh hitting flesh that echoed off the cinder-block walls. This time, Marcia added a convincing shriek of pain.

R.J. replied with a roar and a vicious backhand. As before, his hand never came anywhere near her face, and the sound of impact was produced by Marcia's own clapping hands. Then he pretended to grab her by the arm but actually just lightly touched it, paralleling her movements as Marcia threw herself down in a controlled roll onto her friend the floor, absorbing the impact with the fleshy parts of her arm and back. When she landed at his feet, R.J. reached down and put his fist against the back of her head.

"I'll show you the kind of man I am!" he screamed.

"No!" cried Marcia, clamping her hands around his wrist. "Billy, no!"

"I'll show you, damn it!"

Though it appeared as if R.J. were dragging her across the floor by her hair, Marcia was actually holding onto his forearm and letting him pull her. Nor was she really trying to scramble away in the opposite direction. With her knees bent and her feet on the ground, she was actually helping to support her own weight while pushing herself along backwards toward him. This time she added some miscellaneous kicking and screaming, which made the illusion complete.

"Perfect, wonderful, fantastic," declared Jane, when the routine was done. Then she clapped her hands, stamped her feet, and added a piercing, two-fingered whistle for good measure. A little positive reinforcement never hurt when you were dealing with performers.

Marcia grinned sheepishly and took a little bow. R.J. shook out his arms and flexed his muscles, clearly pleased with himself. Jane hadn't met an actor yet who didn't get a charge out of dragging a member of the opposite sex across a stage by the hair, even if only in simulation. Perhaps it said something about the species.

The door of the basement studio opened and Sigrid Orthwein entered quietly. A tall, steely-eyed woman in her late thirties, Sigrid was the director of the play they were rehearsing, and the guiding light behind the Cincinnati Repertory Theatre. It was Sigrid who had hired Jane to direct the fights in this production of Hale Lumley's *Eventide in Gilead,* CRT's final play of the season.

"Greetings, Fearless Leader," said R.J. with a flourish and a bow to Sigrid, not having yet recovered from the hormones that flood every man's system when he's pretending to beat up a woman.

"I need to speak with you, Jane," Sigrid said, her voice less imperious than usual. Her gaze was almost sympathetic. "Are you guys finished?"

"Just now," said Jane.

For Sigrid to interrupt one of Jane's rehearsals was unusual. Though Sigrid was responsible for the whole play, the fights were Jane's domain. Sigrid was not one to hover nervously. Tonight was the technical rehearsal, when the actors would try out their costumes for the first time and the light and sound cues would be plugged in. Sigrid had no time simply to drop in and visit. What was this about?

"I'll be watching tomorrow at dress, folks," said Jane, trying to appear unconcerned. "If you have any problems, we can work on Thursday before the opening if you want."

"I don't want," said Marcia, scooping up her backpack and heading for the door. "I hate this play."

"Wait till you see me explode in naked fury tomorrow, Sigrid," said R.J. proudly. "Like you said—Billy Tutridge is a sexual time bomb, just waiting to explode in naked fury. I'll be great."

"Just don't forget your cross in Act Three again or something really will explode," said Sigrid. She waited until the two actors had left the room before she turned and spoke again.

"I'm sorry to barge in like this, Jane, but there's a call for you in the office. It's important."

"What now?" muttered Jane, her eyes rolling upward.

The whole month had been a disaster. First Jane had somehow gotten the notion that, being out here in a city where nobody knew her, this would be a good time to see what she would look like as a blonde. The ensuing experiment with hair color had resulted in a shade somewhere between Golden Egg Yolk and Day-Glo Taxicab. It would be months before her ends unsplit, her roots unfrizzled, and she could come out from beneath the cover of a hat.

Then the entire summer had fallen through. Jane had turned

down several other offers to take a position directing fights for the Denver Free Theatre. It was going to be a gloriously violent season—*Cyrano, Titus Andronicus, West Side Story*—but two weeks ago the theatre had suddenly declared bankruptcy and folded. It was now almost June, and Jane's chances of finding another fight-directing job at this late date were close to nil.

But these catastrophes were nothing compared to her having slept with Dale Kupkin, the lead of *Eventide in Gilead,* the night before rehearsals began.

It had all happened so quickly. Jane didn't have much experience with margaritas. Dale was tall, gorgeous, and charming. The night had been young and the music hot.

In Jane's twenty-nine years there hadn't been many leading men who plied her with compliments and alcohol and asked permission to compare her to a summer's day (did every actor in the world quote poetry?). Between stints of collecting unemployment insurance, Jane spent her life going from production to production at regional reps and summer stock theatres, rarely spending more than a month in any one city—hardly enough time to form lasting relationships.

Lately, the loneliness had been getting to her, bad. After years in which her only physical contact with men was demonstrating how to flip them on their backs and kick them (in simulation) in the crotch, she longed just to touch one of them gently for a change and to be touched.

Then suddenly here was the opportunity, with this big, beautiful specimen who said he wanted her more than life itself. Heart thumping, head spinning, Jane had somehow found herself at Dale's apartment, taking off her clothes within a few hours of meeting the guy. Everything except her hat. Nothing like this had ever happened to her before.

Nor would it again, she vowed. The next day, Dale had treated her like a total stranger. Jane had spent the past weeks of rehearsal squirming and miserable, as he worked his way through practically every woman in the cast, crew, and cleaning staff. How could she have been such an idiot?

"I'm afraid it's bad news," said Sigrid.

"Bad news?" asked Jane. What could be worse than comic-book hair, looming unemployment, and total humiliation? They couldn't very well fire her two days before the play opened, could they? Dale had used a condom. What kind of bad news was left?

"It's a doctor in New York," said Sigrid. "It's about your dad."

"Is he okay?" said Jane quietly. She had known this call would come one day, but there was no way to prepare for it. A strange numbness swept through her.

"I think he's had some kind of accident. They need to speak with you."

Not waiting for Sigrid, Jane grabbed her notebook and raced out the door, then down the narrow basement hall and up the stairs to the office where the business of the Cincinnati Rep was conducted, a small cluster of rooms at the rear of the theatre complex. Aaron Sailor could hardly have had an "accident." Jane braced herself for the worst.

"There's a call for me?" she said, opening the door to the little reception area.

"You can take it in Sigrid's office," said Helen, the theatre's combination secretary, receptionist, and grapevine. "Line one."

"Thanks."

"Bad news?" called Helen eagerly as Jane went into the first room on the right and closed the door.

Sigrid's office, like all the rooms at the back of the theatre, was a windowless cubicle with beige cinder-block walls, most of them covered by bookcases jammed with bound plays and theatre texts. The floor was stacked with manuscripts.

Jane picked up the phone, took a deep breath, and punched the blinking yellow light.

"This is Jane Sailor," she said, suddenly feeling strangely calm, almost detached. "Did my father die?"

"Oh, my goodness, no," came a round voice with a hint of a chuckle in it. "Dr. Contino, Miss Sailor, Benton Contino. From Royaume Israel, I'm the new director. Didn't mean to alarm you. No, your father just had a little accident, that's all."

"What kind of accident?"

"A bit of a fall, actually."

This was too much. Jane pulled off her stupid hat and furiously scratched her poor, bleached-blond head.

"How could my father have fallen, Doctor?" she demanded angrily. "It's not like he can walk around and find things to trip over."

"This is true," acknowledged Dr. Contino. "It was most unfortunate. One of our new aides was rotating him—we like to rotate the patients several times a day here at Royaume Israel. Turn them over, you know. That's why the safety braces on the bed were down. She's a very capable young lady, fully qualified, but these things happen. I'm sure you can understand."

"Just give me the bottom line, Doctor. You wouldn't be calling me if my father just fell out of bed. The aide would have put him back in, and nobody would have been the wiser. Did he break his leg? An arm? Jesus, as if the poor guy doesn't have enough troubles."

"No, no, Miss Sailor," said Dr. Contino with another annoying little chuckle. "You don't understand. It's nothing like that. It was just a little bone in the wrist."

"Oh. Just a little bone in the wrist."

"We're terribly sorry, but it really isn't very serious at all. And it seems that the incident actually has had some therapeutic effects."

"Therapeutic? That's rich."

"Yes, indeed. You see, your father has begun to talk."

Jane nearly dropped the telephone.

"You mean he's conscious?" she exclaimed.

"Well, not exactly. The brain is a very mysterious organ, Miss

Sailor. Sometimes it's hard to know exactly what's going on in there."

"What is my father saying?"

"That's rather hard to describe," said Dr. Contino carefully. "I would hate to characterize it as delirious ravings. He has mentioned your name several times. He repeats certain words, phrases."

"Is he waking up? Do you think he's going to wake up?"

"I don't know, Miss Sailor. Even in cases where there has been substantial brain damage, surprises can occur. It is conceivable that your father could awaken, but then he may also quickly relapse into his previous state. If he does wake, it is likely that he will be profoundly handicapped, but it's impossible to know for sure. Miracles are known to happen, even at Royaume Israel. As your father was not expected ever to speak again, already we are in unknown territory."

"I'll be there as soon as I can."

"Oh, how nice. I'll look forward to meeting you."

Jane hung up the phone. Then she sat in Sigrid's big chair, trying to feel something.

Tears used to come easily for Jane when she thought about her father. When Aaron Sailor had fallen down the steep stairs of his loft building in SoHo eight years ago, Jane had still been in college. She had come home and gone through the horrible process of American medicine in a state of panic and determination, barely able to fight down the emotions roiling inside her and articulate the decisions that had to be made. Many nights she had just sat by his bedside weeping, overwhelmed by it all.

As the days turned to weeks and the weeks to years, Jane had had nightmares and their daytime equivalents, haunted by her father's blank face, his sightless eyes, his broken mind. The loft and all Aaron Sailor's possessions had had to be sold to satisfy medical debts before he could be taken into the Royaume Israel nursing home. Only Jane's scholarship and the salaries from two jobs had enabled her to finish college.

Now virtually nothing of her father remained except his paintings. These had been in the basement locker of Jane's Manhattan apartment building until a few months ago—his most precious possessions, ironically judged to be worthless by his creditors.

But now Aaron Sailor was speaking for the first time in eight years. Though the doctors had said that he would live out his life with no more awareness than an eggplant, he could even be waking up.

Why, then, didn't Jane feel anything? She had loved this man more than she could dream of loving another human being, and she had cried her heart out for him over years and years. Was her father already so dead in her mind that there were no feelings left for him? What would happen if he did come out of his coma, if he spoke to her again as he used to, in that kind voice with his roguish smile? Or would he just drool and make noises like an animal? What would she feel then?

Jane rose from the chair. If she gave herself the rest of the day to tie up the loose ends here, she could be on a plane back to New York tomorrow morning. There was no real reason to stay in Cincinnati for the dress rehearsal. The fights were in as good a shape as they were going to get. The last class in stage combat she had agreed to teach at the University of Cincinnati had been yesterday. Sigrid would understand, Jane told herself. She might even prefer that Jane bow out now and go to her family medical emergency rather than stick around like a good trouper, making everyone uncomfortable.

Besides, Jane had no choice. She had to go home and see this man who had died, yet lived on. After all the years and all the heartache, her father still had no one else, and she had no one but him. Once again she would have to look upon the shell of his body. This time, she would also have to hear the echo of what had been his voice.

Whether she could find anything left to feel, however, she did not know.

Two

The ride out to Great Neck on the Long Island Railroad was not nearly as horrible as Jane had anticipated.

Maybe the morning's travels had served as some kind of vaccination, she thought, staring out of the scratched-up window as the drab little houses of Queens whizzed by. Just as a slight case of smallpox or diphtheria conferred immunity against those diseases, so too, perhaps, the nine a.m. flight from Cincinnati, the cab from LaGuardia to drop off her bags at her apartment, and the subway ride down to Penn Station had conferred upon Jane some strange immunity against the LIRR. The cheesy, pus-colored cars full of smug suburbanites, the smells of stale smoke and cheap perfume, and the bone-wrenching bumps and screeches for which the commuter train was famous had hardly bothered her at all.

Being faint from hunger probably had some positive effect as well, Jane decided, making a mental note to try another breakfast of airplane peanuts washed down by a plastic cup of lukewarm coffee-colored water the next time she was faced with a difficult day.

At least there hadn't been any unforeseen problems escaping from Cincinnati. Sigrid's assurances that the show could easily go on without her had been almost too convincing. The actors and techies had all been properly solicitous. Even Dale Kupkin, primping in the green room, had shot Jane an encouraging wink as she phoned to change her plane ticket and make arrangements to vacate a day early the apartment the theatre had provided for her stay.

The LIRR train rattled into Great Neck too soon. Jane got out with a bunch of giggling teenagers and stood on the platform trying to orient herself. The clocktower across the tracks told her it was twenty after one. The crystalline sunshine and balmy air shouted that it was May. Somewhere about a ten-minute drive north of here, the man who had been her father lay restrained in a hospital bed.

It had been more than two years since Jane was last out to Great Neck. That was when she had finally accepted that her father wasn't going to come back, that the man with the laughing eyes was dead and only an insignificant shadow lived on. There was no more reason to come to Royaume Israel than there was to visit the marble headstone in the Bronx under which the body that had once served her mother was buried. Being at the nursing home brought Jane no closer to her father. He was not there.

Or was he?

Across the street from the platform Jane could see several yellow taxis. Though shinier than their Manhattan counterparts, they looked strangely out of place in the suburban setting. Suppressing the urge to find a place to get something to eat, Jane made her way to them. The sooner she got this over with, the better.

"2600 Blesner Boulevard, please," she said, getting into the last cab in the line, the only one in which the driver looked to be alive.

"Yes, please," said the cabby, an olive-skinned man with a huge nose and a dashboard full of pictures of children. "It is to the Jewish nursing home you go, yes?"

"Yes," said Jane. "Royaume Israel."

"I know this place well," said the cabby, starting his engine and studying her in the rearview mirror through the open section of the bulletproof partition. "I take many from the city there to see their *bubbes*. This is a Jewish grandmother, a *bubbe*. You see, I have learned your language. I am Syrian myself, but I hold no animosity toward the Jewish people. In America, it is different. Here it is not necessary to hate and kill one another. Here we can all live together and be happy. You are Jewish, yes?"

"No," said Jane, pressing down on her stupid hat as the cab darted into traffic. The last thing she wanted right now was to get into a discussion of Middle Eastern politics.

"But do you not go to visit a relative?"

Jane hoped that if she didn't answer, the man would get the message. He didn't.

"Which relative is it who you go to visit?" he asked eagerly. "Your *bubbe*?"

It was going to be another one of those New York cab rides, Jane knew. Even in the suburbs, a significant percentage of drivers believed that possession of a hack license was the same as having your own talk show. Better, even. Your audience couldn't change the channel.

"I'm going to visit my father," muttered Jane coldly, sending out "Shut up!" body language at what she hoped was very high volume. Didn't she have enough on her mind right now? Did she really have to tell a cab driver her life story?

"So your father is Jewish," said the cabby triumphantly.

Jane couldn't believe it, but she found herself missing Cincinnati. People didn't put you on the spot like this in the Midwest. In the Midwest you didn't have to talk to strange cab drivers. You didn't have to talk to anyone. You could live your whole life sealed up in a car, safe from all human contact—especially the international relations variety. She suddenly felt very much back in New York.

"Your father is Jewish, yes?" persisted the cabby.

"No."

"But do you not have to be Jewish to get into this place? That was my understanding."

"My father's mother was Jewish," explained Jane, between clenched teeth. Maybe the simple truth would satisfy the man. "She died in childbirth. None of us ever knew her. Dad was raised by my Catholic grandfather. We're about as Jewish as you are, okay?"

"You should not be ashamed to be Jewish," said the cab driver, nodding in the rearview mirror, "even in light of your people's illegal occupation of Palestine. We are all the children of Abraham. So, he is old and sick, your father?"

Suddenly all the feelings that Jane had been bottling up since she had gotten the phone call yesterday exploded.

"He's a goddamned vegetable," she shouted, unable to stop herself. "He's been in a coma for years! If there were any mercy in the world, he'd be dead! Is that good enough for you? Are you satisfied now?"

"So sorry," said the cabby, slinking down in his seat and careening through a red light. "Very sorry."

They drove for another few minutes in blissful silence, finally pulling into the driveway of Royaume Israel, a squat building of redbrick. Feeling guilty for her outburst, Jane dug into her wallet for the fare and added a thirty percent tip that she couldn't afford. The cab driver had meant no harm. It was a rough enough way to make a living, without having to deal with hysterical passengers. At least she hadn't exposed him to her hair.

"Thank you very much," said the man, taking the bills and bending forward to see her better as she opened the door. "Each of us must accept the destiny that Allah in His infinite wisdom has determined. Just as Allah brought you to my cab, so in His perfect time will Allah release your father and give him peace. That time will come soon, you will see. *Salaam aleikum.*"

Jane stood in the drive, murmuring thanks, as the cab screeched away. Strangely enough, she felt comforted by the driver's words. Maybe God *had* brought her to this particular taxi and selected the chatterbox driver to give her a message. Maybe the limbo in which her father lived and which she shared was finally drawing to an end.

The feeling lasted only an instant. Then the familiar curtain of hopelessness crashed down over her again. Who was she kidding? The doctors had said that Aaron Sailor could live on for decades. So what, if he had started raving deliriously. It didn't mean he was coming back. It didn't mean anything.

Jane suddenly wanted to get the hell away from this place. She hated Long Island. She hated nursing homes. She hated having taken advantage of the generosity of the Jews. She'd gotten her father into Royaume Israel on a technicality—the nursing home had been founded after World War I for Belgian Jewish refugees, and Aaron Sailor's mother had grown up in Antwerp. Jane had taken little comfort when the interviewing rabbi had suggested that for her to feel such guilt about using an obscure connection to get her father into the home perhaps meant that she was more Jewish than she gave herself credit for.

There were no taxis in sight on the suburban horizon. Jane was trapped. She'd have to go into the nursing home just to call a cab back to the train station. Resigning herself to the inevitable, she mounted the short steps and walked through the front door.

It was another world inside. The beautiful May sunshine was replaced by stiff, cold fluorescent light, the azure sky by pea green wall paint. The lobby of Royaume Israel was a small space that smelled of bodily functions and antiseptic. The walls were plastered with official memoranda, government health regulations, and travel posters of Tel Aviv.

"Jane Sailor to see Dr. Contino," said Jane at the reception window, pulling herself together, and becoming—at least on the outside—the confident young woman that everyone who saw her thought her to be. It was amazing what good posture and a strong, clear voice could do.

Behind glass, a bored receptionist in a shapeless blue jumpsuit picked up a telephone and motioned Jane to a plastic chair to wait. After a few minutes the door next to the reception window opened and a man emerged, apparently direct from an aspirin commercial. He was tall, stout, and distinguished-looking, with a theatrical halo of snow white hair, wire-rim glasses, and a jaw squared like a milk carton. He wore a white lab coat in the pocket of which was a pen-sized flashlight. A stethoscope hung from around his neck. As if the studied costume could leave any doubt, he sported a large nameplate over his heart: "Benton Contino, M.D., Director."

"Miss Sailor," he said in a smooth, well-oiled baritone, extending a large hand. "Benton Contino. Welcome. Welcome to Royaume Israel. So happy you could join us."

"How's my father?"

"Fine, fine," intoned Dr. Contino. "We've taken care of everything. Nothing to worry about. Nothing at all. I expect you want to see him?"

"That's what a good daughter does, isn't it?"

He led her through the door down a long green hall, chattering convincingly about the weather and the expert level of care at Royaume Israel. They passed room after room, the doors of some of which were open to reveal elderly men and women. Assisted by white-uniformed young people from a selection of minority groups, the residents ran the gamut of nursing home activities: watching television, eating cost-effective food, staring blankly into space.

All the way down the hall at the back of the building was a pair of double doors. Dr. Contino opened them and flipped on the lights. Jane found herself in a large, windowless ward with more than a dozen beds, each of which contained a still form. Some had IV lines connected to their bodies, some were attached to respirators, all were fenced in by metal safety gates.

"You keep them in the dark?" Jane asked, incredulous.

"Just saving a bit of electricity," said Benton Contino with a nervous chuckle. "One of my little innovations. You know how expensive utilities are on the Island. The patients can't tell the difference."

It was true enough. The room was uncomplaining and silent except for the rasps of labored breathing. There were also faint sounds of words that Jane could not make out, coming from a bed in the back corner. It was to this bed that they made their way.

It was as Jane had feared. She felt nothing as she gazed down at the expressionless face, which bore only slight resemblance to Aaron Sailor's. The man who had animated this mask had not returned. The remains of the human being he had been were nearly as Jane remembered. Yet there were two differences now from the last time she had been here: the body bore a white plaster cast on its left arm from knuckles to elbow; and it was speaking.

"No, Perry, no. Don't do it, Perry, don't do it. No, Perry, no."

The words came softly in a dull monotone, without inflection.

"Is that what he's been saying?" Jane asked.

"Yes, basically," said Dr. Contino. "With a few variations."

"No, Perry, don't. No, Perry, no," said Aaron Sailor.

"Who's Perry?" asked Jane. "The aide who dropped him?"

Dr. Contino's big pink hand rose to his throat.

"Heaven forfend!" he exclaimed. "Reema is one of the most conscientious young women it has ever been my privilege to know. She feels absolutely terrible about this whole thing. Accidents happen, as I'm sure that you of all people can understand."

Jane gazed at the cast that covered practically the entire arm of the inert body on the bed.

"I thought you said it was just a little bone in his wrist."

"Indeed, it was," said Contino rapidly, beads of sweat breaking out on his expansive lip. "Totally insignificant as fractures go. As you see, we are taking every possible precaution so that it heals properly."

Contino made a dry little laugh. His smile whispered, "There's nothing to worry about," but his eyes screamed, "Please, God, don't sue us."

"No, Perry, no."

"Why does he keep saying that?" asked Jane, fighting down a wave of nausea. "There's no one here named Perry?"

"No one," said Dr. Contino. "I assumed that Perry was a friend of your father's, perhaps someone who was with him just before his accident. Sometimes a last conversation is frozen in the mind and the patient keeps repeating it like an old broken record. Was this Perry driving the car when it happened? Perhaps your father was trying to alert him to some danger ahead of them in the road."

"It wasn't a car accident," said Jane. "My father fell down the stairs."

Dr. Contino whipped out a white handkerchief and serviced his damp brow.

"Well, I'm new here, as I said, and there isn't much about the case in the files. Perhaps this man Perry and your father were arguing about something. 'No, Perry, no,' your father could have been saying just as he lost his footing."

"My father was alone."

"Are you certain?" asked Contino.

Jane didn't answer, just stared at him.

"Yes, the mind is a mysterious organ, mysterious indeed," said Contino, grabbing a straight-backed chair from the bedside of a tiny old lady, who may or may not have been breathing, and placing it next to Aaron Sailor. "I'm sure you and your dad will want some time alone."

"No, that's not . . ." said Jane weakly.

"Yes, of course," said Contino, hustling toward the door. "You take as long as you like. I understand completely."

In an instant he was gone.

Jane wanted with all her heart to run after him, to escape from this warehouse of the living dead. It would look uncaring, she knew, but so what? She wasn't a bad person, she told herself. It wasn't that she didn't want to see her father. Her father just wasn't here.

"No, Perry. Perry, no. No, don't do it."

Jane stood by the bed for a moment, then sat on the chair that Dr. Contino had brought over.

"Hi, Daddy," she said unconvincingly.

"No, Perry, don't do it. No, Perry, no."

"Who's Perry?"

"Don't do it, Perry," said the body that had been Aaron Sailor's, this time a little louder. "Please don't. No, Perry, no."

Jane looked around the ward, half expecting someone's ancient *bubbe* to shout, "Pipe down over there, some of us are trying to catch some z's." The other residents of the ward were silent, however.

"So how do you like the accommodations?" she asked. There was no answer from the still figure on the bed.

Jane reached over and took his limp hand. She began drawing tiny circles, trying to focus on his smooth cool skin and calm her thoughts.

What did Allah have in mind when He came up with places like this? she wondered unhappily. Wasn't life puzzling enough on its own, without dark rooms full of unconscious men and women in disposable nightgowns? The coed sleeping arrangements struck her as dreadfully improper, too, though none of the patients seemed to mind.

"Jane, Jane, Jane."

Jane looked up in amazement. For an instant, she was a little girl again and her father was calling her. Had Aaron Sailor returned? Was he waking up? She waited a moment, afraid to breathe, feeling gooseflesh raising on her arms and legs.

But there was no further sound. There was no movement. The gaunt figure on the bed was no more sentient than it had been a minute before. Jane let out a deep sigh. Her father had simply repeated a word he once knew, not really called her name. Now he returned to a more familiar refrain.

"No, Perry. Don't do it. No, Perry, no."

Jane returned to her chair and sat for another few minutes, until she couldn't stand it any more. She had stayed only for the sake of appearances, and she had stayed long enough. She no longer felt ready to run off screaming into the bushes, but her appetite, which had disappeared the moment she had entered the nursing home, had now returned with a vengeance. Was there a pizza place near the Great Neck station, maybe? Could she hold out until she was safely back in Manhattan? Was it horrible of her to think about her stomach at a time like this?

"Jane, Jane," murmured her father again, as if he knew she was going to leave.

Jane reached into her purse for a felt-tip pen and carefully drew a little heart on the cast that covered his arm. Inside the heart she wrote "Love Janie" in the tiniest of letters.

"No, Perry, no," he said in response, oblivious. "You're a liar, Perry. I know the truth."

"The truth about what?" Jane asked.

"No, Perry. Please don't do it. Please."

Jane left the room dry-eyed, but with a lump in her throat. Benton Contino was waiting for her in the hall. He wouldn't let her escape into the light of day until she had assured him that she didn't intend to sue.

An hour and a half later, hands deep in her pockets, stupid hat squished on her head, Jane climbed the front stairs of her brownstone on West Ninetieth Street.

Automatically she checked the mailbox, but of course there was nothing in it. The forwarding order she'd filled out at the Post Office before leaving town last month would be in effect until tomorrow. Nothing of any interest had reached her in Cincinnati anyway. Who but catalogue companies would care that she was now back in New York?

Jane stared up the long staircase that stood between her and her apartment on the fifth floor. She hadn't been gone long enough this time to sublet, and it was amazing how much dust a New York apartment could accumulate in a month just sitting empty.

The prospect of a lonely unpacking session followed by an hour of dusting wasn't much motivation to climb four flights of stairs. On the way home, she had stopped for some gyoza and a California roll at one of the zillion Japanese places on Broadway, then grazed for half an hour at the huge Barnes & Noble at Eighty-third Street. What else could she do to postpone the inevitable?

Jane's keys were still in her hand from opening the mailbox. A small steel one at the end of the ring caught her eye. It was the key to her storage space in the basement. Was there an address book somewhere in the boxes of Dad's personal things that she had stored down there? Could it tell her who this Perry was that Aaron Sailor was suddenly mumbling about? "No, Perry, no." Jane had tried to push her father's words out of her mind, but they kept coming back. "No, Perry. Please don't do it." Who was this guy?

Not needing further encouragement, Jane unlocked the basement, which took the same key as the front door, turned on the switch that lit a dangling naked bulb, and descended the stairs.

The basement of the brownstone consisted of a narrow central passage, off which six storage spaces had been created out of metal link fencing. Jane's cubicle at the back was triple the size of the others (and as expensive as an apartment in many cities), its cement floor covered with plastic milk crates that she had appropriated from outside a Gristede's supermarket when she had moved in.

Until three months ago, the milk crates had kept eighteen Aaron Sailor paintings off the floor in case the basement flooded. Thankfully, it never had, but Jane wasn't going to take chances with her father's work, no matter how many people had told her it was worthless.

Ultimately, she had been proven right. The paintings had gone off in February to the Fyfe Museum in San Francisco as the centerpiece of their show on Contemporary Realism. After all these years, Aaron Sailor was finally gaining acceptance from the art establishment that had virtually slammed the door in his face a decade back. For all the good it did him.

Jane applied the key on her ring to the padlock and opened the wire door of the cubicle.

Without the paintings, the space looked smaller somehow. The lights, ornaments, and the base for the trees that Jane bought herself those few Christmases she was in town (and which took up virtually half her apartment) were stored on the far left side. At the far right were the big garment bags of winter clothing she brought down each April to exchange for her summer stuff—her apartment had less storage space than a Toyota.

Four large cardboard boxes of Aaron Sailor's personal effects sat on a brick ledge protruding from the basement wall. Jane had only vague recollections of what she had taken from the loft before leaving eight years ago. She had tried to push that whole year out of her mind.

Having this stuff upstairs would have been too painful, always reminding her of the man who had drunk invisible tea with her at childhood parties, the man who had taught her how to play poker, the man who had taken her to Bergdorf Goodman a month after Mom died and bought her the most beautiful dress she had ever seen. It was too much to bear that she would never see that man again.

Jane reached up and took down the first of the boxes, pushing the feelings back before they overwhelmed her. Years of dust had hardened on the top of the box into a gray patina. Inside was a neat stack of sketchbooks, more than a dozen in all. She sat down on a milk crate and leafed through them one by one, amazed after all these years at the subtlety with which her father had seen his world, and the delicacy with which he could render it.

One book was filled entirely with drawings of wrists and fingers. Another contained studies of stern-faced men and women from the days when Aaron Sailor had made his living as a portrait painter, before he started doing "real" art. A third had sketches of their old loft, a huge space on Greene Street that Jane still had dreams about, dreams in which she would discover whole new rooms that she had never seen before and find her mother practicing her cello. None of the pads, however, held a clue to the identity of Perry.

Jane returned the box to the ledge and took down the next,

which contained financial and tax records. Nothing here about anyone named Perry either, just monetary details that had no relevance
to Jane or her father or probably even the IRS any more. Each
successive 1040 recounted the descent of her father's earnings after
he had given up doing portraits.

How long did you have to keep stuff like this, Jane wondered,
packing the tax forms back away. Seven years? She probably could
throw most of it out now. One of these days she would.

The third box was the biggest and heaviest of the four. Jane
had only to open the top flap to know what was inside. It was the
ceramic monstrosity that Jane's Jewish grandmother, Sylvie, had for
some incomprehensible reason brought out of Belgium with her
when the Nazis invaded.

Even after all these years, Jane still remembered exactly what
it looked like. It was truly hideous: a solid chunk of fired clay
slightly larger than a cinder block. Trompe l'oeil clocks were de-
picted in colored glazes on front and back. The dial of one clock
was marked with Roman numerals, the other with Arabic numbers.
Neither had hands.

Handless clocks were strangely fitting somehow. Time had
never really begun for Sylvie. Her father had been a well-to-do
doctor, but he and the rest of the family had perished in the con-
centration camps. Only Sylvie had managed to escape. Somehow
she made it to New York City, where she had met and married
Jane's Catholic cabinetmaker grandfather, only to die a year later
giving birth to Jane's father.

A feeling of being totally alone in the world suddenly swept
over Jane. She wrestled the box with the garish ceramic back onto
the shelf, fighting a cloud of dust and self-pity. She knew that
looking through this stuff was going to upset her. She should have
left it alone.

Jane sank down on one of the plastic crates and tried her best
to cry. She managed a few sniffles, but no tears would come. Feeling
a little better nevertheless, she took down the only box that re-

mained on the ledge. In it was the hodgepodge of stuff that every man had in a drawer somewhere: cufflinks and collar stays; silver quarters and wheat-back pennies; old lighters, high school medals, old passports, fountain pens, and souvenirs.

Jane fingered the gold watch Aaron Sailor had been wearing the night he fell down the stairs, its crystal shattered. She sighed as she paged through an album of photographs and stared at the banded letters from her mother to her father. Jane had read them once and couldn't bear to again, so tender and loving they were. He must have been heartbroken when the cancer had taken her, Jane knew. As heartbroken as Jane had been.

In the back of the box was her mother's dragonfly cross. Jane hadn't seen the cross for years and didn't even remember that it was down here.

It hung on a simple black ribbon: a stylized insect consisting of two open-ended tubes—the short top one about the diameter of a drinking straw, the long tapering bottom piece narrowing to a bulb the size of a capital O. The tubes were joined together three-quarters up by a pierced pair of wings which served as the cross-piece. It had once been gilded but this had mostly worn off, revealing the dull yellow brass beneath.

Ellen Sailor wasn't a religious woman. She had worn the cross only to funerals and to the Episcopal Christmas and Easter services uptown at St. Thomas's to which she took Jane. Aaron Sailor had always refused to come.

The cross was three inches or so long—too big and heavy to be stylish, but it had a vaguely Art Nouveau/Art Deco look and wasn't unattractive. Jane didn't know when she would ever want to wear such a thing—she hadn't been to church or a funeral for years. Still, the cross was a connection to her mother, and the memory didn't hurt so much any more. As she put it in her pocket to bring upstairs, a black leather book no larger than a playing card caught her eye. She grabbed it greedily and riffled through it.

This was exactly what she had been looking for. The book

was filled with names and phone numbers divided alphabetically. Jane recognized some of them. Imre Carpathian and a few other artist friends of her father. Elinore King, Dad's art dealer. Jane's own dorm address and phone number from Lewis College in New Hampshire eight years ago.

To her disappointment, there was no one named Perry, but there were plenty of women, some with brief descriptions beside their phone numbers: "Nice hips, heart belongs to her schnauzer"; "Smells like a salad, not many brains"; "Tall, blonde, cooperative."

"Jesus," muttered Jane. "Daddy had a sex life."

She tossed the little black book back into the box. Today was not the day Jane wanted to hear about sex. She could take only so much irony in a twenty-four-hour period. She was ready to call it quits when a small, cream-colored card sticking out of a well-worn copy of Marcus Aurelius' *Meditations* caught her eye.

Jane pulled out the card and found herself looking at a drawing of a little man with a big white mustache, a top hat, and a cane. Underneath it bore the inscription: "Get Out of Jail Free."

Smiling involuntarily at the image, familiar from myriad childhood games of Monopoly, Jane turned the card over. On the back, above a date just before her father's accident, was a signature scrawled in blue letters. It was not her father's handwriting.

"Peregrine Mannerback," Jane read out loud.

It was a totally unfamiliar name, but then Jane didn't know many of her father's friends, having been farmed out to boarding school after her mother's death and then off at college in New Hampshire.

"Peregrine," she repeated. "Perry. Is he the one you were raving about today at the nursing home?"

Jane studied the card and spoke again to the empty walls.

"So what didn't you want Perry to do, Daddy? Borrow a hundred dollars, maybe? Fix you up with a girl who smelled like a salad? Push you down the stairs?"

Jane's hand came involuntarily up to her mouth, but it was too late. The thought that Perry, whoever he was, might have pushed her father down the stairs had been just beneath the surface of Jane's mind ever since Benton Contino had delivered his theory this morning.

Was Aaron Sailor simply repeating mindlessly the last words he had spoken? Had he been arguing on the third-floor landing outside the door to their loft with a man named Perry who had pushed him? Was a final plea, "Don't do it, Perry," blazoned into her father's brain as he plummeted down the stairs and crashed headfirst into the vestibule floor?

"No," said Jane, shaking her head determinedly. "No way I'm going down that road."

No one had ever suggested that Aaron Sailor's fall was anything other than an accident. Though the police had asked routine questions, the facts had spoken for themselves. Her father had had sixty dollars in his pocket and a gold watch on his wrist when he was found on the vestibule floor. That ruled out robbery.

Also, the stairs were treacherous. The loft was an industrial space, built long before the days of building codes. The treads were a good two inches higher than modern steps, making them dangerously steep. Everyone had worried about them. And Aaron Sailor had been drinking that night. His blood-alcohol level would have been high enough to get him arrested had he been driving. There had been no witnesses, and without a statement to the contrary, there was no reason to assume that he hadn't simply tripped and fallen down the stairs.

But now there was a statement from Aaron Sailor. "No, Perry, no. Don't do it, Perry."

Unsettled, Jane put the "Get Out of Jail Free" card in her pocket with her mother's cross and placed the box with her father's things back up on the ledge. Then she locked the storage cubicle, walked up the basement stairs, and turned out the light.

By the time Jane had gotten up to her apartment on the fifth floor, the suspicions she had been trying to dismiss as absurd and unsupportable had jelled against her will into a full-blown scenario. This Perry Mannerback could indeed have been with her father that night eight years ago. "You're a liar, Perry," Dad could have said, angry, intoxicated, unpredictable. "I know the truth." Perhaps Perry couldn't afford for anyone to know that truth, whatever it was.

Unlike modern buildings, where you couldn't fall further than the next landing, the staircase descended diagonally in a straight, unbroken path from the Sailor loft on the third floor at the very back of the building all the way down to the ground-floor doorway at the front. Pushing someone intentionally from the top of those stairs was the same as hurling him out of a window.

In a way, such a scenario was somehow less horrible than Aaron Sailor just getting drunk and falling. To lose her father in such a stupid accident had always been almost the worst thing about the whole tragedy. The shame of it, the pointlessness. But if he had been pushed . . .

"No, this is nuts," muttered Jane, turning on the faucet in the kitchen sink to wash the basement grime off her hands. "Don't I have enough troubles? There's nothing to this. There can't be."

Twenty minutes later, her socks and underwear out of suitcases and safely back in their drawers, her slacks and blouses hanging in the tiny closet, Jane put down the dustcloth and reached for the telephone book. Instead of disappearing as she had hoped, her questions about Perry Mannerback had only multiplied.

There was no Peregrine Mannerback in the phonebook, either in the business listings or in the personals. Perhaps he had moved. He could even have died. He might not even be a he. For all Jane knew, Peregrine Mannerback could have been some hot little chickie that Dad had been playing Monopoly with. Or a law firm with a clever marketing gimmick. Or the name of a toy store.

Who would know if there had been a Perry Mannerback in Dad's life eight years ago?

Jane went to the desk, got out her own address book, and flipped through the pages until the listing for Imre Carpathian appeared. Imre's loft on Broome Street was only a few blocks away from where she had grown up. For all Jane knew, Imre might have moved or died. She hadn't spoken with him for years.

"What?" answered an enraged voice after the seventh ring. "Who is calling Imre when he works, you stupid fool?"

"Hi, Uncle Imre, it's Jane. Jane Sailor."

"Jane?"

"It's been a long time."

"Dear little Jane," the voice softened to a roar. "Why you never call me? You are still making with the sword fights?"

"That's me," said Jane. "Fencing, fisticuffs, and fearlessness. I'm not in New York too much. Most of the work is in regional theatres."

"Good for you. We get together some time, make palacsinta, sing dirty Hungarian songs. Not now, though. I am creating. I am blue. I am paint. I am this stupid can."

Jane heard a clattering that might have been a paint can being kicked across the room. It was nice to hear the crazy old artist's voice again.

"Just answer one quick question, Uncle Imre. Do you remember a friend of my father named Peregrine Mannerback? Perry Mannerback?"

"Never heard of no such person. Ridiculous name. Call me later sometime. I am working now. Good-bye."

The phone went dead. Imre hadn't changed at all.

The only other person Jane could think of who might know her father's friends was Elinore King, his dealer. Was finding out about Peregrine Mannerback worth a call to the woman her father referred to as "greed on legs"?

Jane looked at the "Get Out of Jail Free" card again. Then she found Elinore's number in her book, picked up the telephone, and began to punch out numbers. Ever since the show at the Fyfe had been announced, Elinore had been calling about Aaron Sailor's paintings. Jane knew she would have to have it out with Elinore sooner or later. Why not kill two birds with a single stone?

"Galerie Elinore King," said a soft, melodic voice.

"Is Elinore available? This is Jane Sailor."

"Janie, darling, honey," screeched Elinore a minute later. "I've been calling and calling, but you never return my messages. You're okay? Nothing's the matter?"

Her voice was a cross between a steam whistle and a myna bird, with a touch of cat being castrated thrown in.

"I'm fine," said Jane. "I've been out of town on a job. I only just got back."

"Hold on, hold on," shouted Elinore. "I'm in middle of eighteen things. Hold on."

A stream of invective followed that was not as loud by a few decibels because it came through a set of fingers. "No, no, not there. Why are you so stupid? I told you where I wanted it. Can't you do anything right? All right, fine, now get out."

Elinore's voice changed again when she returned to Jane on the receiver. Now it was coquettish and giggly.

"So Janie, honey, sweetie, it's so wonderful to talk to you. You know, I'm hearing fantastic things about the show in California at the . . . you-know museum . . . what's it called?"

"The Fyfe."

"They love your father. Absolutely love him. It's incredible. Did you see the article in *ArtNews* that I sent you? Isn't it fantastic?"

"Yes," said Jane. "It's nice to see that Dad is finally getting some of the credit he deserves."

"And it's about time," Elinore said smugly. "I mean, I feel so proud. I'm the only one who believed in your father, you know. I sweat blood for that man. It cost me a fortune to promote him, a fortune!"

Jane felt her jaw tighten. She hadn't seen her father's dealer in eight years, but could still picture Elinore's delicate features, her long blond hair, her self-serving smile. Most people thought Elinore was pretty. Jane knew what she really was.

"If you believed in him so much, why wouldn't you buy Dad's paintings from me after his accident?" said Jane, her voice exceedingly cool.

"Janie, Janie . . ."

"You could have had them for next to nothing, but you weren't interested. You wouldn't even store them."

"Janie, listen to me . . ."

"It would have made a real difference."

"Janie, sweetie, please," cooed Elinore, "let's not get back into this, okay? Nobody wanted Realism back then. That wasn't my fault, was it? God, everybody thinks it's so easy, but believe me, it's not. You were too young to understand, but I promise you, honey, that this was . . . that I didn't . . . you know what I mean? Okay? It's all water over the bridge. Okay? I mean, you really hurt me when you talk that way. Now that things are going so well. Did I tell you about the *New York Times?*"

"No. What about the *New York Times?*"

"They're doing a piece in the *Sunday Magazine.* A feature. I've sent them transparencies and everything. It's fantastic. This is what I've been working for all this time, to get Aaron the recognition he deserves. You'd be amazed at what has to go on behind the scenes to get this kind of publicity. Oh God, you don't know what I've gone through to get this show at the what-do-you-call-it museum, and this article in the *Times.* You owe me, you know. You really do."

Jane took the phone away from her ear and tried to stay calm. What she owed Elinore was seventy percent of the proceeds from any sale of her father's paintings because of the overreaching contract he had signed when he was desperate for gallery representation. Jane had talked to three different lawyers about it over the years. The bottom line was that trying to break the agreement could cost thousands of dollars in legal fees with only the tiniest possibility of success.

But if Jane were stuck with Elinore, Elinore was also stuck with her. Elinore couldn't collect her percentage unless Jane agreed to a sale, which of course was the reason for all this sudden interest.

"I'm not calling to argue with you, Elinore," said Jane in a quiet voice. "I just want to ask you something."

"That's fine, sweetie. Ask me, ask me anything. That's what I'm here for. That's what a dealer does. I'm just here to serve. I'm just here for you. I'm like your personal servant. Your wish is my command."

"Have you ever heard of Peregrine Mannerback? Perry Mannerback?"

"Perry Mannerback, of course I've heard of Perry Mannerback," declared Elinore. "Why? What about him?"

"Who is he?"

"He's a client of mine. Very difficult. I've tried a million times to get him on the phone to tell him about opportunities, but he never returns my calls. He's very rich but strange. A real problem."

"Did he know my father?" asked Jane.

"Yes, of course he knew your father. Mr. Mannerback . . . Peregrine . . . Perry . . . was the man who bought that big painting of Aaron's, the only thing we ever sold. I put a photo of it in the window downstairs and he came up and bought it before we opened the show, before anyone else even saw it. It was one of the transparencies I sent to the *Times*. Has Perry Mannerback contacted you? Is he interested in another piece?"

Jane wondered if it was her imagination or whether you could actually hear someone salivating over a phone line.

"I just found his name in some of my father's old papers and was curious, that's all," Jane said, not wanting to share any more with Elinore than she had to. "Did Perry Mannerback and my father know one another well?"

"They met when he bought the painting," said Elinore. "Then he came to my opening vernissage. I don't know what happened after that, but listen to me, honey. If Perry Mannerback wants to buy another painting, you can't fuck around with him. He's an important man and the only one who supported Aaron's work back then. You have to let me sell him whatever he wants. You just have to."

"We've been all over this, Elinore," said Jane evenly.

"But Perry Mannerback—"

"I've told you, I don't want to do anything right now."

"Okay, okay," muttered Elinore. "That's your privilege. If you want to be this way, I'm not going to argue. You're your own woman. You can do what you want, now that Aaron is beginning to get a little success. I just happen to think that you have a moral obligation to your father, that's all. Sales are what he would have wanted. This isn't about money, it's about Aaron. His work, his art. Okay, now I've said my piece, and I won't bring it up again. You'll never hear another word from me on the subject, I promise. I swear to God."

"Don't worry, Elinore," said Jane. "You'll get paid if I do anything. I'm just not ready to sell anything to anybody right now."

"Janie, darling, sweetie," said Elinore, her voice growing dewy. "Of course I trust you. After all we've been through together. We're just alike, you know. We're like sisters. That's why you have to trust me, too. You do trust me, don't you?"

Jane didn't say anything. What do you say to a sister who would probably charge you a commission for selling you into slavery?

"So when can I see you?" Elinore resumed, the ground glass returning to her voice. "Greg and I would love to take you out for dinner, get reacquainted. There's this fabulous new place in the Village that everyone's talking about, *Les Matins*. It's all the rage.

The 'in' place. And you know that I'm an 'in' girl. So when would be good? Saturday? This is absolutely the top place in the city. You're going to love it."

"I just got back to town. Maybe in a few weeks."

"Next Saturday then. Please, pretty please?"

"I'd like to, Elinore, but there's so much I have to do."

"Sure, darling. I understand completely. That's why we want to take you out, so you can relax among friends. Then it's a date? Next Saturday? Please say yes, I absolutely won't take no for an answer."

Jane gritted her teeth. Elinore's strategy was to make herself so difficult that most people ultimately gave up and just let her have her way. Jane really didn't want to have anything to do with the woman, but getting rid of her would probably require a silver bullet. And a wooden stake through her heart. And perhaps burial at a crossroads at midnight. Maybe if Jane saw her in person she could get Elinore off her back for a while.

"All right. Next Saturday."

"See?" said Elinore, laughing happily. "That wasn't so hard. I'm going to mark it in my calendar right now. You can't know what I'll have to go through to get a reservation, but it will be so great to see you. I'm going to win your trust, you'll see."

"Do you have Perry Mannerback's telephone number?"

"Why don't you let me call him for you?"

"I thought you said he didn't return your calls."

"Can you believe that?" shrieked Elinore, remembering her outrage. "I don't understand that man. I really don't. And I suppose it's your business if you don't want to tell me what this is all about. That's okay. I'm not hurt. Really, I'll be fine."

Jane didn't say anything.

"Martha!" Elinore yelled. "Get me a phone number. Where is that stupid girl?"

It took another five minutes for Jane to extricate herself from the conversation. Then she dialed the number that Elinore had gotten from her secretary. As Jane did so, she caught a glimpse of herself in the little mirror on the back of the kitchen door and shook her head in disbelief. She should have left her hat on. She looked like a dandelion.

"You have reached the offices of OmbiCorp International," answered a mellow, recorded female voice. "If you know your party's extension, you may dial it at any time or select from the following menu . . ."

It took several minutes to get from this point to a human being, but Jane eventually succeeded.

"Mr. Mannerback, please," she said in her best command voice, the voice she employed to order self-important actors and narcissistic actresses to perform summersaults and sit-ups.

"Thank you," said the operator. "One moment, please."

"Chairman's office," said another voice after a moment.

"Mr. Mannerback, please," Jane repeated.

"I'll connect you."

"Mr. Mannerback's office," said a third voice in due course.

"Is he available?"

"Who's calling?"

"Jane Sailor."

"Is this a foundation matter or corporate?"

"It's personal."

"One moment, please."

There was a longer wait this time. Eventually, still another voice came on the line. This too was female, as all the others had been. She spoke with a clipped, efficient British accent. Her voice was as cold as the concrete floor in Jane's basement.

"Miss Barbara Fripp. May I help you?"

"I'd like to make an appointment to see Mr. Mannerback," said Jane, trying to sound equally efficient.

"To what is this in reference?"

"It's personal," said Jane. She had no idea of what she would say to Perry Mannerback, but figured that just meeting him would give her an idea of how to proceed.

"Mr. Mannerback is a very busy man," declared Miss Fripp. "If you would care to put your problem in writing and send it along, I will be happy to bring it to his attention."

"I'd prefer to see him in person."

"Then you will have to tell me what this is about."

"I believe that Mr. Mannerback bought a painting of my father's," said Jane. "My father was an artist. I believe they were friends."

"And your father's name would be?"

"Aaron Sailor."

"No, it is not a name with which I am familiar. Mr. Mannerback makes the acquaintance of many individuals during the course of his travels. His time is very valuable. I am afraid that a meeting is out of the question. Impossible. You are welcome to send us a letter."

"I see," said Jane, her spirits sinking. What could she write under the circumstance? "Dear Mr. Mannerback, do you happen to remember if you pushed my father down a flight of stairs eight years ago?"

"Our address is 1381 Avenue of the Americas," said Miss Fripp, "New York, New York, 10020."

"May I ask you a question?" said Jane.

"Certainly," replied the chilly voice.

"Why would Mr. Mannerback give my father a 'Get Out of Jail Free' card?"

"Get Out of Jail Free?"

"From Monopoly. The board game. Mr. Mannerback signed it on the back."

"And you have this card?" said Miss Fripp, amazement flooding into her voice. "It is in your possession?"

"I'm looking at it now."

"Well, why didn't you say so?" demanded the secretary. "How about tomorrow morning?"

"How about tomorrow morning for what?"

"For your appointment, of course. Mr. Mannerback takes his 'Get Out of Jail Free' cards very seriously. Would eleven o'clock be convenient?"

eeeeeeeeeeeeeeeeeeeeeeeeeee Four

The Avenue of the Americas—or Sixth Avenue, as New Yorkers still called it generations after its renaming—was one of those places, like the city's financial district, where skyscrapers had triumphed entirely over human beings.

Buildings that touched the clouds lined both sides of the busy thoroughfare from Forty-second Street all the way up to Central Park. While a few were architecturally distinguished, like Radio City Music Hall and CBS's Black Rock Building, most were just the anonymous glass cigar boxes that Corporate America required of its big league players.

The headquarters of OmbiCorp International was one of these behemoths, a towering gray structure at Fifty-sixth Street, complete with the requisite fountain-strewn pedestrian plaza in front and half-acre Frank Stella tapestry hanging in the lobby.

Jane sat on a beige suede sofa in the fifty-first-floor reception area of OmbiCorp's executive offices. Directly across from her, behind the receptionist, was an enormous window that looked out over the long green postage stamp of Central Park far below. From up here, the exclusive apartment buildings of Fifth Avenue and Central Park West looked like dollhouse furniture, and the people on the sidewalks weren't even the size of ants. That was the point of all this. A skyscraper was about perspective. This was the top of the world, or so the inhabitants of such aeries would have you believe.

Jane was dressed in her best gray Bonnie Businesswoman suit, complete with white silk blouse and a string of Jackie Kennedy–style fake pearls. Being of the theatre, she knew the importance of costume as well as OmbiCorp knew the importance of sets. From the address Miss Fripp had given her, Jane had expected something like this. The reality, however, was beyond intimidating, it was positively scary. She again thanked the hair gods that Chop Sui had managed to squeeze her in for a nine a.m. appointment.

At least she wouldn't face Perry Mannerback looking like an advertisement for bad hats or rebellious teenagers, thought Jane, gazing at her reflection in a chrome end table. Romero had assured her that Raphael Renaissance Red was the only way to neutralize the blond mess she had made of her hair, and he had been right. At the cost of a mere two hundred and fifty dollars, she no longer looked like a dandelion. Now she looked like a marigold.

Jane twiddled her thumbs and tried to move her thoughts from how stupid she looked as a redhead to what she was going to say. Unfortunately, there was no real way to plan for a situation like this. You had to let things unfold naturally. From what Peregrine Mannerback looked like, however, Jane suspected they would end up screaming at one another. She had seen him twice now in the half hour that she had been kept waiting. The first time was when he had arrived off the elevator.

He was unmistakably the man in charge here: thin, tan, and six foot four—a ramrod-straight military type, with short-cropped salt-and-pepper hair, cold gray eyes, and thin lips. He wore a two-thousand-dollar black suit, a starched white shirt with monogrammed cuffs, and an "I take no prisoners" expression. He not only seemed perfectly capable of pushing someone down a flight of stairs, he looked like he would enjoy doing so.

The receptionist had shot to her feet in fearful silence and practically saluted when he entered. He had breezed past her without even a glance of acknowledgment, moving through the space as if he owned it and everyone in it as well. About ten minutes later, he had crossed back through the reception area with a train of deferential associates in tow, all clamoring for his attention.

This must be the chairman of OmbiCorp, Jane had decided immediately, the man who needed four levels of secretarial protection, the man who may have destroyed Aaron Sailor's life.

Jane found herself planning for the coming confrontation. Should she begin with guns blazing? "Why did you push my father down the stairs eight years ago, Mr. Mannerback?" Or should she first lull him with small talk, then take him by surprise? "My, what a lovely tie. Is that what the well-dressed murderer is wearing this season?"

And "murderer" was the right word. If Peregrine Mannerback had in fact pushed Aaron Sailor down those stairs, then he had murdered him, murdered him as surely as if he had plunged a knife into his heart. In a way, it was worse than murder. When a person was dead there was at least finality, the story was over, you could mourn. Aaron Sailor was dead, but his corpse lived on.

At that moment the man Jane believed to be Peregrine Mannerback entered the lobby again. This time he noticed Jane for the first time and stopped abruptly. Jane felt the adrenaline surging into her system as, not taking his eyes off her, he crossed to the receptionist and whispered something that Jane could not hear. The girl turned pale and whispered something back. The man listened, then turned on his heel and exited without another glance at either of them.

Jane knew she was having an involuntary fight-or-flight response. Her pulse was racing. Her hands had become cold. That would never do, she thought angrily. She took a deep breath from her diaphragm, counting to ten as she did, then let it out twice as slowly. Her center of gravity had leaped into her chest, which was absolutely the worst thing you could have going into a fight.

Jane took another deep breath. She didn't have to be thrown off balance, she told herself. Perry Mannerback couldn't intimidate her, no matter how cold his manner or rich his stage set, unless she let him. He could let her cool her heels for another hour if he wanted to. She would begin their meeting with a calm heart and a low center. She would find out the truth.

"Gummy bears, gummy bears," muttered a voice. "Very important. Very important."

Jane turned toward the voice in time to see a man getting off the elevator. He was a slight, wild-looking fellow, with a long, thin nose, a high forehead, and big, startled brown eyes. His tangled brown hair swept back in all directions as if he had just stepped out of a race car or a centrifuge. Under his rumpled raincoat he wore a navy blue blazer with gold buttons, a butterscotch-colored vest, and a big polka-dotted bow tie. He was about five foot seven and walked with the spastic energy of a teenager, though the bags under his eyes and wattle beneath his pointed chin suggested an age approaching sixty.

The receptionist smiled and shook her head, the way you might at the sight of a little boy with his best Sunday clothes covered in chocolate.

"Good morning, Mr. Mannerback," she chided, as he sped by her.

"Gummy bears, very important," said Peregrine Mannerback, the chairman of OmbiCorp International, oblivious to her greeting. "Gummy gummy gummy gummy bears."

Jane knew she must look ridiculous with her mouth open, but she was still too shocked to have gotten it properly closed by the time he returned a few seconds later. This is what happened when you tried to anticipate! Jane had been so certain that the tall man with the military bearing was Perry Mannerback that now she had no idea what to do. Her brain had stopped functioning entirely.

"Mr. Mannerback, wait," said the receptionist, bolting from her station and chasing after him to the elevator. She whispered into his ear and pointed to Jane. He listened intently, nodded, and marched over.

"Perry Mannerback," he announced, extending his hand. "How do you do? Very pleased to meet you."

"Jane Sailor," said Jane, shaking hands. His hand was cool, his grip was firm.

"Come on," he said. "We'll talk on the way."

"Where are we going?" asked Jane, following him into the elevator."

"Sailor," said Perry Mannerback, pushing the lobby button. "I know someone with that name."

The elevator doors closed.

"You bought a painting by my father, Aaron Sailor," Jane said.

"Oh, yes. That was ages ago. Ages. Do you like gummy bears?"

He pulled out a large bag from one of the bulging pockets of his raincoat and struggled to pull it open.

"No, thanks."

"Of course you like gummy bears, don't be shy," said Perry Mannerback. "Everybody likes gummy bears. Gummy bears are very important to a person's overall happiness. That's why my secretary always makes sure I have some in my office. We're going to have a good time."

What kind of good time could you have in an elevator? Jane was eyeing the alarm button when mercifully the car stopped at the forty-third floor and a pair of witnesses got in.

"I like the orange ones," said Perry Mannerback, unconcerned. "The orange ones are my favorites. Which ones do you like?"

"I like the orange ones too," said Jane cautiously.

"No, those are mine," said Perry Mannerback. "Here. You can have a green one."

He placed one in her hand. The elevator stopped again on its long descent. Jane's ears popped as they had on the way up. More people got in. Perry Mannerback dug into his bag and distributed gummy bears to everyone. Some people took them with amusement, others looked annoyed, perhaps because he had reserved all the orange ones for himself.

When the elevator finally reached the ground floor, Perry Mannerback grabbed Jane's hand and practically dragged her through the crowded lobby and outside to a long black limousine parked in front of the building next to a "Don't Even THINK of Parking Here" sign.

"Let's go, Leonid," said Mannerback, closing the door. "Let's go, let's go."

"Yes, sir, Mr. Mennerbeck," answered the chauffeur, a compact, Slavic-looking man in his thirties, who wore a well-pressed suit, a black chauffeur's hat, and a resigned expression.

"Okay!" said Perry Mannerback, bouncing up and down on the soft leather backseat with excitement. "Okay!"

"Where are we going?" asked Jane, feeling strangely calm. Her center was low. Her breathing had returned to its proper rhythm. She was ready for anything (she hoped).

"We're going to have a good time," said Perry Mannerback again with a satisfied expression, studying her for the first time. "Who did you say you were?"

"Jane Sailor. You bought a painting from my father, Aaron Sailor."

"Oh, yes. Very nice chap. How is he?"

"He's been in a coma for the past eight years since somebody pushed him down a flight of stairs."

Jane had decided on going intentionally for shock value. It worked. Perry Mannerback reeled back as if struck with a fist. He placed his hand on his heart, then brought it up to his forehead. Then he leaned across the long leather seat and clasped it over Jane's with surprising gentleness.

"You poor thing, you poor, poor thing," he declared with what appeared to be sincerity. Then he sat back. His eyes filled with tears. "Terrible to hear this. Yes, I remember him. Your father. A nice man. Very nice man."

Mannerback wiped his eyes, then pulled out a silk handkerchief and blew his nose with a honk.

"Thank you," said Jane, taken aback.

They stared at one another for a few moments. Up close, she could see the white-on-white pattern of his shirt and the faint age spots on his neck and hands. Part of what gave his big eyes their earnest expression was that his eyelashes were unnaturally long and silky. He leaned forward again and spoke.

"So why are we meeting?"

Jane didn't have a clue what to say. Instead, she just opened the little black purse she had brought along, took out the "Get Out of Jail Free" card, and handed it to Mannerback.

"Of course," he said, turning it over and noting his signature. "I remember giving that to your father. The painter. Nice chap. I didn't know. Really, I didn't. So what would you like for your favor?"

"My favor?"

"Yes. I give those cards when I owe someone a favor. A big favor. Very big favor. Anything you want, just name it."

Jane paused for a moment and studied him, wondering whether the monogrammed gold buttons on his blazer were in fact actual gold. He looked back with the eager smile of an eight-year-old.

"I'd like to know who pushed my father down those stairs," she said softly.

Perry Mannerback's eyebrows scrunched together and his lips screwed into a frown.

"Terrible thing. Terrible thing. But I don't know how I can help you with that one. I really don't. I can only do what I can do, you know? Would you like a job?"

"A job?"

"Sure," declared Mannerback. "I've got plenty of those. That's what people usually ask for. A job. Or money, sometimes they just ask for money. Perhaps one day someone will actually ask me to get him out of jail. Are you an accountant?"

"No. Why? Do I look like an accountant?"

"A little."

"Please don't tell me that."

"We're always looking for accountants. Count all our money, we've got plenty. I know, you're a lawyer!"

"God forbid!" said Jane.

"Not an accountant. Not a lawyer. No matter. We employ all kinds of people. Programmers. Analysts. Executive types. Secretaries. So what are you?"

"I'm a fight director."

"A what?"

"A fight director. I choreograph fights. For the theatre."

"I don't think we need any of those. No, indeed. Fight director. What a curious profession. How on earth did you get into that?"

"It's a long story," said Jane.

"Good. I like long stories."

"I'm sure you wouldn't be interested."

"But I am," protested Perry Mannerback, clenching his little fists. "I am, I am, I really am. I want to hear. Please, tell me. Please."

"I have this funny talent," Jane said with a shrug. "I don't know how to really describe it. It's like I can see the relationships between moving objects from different angles in my mind. Since I was a kid I've been able to do these weird things, like toss a milk bottle in the air and as it's falling back down, end over end, I can throw a clothespin right into it. You know how people make shadow animals with their fingers?"

"I love that!"

"When I was in college, I did something like that but with my whole body. My roommate would set up a sheet and project a light behind me, then I would jump around like a lunatic but to the people sitting on the other side of the sheet it would look like mating elephants, dancing fish, Mickey Mouse—all kinds of strange things. I never planned anything, never rehearsed—I could just see in my mind what my movements would look like from out front."

"That's fantastic!"

Jane shrugged.

"It was just this funny talent I had, this party-trick kind of thing. It never occurred to me that it was good for anything but some laughs. Then a girl in the drama department saw one of my little performances and asked me to help her with the fights in this play she was directing. She said I'd be able to do it easily. I thought she was crazy, but she was right. From the first rehearsal, I could see exactly what two people on stage could safely do so that it would look like they were beating one another's brains out from the audience. And of course I've been fencing competitively since I was eight, so the sword fights weren't a problem. A producer came to the opening night and in one of those million-to-one shots brought it to New York. You might have heard of it—*Tillabuck*."

"About the man with the mustache!" said Perry Mannerback. "I saw that on Broadway. It was great!"

"It ran a few years," said Jane, nodding. "It was probably the luckiest break anyone ever had—for all of us. Half the company are now on television or in the movies. The director did the new Wendy Wasserstein. I made some money and some connections in the New York theatre. I ended up with a boyfriend who was one of the handful of guys in the world who actually make their living as fight directors. I learned so much from him that pretty soon I was getting jobs on my own, which was one of the reasons we broke up."

"And you actually make your living like this? Choreographing fights?"

Jane nodded.

"I'm one of the few women working in the field," she said, "so I'm a very politically correct hire for nonprofits and regional theatres. It doesn't hurt that I know what I'm doing, either. When I get through with a production, the actors really look like they're killing one another. And if I need to, I can skewer a full-grown egomaniac with épée, foil, saber, or dirk."

"Marvelous!" said Perry Mannerback, clapping his hands together. "I know. You could be my bodyguard."

"Right," Jane said with a laugh.

"No, I'm serious. You look like a bodyguard. Professional. Fit. And redheads are supposed to be very fiery. You could scare people away just with your looks."

"That's very comforting to hear," murmured Jane. "The fact is that I've never been in an actual fight in my life. Only pretend."

"But you would know what to do, I'll bet, if I got kidnapped by pirates or something."

"That doesn't seem likely."

"It could happen," said Perry Mannerback indignantly. "Just look at all those terrorists out there. And serial killers. And out-of-control journalists. Besides, I need an assistant."

"Mr. Mannerback, I didn't . . ."

"You can be my bodyguard assistant. This will be grand."

"Mr. Mannerback . . . "

"Come on," he pleaded. "I haven't had an assistant for a long time. They always quit. I'll pay you. I have plenty of money."

Then he named a weekly figure so much higher than most people in the arts could make that Jane wanted to cry.

"And benefits," said Perry Mannerback, adding injury to insult. "Health insurance with dental. Profit sharing. OmbiCorp employees get all kinds of neat stuff, and we don't care because the stockholders pay."

Jane tried to catch her breath. Health insurance, too. Practically nobody she knew in New York had health insurance. To get health insurance, you had to sign a long-term contract with a LORT theatre and move to some place like St. Louis or Minneapolis.

"What did my father do that you owed him such a big favor?" she asked.

"Gosh, it's a nice day," replied Mannerback, turning away and staring out the window as the limo inched up Broadway.

"What did my father do that you owed him such a big favor?" repeated Jane.

"I don't know," he said, his voice suddenly louder than necessary. "I can't remember."

Jane almost laughed aloud, the man was so obviously lying. They sat in silence for a moment. Then Mannerback turned back and looked at her like a bad puppy.

"So what do you say? Will you do it? Will you let me give you a job? I always pay my debts."

Jane's instinct was to open the door of the limousine and dive into traffic, but this was one of those times you had to use your head, not your emotions, to decide.

She didn't have a job for the summer, and the money Perry Mannerback was offering beat unemployment by a long shot. It wouldn't be forever, Jane told herself. By next fall she'd be back in Omaha or Austin teaching punch-ups to actors again. Besides, how else could she find out why Perry Mannerback owed her father such a big favor? Or if he had pushed him down the stairs.

"Okay," Jane said. "Why not?"

"Hurrah!" her new employer declared, pumping her hand and slapping her back. "This is great. Wonderful. Welcome aboard."

Just then the limousine glided to a stop at the side entrance to the Lincoln Center complex on Sixty-second street, across from the Fordham University Law School. The chauffeur cut the engine, then got out of the car and opened the backseat door.

"Where are we going?" asked Jane, following Mannerback, who had jumped out and was bounding up a walk toward a large tent that had been set up in an area where they usually had outdoor concerts.

"We're going to have fun!" shouted Mannerback over his shoulder.

As Jane chased after him and rounded the corner, a huge banner stretched between two posts came into view: THE BIG APPLE CIRCUS.

Her first duty as Perry Mannerback's bodyguard-assistant was to get them both popcorn.

Five

"You'll be surprised," said Perry Mannerback in his earnest, excited way as they got into the small, mahogany-paneled elevator. The elderly, white-gloved attendant closed the door and pressed the button marked "PH." "It's not what you expect, I bet. I bet it's not what you expect at all."

Nearly a week had now passed since Jane had come to work for Perry Mannerback. This was the first time she would have the opportunity of seeing his penthouse apartment, but if it turned out that he lived with a family of elves in the exclusive Fifth Avenue building that he had brought her to, she wouldn't be surprised. Perry Mannerback was the most remarkable man Jane had ever met.

There were other men who were like children (practically every guy Jane knew was childish to one degree or another), but Perry Mannerback truly *was* a little boy: a fifty-six-year-old with all the good and bad aspects of a third-grader. He was innocent, yet he was naughty. He was rough, yet he was gentle. He was boisterous and shy, selfish and thoughtful, silly-looking but somehow cute. He could be hateful and stupid one moment, sensible and incredibly sweet the next.

If Perry Mannerback had been born into a poor or even a middle-class family, Jane didn't know what would have become of him. He certainly wouldn't have been able to hold a job. He had no useful skills, was totally irresponsible, and had the attention span of a tropical fish. However, in the same way that God seemed to look out for mothers, drunks, and little dogs, the Almighty had provided Perry Mannerback from birth with everything he needed for a happy and productive life—namely, money.

Perry Mannerback, as Jane had learned over the past few days, was the great-great-grandson of Otto Mannerback, an industrious German immigrant who had arrived in New York City in 1869 at the age of eleven without a cent in his pocket. Otto had eventually found work in a factory that made buttons from discarded oyster shells. Within ten years he had founded his own company in a lightless tenement on Grand Street—Otto Mannerback Buttons.

By the time Perry was born, several generations of shrewd and hardworking Mannerbacks had built Otto Mannerback Buttons into the largest buttonmaking concern in the world. Perry's great-grandfather had diversified into other unglamorous yet profitable businesses that had assured Ombicorp's profitability in bad button years as well as good. Perry's grandfather had taken the company public and continued its expansion. His father had built it into an international conglomerate.

Perry Mannerback had thus entered the world wrapped in a safety net of trust funds and privilege, his childlike qualities valued rather than condemned, his interests viewed as eccentric instead of crazy. Because of his wealth he was accorded opportunities that most men could only dream of.

To her astonishment, Jane had learned that this man who made "vroom-vroom" noises when he played with toy cars had graduated from Harvard University (albeit not at the top of his class), had made his way through three marriages to beautiful and well-bred women (presently all happily divorced), and was now an actual grandfather. He was a respected member of New York society, a trustee of the Metropolitan Opera and the Museum of Modern Art, and served on the boards of directors of several major banks, corporations, and charities. Perhaps most surprisingly of all, under his leadership OmbiCorp International had flourished beyond anyone's wildest dreams.

Perry Mannerback's shrewd tactics and unorthodox style had become a business legend. Competitors and journalists alike were always trying to figure him out, but to no avail. When OmbiCorp had bought out a small plastic toy producer whose Arizona factory complex turned out to be sitting on top of the largest palladium deposit ever discovered in the Western Hemisphere, all Perry Mannerback would say was, "Yellow stegosauruses. They make yellow stegosauruses. Who wouldn't buy a company like that?"

When *Forbes* asked how OmbiCorp had thought to snap up a biotech company involved in recombinant DNA before the field got hot, the enigmatic chairman replied, "I thought it had something to do with combs. Everybody needs a comb."

Stock market analysts were so pleased by the synergy when OmbiCorp took over Armex Patterson, the Canadian electronics conglomerate, that OmbiCorp's stock shot up eight points. Perry Mannerback, however, claimed that all he had been interested in was a small string of movie theatres that Armex Patterson owned in Manhattan. "Now I can go to the movies right around the corner from my office any time I want to," he boasted to the *Wall Street Journal,* "and I get in for free!"

Not only did everything that Perry Mannerback touch turn to gold, he had a talent for attracting loyal, talented employees besides.

His executive secretary, the fiercely protective Miss Fripp, typed a hundred and ten words a minute, kept him stocked with gummy bears, and wouldn't let him go out without buttoning up his coat.

Leonid, the Russian chauffeur, was so grateful for Perry Mannerback's kindnesses to him and his family that he would regularly stop the car in the middle of a busy avenue, rush into a store, and come back with an ice cream cone or lollipop for Perry that he had bought with his own money.

But perhaps the most valuable employee of all, Jane had discovered to her surprise, was the tall, unpleasant man whom she had mistaken for Perry Mannerback that first day. His name was Theodore B. Danko. He was OmbiCorp's president and chief executive officer, the man who actually ran the company.

According to the Gang of Five—a group of OmbiCorp secretaries who were happy to have someone new to gossip with around the water cooler—Danko had started in sales and risen to vice president of the North American marketing division under Perry's father. When Reginald Mannerback died twelve years ago, Perry had selected Danko over several more senior people to run the company, "because he looked like a quarterback," Perry had once said.

It turned out to be yet another brilliant decision for all the wrong reasons, in typical Perry Mannerback fashion. Ted Danko was a shrewd, efficient, and utterly ruthless executive, enough of a buccaneer to navigate OmbiCorp through the treacherous waters of international business, yet enough of a politician to deal with a loose cannon like Perry Mannerback.

Jane had met Danko formally for the first time yesterday, her fourth day on the job. Up to this point, she and Perry had stopped by OmbiCorp's Sixth Avenue offices only briefly each morning for gummy bears and grant checks. It seemed that Perry Mannerback hated business and spent most of his time having adventures and giving away money through his foundation. The past week had been a blur of fun, feature films, and selfless philanthropy (at one point Jane had watched in amazement as Perry Mannerback spent three hours reading stories to toddlers in a Harlem day care center, and then, unable to find his pen, wrote a fifty-thousand-dollar check with a crayon).

Finally, though, Perry had had to spend a few hours at OmbiCorp's Sixth Avenue offices with Miss Fripp, signing documents and correspondence, about the contents of which he didn't seem to have a clue. As he and Jane were escaping they had run into Danko accidentally in the hallway outside Perry's enormous office.

There had been an awkward moment of silence. Clearly, the two men didn't see one another often. Perry had then introduced Jane to Danko as his new assistant and inquired how things were going with the business, crossing his arms and assuming a very serious businessmanlike expression for the occasion—rather like a little boy putting on his father's hat and frown.

"I'm glad you asked, Perry," Danko had replied smoothly. "Things are doing very well. Sales are up in Europe and we're taking advantage of the monetary problems in the Far East to buy raw materials. Happily, Asia has never been a market for our products, isn't that right?"

"Oh, yes," Perry had said. "Absolutely."

"So you don't think we should try to penetrate the Asian markets?"

"Well, I don't know about that."

"You mean, then, that we should?"

"Gee. Is this something I have to decide right away, Ted?"

"No, Perry. Take your time. Take as long as you want. You're the boss."

Danko's face hadn't changed in any aspect as he spoke. His voice carried no inflection. However, his cold gray eyes betrayed him, at least to Jane. There was more than cruelty in those eyes. There was contempt. And something else, something frightening. Danko did not merely think Perry Mannerback a fool, he despised him. He hated him with a passion.

"What do you think we should do, Ted?" Perry had asked, oblivious.

"I can study the situation, if you like, and make a recommendation."

"That's good. That's very good, Ted. Make a study and recommend something."

"I'll do that," said Danko without a trace of emotion in his voice. "Thank you, Perry. I don't know how we'd manage without your guidance. Now, if you'll excuse me, I have a meeting. A pleasure to meet you, Ms. Sailor."

Then he turned on his heel and marched away.

"Nice man," Perry had said, beaming, clearly delighted to think he had solved another problem.

The incident had left Jane with an unsettled feeling in the pit of her stomach. Certainly, Perry needed someone like Danko to run his business. Perry couldn't match his socks on a regular basis, let alone make the kinds of day-to-day decisions that a huge corporation like OmbiCorp depended on.

But Jane knew instinctively that Danko's animosity posed a real danger for her new employer. Perry seemed so vulnerable and helpless against such a man—and this was what had left Jane feeling so unsettled. She had taken this job to learn if Perry Mannerback might have destroyed her father. Now, after only a few days, she was beginning to feel as protective of him as Miss Fripp!

"I live in the penthouse," said Perry proudly as the elevator came to a stop, jolting Jane back to the present. He was wearing a plaid vest today, which was too busy a combination along with his striped shirt and patterned bow tie, but on Perry it all somehow seemed to fit. "Mine's the best apartment in the building, isn't it, John?"

"Yes, it is, Mr. Mannerback," said the white-gloved attendant with a smile.

"I have to get that article in *Time* magazine for Aunt Eunice," Perry continued, fixing the elevator operator in his eager gaze. "The one all about sex chat rooms on the Internet. Did you read that article, John?"

"No, Mr. Mannerback."

"But you remember Aunt Eunice, don't you? The one who gets stoned out of her gourd every year at Thanksgiving? She's always telling everyone what a sex maniac she is, which is why I think she'll be interested in this article."

"I'm sure she will be, Mr. Mannerback," said John. He opened the metal gate, then the outer door.

"Come on, we're here," announced Perry Mannerback, urging Jane out of the elevator and directly into the vestibule of the most spectacular apartment she had ever seen.

A huge silver chandelier carved with stags' heads and grape-leaves was suspended into the room from a ceiling at least twenty feet high. The floor was alternating squares of black and white marble. An elegant limestone staircase wound its way to a second floor. Eight superb grandfather-type case clocks, graduating in size from three feet to eight, flanked one wall. An antique Brussels hunting tapestry graced another. A ballerina painted by Degas posed *en pirouette* above a walnut hall table.

In the rooms ahead Jane could see a center table with an enormous arrangement of fresh flowers, stunning Oriental carpets, important paintings, and windows looking out onto the grand buildings of Central Park West across the green expanse of the park itself.

Amidst this glory, however, all Jane could focus on was the sound.

It seemed to come from everywhere and nowhere, high and low, near and far: a pervasive rhythmic pulsating, like a million butterflies beating their wings or an ocean of bubbles bursting in time with one another. Jane turned to the right, then the left, but still couldn't grasp what it was or its source until one of the grand-father clocks began to chime the hour with a low *dong.*

"Isn't that a beautiful sound?" said Perry Mannerback, tilting his head up and closing his eyes.

Jane looked at her wrist. According to her watch, it was a

little before six o'clock. Perhaps she was a little slow. The days with Perry Mannerback sped by, though Jane still didn't know exactly what she was supposed to be doing to earn her extravagant salary.

A second grandfather clock began to chime. Then from the other room, a clear bell began to ring. Then another, and suddenly the air was vibrating with what a poet had once needed to coin a word to describe: tintinnabulation. The ringing and the singing of a hundred different bells and gongs. More joined in. And still more. On and on it went.

Jane looked over to Perry Mannerback, who was standing in the center of the elegant entryway, his eyes closed in bliss. The tolling of the hour went on for nearly a minute, then began to taper off until all that was left was the rhythmic pulsing that Jane had noticed before. Now she knew what it was—the ticking of a thousand clocks!

"I hear you collect clocks," said Jane, pointing out the obvious.

"Come on, I'll show you," said Perry, bursting with excitement. "Come on!"

Jane followed him past the huge flower arrangement in the inner hall to the living room. If the vestibule had been spectacular, this room was positively incredible, a good fifty feet long and another thirty wide, furnished exquisitely with English antiques, plush sofas, Tiffany table lamps. It was the clocks, however, that dominated everything.

Clocks sat on the marble ledge above the huge fireplace. Clocks crowded the Delft-tiled windowsills. Clocks packed the enormous breakfront. Clocks filled the shelves between the windows looking out over Central Park.

One corner of the room had a collection of old-fashioned "anniversary" clocks under glass domes. Another corner teemed with carriage clocks of every size. The walls were hung with regulator clocks. Scores of brackets held scores of bracket clocks. Table clocks sat on every table. Mantel clocks occupied every mantel. There were clocks with human faces and clocks with painted scenes. There were big clocks that had pendulums and tiny clocks that fit into nutshells. There were ormolu clocks, lantern clocks, cartel clocks, and skeleton clocks. Against every inch of wall space not taken by a window or a Renoir were fine long case clocks with gold and silver faces standing at attention, like an army awaiting orders.

"Do you like clocks?" asked their general.

"I sleep next to one," said Jane weakly. "He wakes me up in the morning."

"Me, too!"

"Why am I not surprised?"

A door on the far side of the room opened and a squat woman in a white uniform marched out.

"Perry Mannerback, what you doing here?" she demanded angrily, her hands on her hips. "You supposed to be having cocktails with Aunt Eunice. You supposed to be there for dinner. She call twice."

"I'm just here to pick up something, Olinda. This is Jane Sailor, Olinda. Jane's my new bodyguard-assistant. Olinda winds all the clocks. And she takes care of me, don't you, Olinda?"

"Olinda going take care of you with a skillet, one these days," said Olinda, shaking her fat fist. "You get out fast and go see Aunt Eunice."

"Okay."

"And you eat your vegetables tonight at dinner. You hear me, Perry Mannerback?"

"I will, I will."

Olinda muttered something in Spanish that sounded unmistakably like a curse, then huffing with disgust disappeared back behind the door through which she had come.

"Come on," said Perry, laughing. "We better get that magazine and scram out of here before you have to give Olinda a karate chop or something. I think it's in my study."

He was already in motion. Jane followed her employer though

the long room. At the far end, he opened a pair of double doors. Two big, beautiful Irish setters excitedly rushed up to meet them as they entered a smaller room (this one only four times the size of Jane's entire apartment). Perry squatted down, gave the dogs hugs, and happily let them lick him all over.

There were clocks here, too, though not as many as outside. Mostly they sat on end tables and on the gigantic Louis XV rococo and gilt bronze desk that dominated the room. On three walls were floor-to-ceiling bookcases filled with leatherbound books. The ceiling was elaborately detailed plasterwork, and the wood of the bookcases matched the paneling on the single exposed wall behind the desk.

It was the painting on this wall that took Jane's breath away. It was about six feet high and perhaps seven feet across. The subject was a naked woman sitting on a staircase. She stared out defiantly at the viewer, her bare chest arched forward. In between her carelessly parted legs was a garishly glazed ceramic clock without hands that Jane recognized right away.

It was Grandmother Sylvie's clock. It was just as hideous as Jane remembered: blue columns, red base, yellow central dial. No wonder she had decided to keep it in the basement. And she knew very well the worn wooden stairs with too-high treads on which the nude sat, too. They were the stairs from Aaron Sailor's loft on Greene Street, the stairs he had fallen down eight years ago.

"My father painted this," said Jane in a subdued voice.

"Isn't it great?" demanded Perry. "A clock with no hands. It says something about the fleeting nature of existence, don't you think?"

"I suppose so," said Jane, somehow doubting that philosophy was why this painting had appealed to Perry Mannerback. Was he one of those guys who bought *Playboy* for the stories? Perry might be a little boy, but he was a little boy who had been through three wives, Jane reminded herself. She was a little disappointed with him for wanting such a painting. And perhaps with her father for having painted it. There was something blatantly sexual about this nude that Jane had never seen before in Aaron Sailor's work. It was almost a portrait of lust.

The two dogs came over to sniff Jane's scent and lick her hands as Perry rummaged through his desk for the magazine he was looking for.

"I've never seen this painting before," Jane said after a moment, unable to take her eyes off the nude.

"I was just walking down the street and saw a picture of it in the window of this gallery on Madison Avenue," said Perry, closing the final drawer of the desk and turning his attention to a basket of papers underneath a gilded French library table. "I went right upstairs and bought it. That's when I met your father. He was there with the dealer lady, and we discussed art and everything. And the fleeting nature of existence."

"I wonder who the model is. She's very beautiful."

"I don't know her," said Perry, suddenly shooting bolt upright. "I have no idea who she is. No idea whatsoever."

"I didn't say . . ."

"It's just a painting of a woman," Perry declared indignantly. "It was the clock I was interested in. Only the clock. I never met her. I have no idea who she is, none at all."

His denial was so overstated that Jane again wanted to laugh at what a dreadful liar he was. Only this wasn't funny.

"Those are the stairs of my father's loft that she's sitting on," Jane pressed. "The stairs he fell down."

"Oh really?" said Perry Mannerback, his voice even louder and more unnatural. "Is that so?"

"Yes, that's so."

"Come on," he said, abandoning his search and walking hastily to the door. "Aunt Eunice is probably having a conniption. She'll have to find out about sex chat rooms on her own. I'll have Leonid take you home after he drops me off."

Jane followed him back through the vast living room filled

with clocks, the smiling red dogs bringing up the rear. Perry began chattering about Aunt Eunice, clock dials, Mars Bars—obviously anything to change the subject.

But now Jane knew for certain that Perry Mannerback knew more about her father than he was telling. What did he know? Why was he lying? And who was the woman sitting naked on Aaron Sailor's stairs?

The next day, Perry Mannerback arranged for Aaron Sailor to be brought from the nursing home in Great Neck to the head trauma unit of Yorkville East End Hospital on Manhattan's Upper East Side for tests.

On the way to Aunt Eunice's apartment at the Dakota the previous evening, Jane had mentioned in passing how the aide at Royaume Israel had dropped Aaron Sailor out of bed and that he had mysteriously begun to speak. She had done so merely to make conversation and break the tension that had developed between her and Perry because of the painting in his study. Naturally, she hadn't revealed what her father had been saying, only that he had begun to talk. Perry hadn't even seemed to have been listening.

Jane had arrived at the OmbiCorp office at ten o'clock the next morning—her second Friday on the job, the first being last week at the circus—ready for another day of philanthropy and fun, fully prepared to pretend that the incident with the painting had never happened.

Instead of dashing off as usual, however, Perry had sat her

down on his big office sofa, fixed her in a serious, puppy-dog gaze, and asked if she would permit him to get Aaron Sailor the medical care he deserved.

Jane's first reaction was horror. Aaron Sailor was gone. Nothing would bring him back, certainly not more doctors, more tests. What could she say, however? Please don't try to help my father? Don't even go through the motions, just leave him there in Great Neck, warehoused in the dark?

Dealing with all the bureaucracy that such a move required would take forever, Jane had protested. It was already taken care of, Perry had answered. It would cost a fortune, she had said. Perry had replied that he had a fortune. Miss Fripp then promptly appeared with some papers for Jane to sign. By the time the feature at the Armex Patterson Fifty-seventh Street Cinema got out at three o'clock, Aaron Sailor had been brought in by ambulance from Long Island for a week at one of the foremost cranial-injury treatment centers in the world.

"Now, don't you worry about a thing," said Perry as they pulled up in front of MoMA, where he had a board of directors' meeting that afternoon. "I'm sure the doctors at Yorkville East End will be able to help. They took out my tonsils and Dad's gallbladder. They're the best."

"I'm sure," said Jane uncertainly, as he got out of the car. "I'll see you on Monday."

"Oh, I forgot to ask," he said, leaning in the window. "Can you go out of town with me next week?"

"Go where?"

"Seattle," said Perry excitedly. "I've just learned about a clock there that I may want to buy. Very rare. We have to act fast, before the competition gets wind of it. Seattle's a really neat place. We'll see the Space Needle, Pike's Market, all kinds of fun stuff. We'll stay overnight. Or maybe a few days if we feel like it."

Jane frowned. Perry Mannerback was already paying her a

ridiculous salary to do practically nothing. He was treating her father to a series of exorbitantly expensive medical tests. Now he wanted to take her on what sounded like a vacation. Was a hired playmate allowed to say no? Jane felt obligated and hated it. She had never had a job like this. What were her rights?

"It'll be strictly business," said Perry, misunderstanding her discomfort. "I don't have any ulterior motives, believe me. I'm not that kind of fellow—no, no, not in this day and age. You don't have to come if you don't want to. I just think it will be fun. We'll fly first class. I always fly first class. You'll have your own hotel room and everything."

"Look, Mr. Mannerback . . ."

"Please call me Perry. We're friends now. Everybody calls me Perry."

"Look . . . Perry," said Jane, "I appreciate what you're doing for my father, I really do, but it's just . . ."

"You want to be here when they're doing the tests, don't you?" said Perry, trying to snap his fingers. "Of course you do. How could I be so stupid?"

"No, no, it's not that," said Jane. "My being here isn't going to make any difference. Nothing's going to make any difference."

"You mustn't say that. There's always hope."

But there wasn't. Not for her father. Her father was gone, Jane wanted to scream. Why couldn't anybody admit the truth?

"All right," she said in a quiet voice. "I'll go to Seattle with you."

"You will?"

"I said so, didn't I?"

"Wonderful," said Perry Mannerback, clapping his hands. "We'll have a great time. Leonid, you take Miss Sailor right over to the hospital to see her father, then wait for her and take her home. She's got to rest up over the weekend for our big trip."

"Yes, Mr. Mennerbeck," said Leonid from the front seat.

"We'll pick you up at your apartment on Monday morning, nine o'clock sharp; our flight's at ten-thirty. Pack for a few days in case we decide to stay over. We'll have a lot of fun, you'll see."

Perry marched off into the museum with the same satisfied expression on his face as when he wrote out a check to a struggling Off Off Broadway theatre group or for a child with a leaky heart valve. The limousine inched into traffic. Jane slumped back in her seat.

There had been altogether too much for her to absorb about Perry Mannerback and his strange, frenetic world in one week. Too many new people. Too many facts. Too many questions. She really did need a weekend to rest, but tomorrow was the evening she had promised to go out to dinner with Dad's rapacious art dealer, Elinore King. That would be about as restful as a night in a cement mixer.

Along the way to the hospital, people turned and tried to make out who she was, sitting there in the back of the big black limousine. No, I'm nobody important, Jane wanted to roll down the window and shout. I'm just a poor dope who's in over her head and doesn't have the sense to get out.

Yorkville East End stood out like a castle amidst the elegant apartment buildings of East End Avenue. A few blocks away was the mayor's residence, Gracie Mansion. In Carl Schurz Park across the street, children played, dogs frolicked, and signs warned of rat poison. Leonid dropped Jane off at the front door of the hospital and went to try to find a place to double-park.

If Royaume Israel was medical dead storage, Yorkville East End was the front lines of the war against injury and disease. The central waiting room bustled with the kind of well-heeled visitors you expected to see at one of the most prestigious hospitals in the city. Doctors in business suits barked urgent orders into cellular telephones. Others in green scrubs marched down the halls like soldiers on parade. Nurses and orderlies in starched white uniforms pursued various life-and-death missions.

As instructed by one of the three crisply efficient receptionists at the front desk, Jane followed a yellow line on the floor through a maze of corridors and double doors until she came to a well-lighted wing somewhere at the north end of the sprawling hospital complex. A wall plaque proclaimed this to be the head trauma unit. Here, a nurse at a central station directed Jane to a semi-private room down at the end of the hall, explaining that her father's tests would start in the morning.

It was a small room, painted a cheerful apricot, with a pair of windows looking out over the East River. Curtains attached to tracks in the ceiling could be pulled around each of the two beds to give the occupants an illusion of privacy. A television set was mounted on a large extendable metal arm at one side of the room, though the room's occupants weren't watching anything, both of them being unconscious and hooked up to banks of electronic monitoring equipment. One was a heavyset African American man whose head was turbaned in bandages and who was breathing laboriously. The other was Aaron Sailor.

There was an armchair in the corner of the room, next to a tiny desk—in case a patient made a miraculous recovery and wanted to alert the family by letter, perhaps. Jane sat down and stared at her father's still form. The electronic lines on the monitor attached to various parts of his anatomy moved in lazy patterns that she couldn't interpret. A few new inscriptions now graced the cast on his arm. One read: "Hearty good wishes for a speedy recovery. Cordially, Benton Contino." Another said: "So very sorry for your suffering, Reema."

Her father's roommate suddenly started to wheeze a little louder. The lines on his monitor began to do a tango. This man's injury apparently had been a recent one. Perhaps there was still a chance he could wake up and return to his life and loved ones with nothing more than a big headache and a raise in his health insurance premiums. Jane wondered whether she should call a nurse or something, but the electronic activity soon quieted down.

Jane sat for a few more minutes, wanting desperately to feel something. Love. Pity. Hope. Nothing came except depression and a vague sense of guilt. Her thoughts drifted to tomorrow night's dinner with Elinore and her husband. At least she'd get fed, Jane told herself. She could have a couple glasses of wine and beg off early with a headache. And Elinore might even be able to tell her something about the nude in Perry's painting, the one he had acted so mysterious about. Then, next week, Jane would be on the West Coast with Perry.

Jane had worked in several different cities in California but never anywhere in the Pacific Northwest. She'd once been up for a job choreographing a season of fights at the Oregon Rep, but they'd gone with somebody else. Seattle was supposed to be a beautiful area and one she'd always wanted to see.

A trip with Perry might even be fun. Jane never got the chance to fly first class and they were bound to be staying in a nice hotel. She'd be collecting a salary all the while, besides. What was so terrible about that? And what was wrong with Perry Mannerback paying for some of the best doctors in the country to see what they could do for her father?

As if on cue, a deadened voice from the still figure on the bed interrupted her thoughts.

"Don't do it, Perry," said Aaron Sailor. "No, Perry, no."

"Janie, darling" screeched Elinore King, throwing her beefy arms around Jane and kissing the air. "I'm so happy! Here you are! Here we are! Isn't it wonderful?"

Jane tried not to look shocked. Though she had spoken to Elinore a few times since the Fyfe Museum had become interested in Aaron Sailor's work, Jane hadn't seen her in person for nearly eight years. To say Elinore had changed didn't begin to describe the situation.

Her father's dealer was still a few inches shorter than Jane, but she had somehow expanded to three times her previous size. Elinore's delicate features—the small eyes, little teeth, and tiny turned-up nose that had been pretty the last time Jane had seen her—now looked piggish in her bloated face. What had once been long blond hair was now short and hamster-colored, and so brittle-looking that Jane had to suppress an urge to give it a little squeeze to see if it would break.

Elinore had stuffed herself into a gray silk Mandarin-style tunic, which might have been exotic on a thin young model, but on Elinore looked like someone's bad attempt to gift-wrap a barrel. A fifteen-thousand-dollar Rolex graced her wrist. Great globs of gold dangled from her earlobes. Her fingers sparkled with diamonds and rubies in thick settings.

"Welcome, welcome," said an eager male voice.

Elinore spun around like a three-hundred-pound top.

"I'm saying hello to her, Gregory, just let me say hello. Why are you always interrupting me? He's always like that, Janie, always interrupting me."

"What a wonderful, wonderful pleasure," said Gregory King, reaching over Elinore to sandwich Jane's hand in both of his. "Simply fantastic. Elinore's told me so much . . ."

"Please, Greg, please!" said Elinore. "I'm trying to talk to her."

Jane had never met Elinore's husband and was somehow expecting a sleazy huckster type. To her surprise, Gregory King turned out to be a tall, handsome man who looked like Cary Grant had at fifty: sensitive brown eyes, a strong chin, thick black hair with a distinguished touch of gray at the temples. He wore an elegant blue suit, a quietly patterned tie, and a white handkerchief in his breast pocket. His hands were warm and strong.

"Come on, let's sit down," said Elinore, grabbing Jane by the arm and leading her another two steps into the room. "They better have our table ready. Greg, tell them to give us our table. You're going to love this place, Janie."

"You're going to absolutely love it," echoed Gregory King happily, motioning to the hostess.

Jane smiled politely as the woman led them to their table and Elinore rattled on nonstop about how nice it was to see Jane and what a wonderful place this was and how she and Gregory were such an "in" couple, always on the prowl for wonderful new restaurants to take out all the important people that they knew.

*Les Matins* was an intimate, one-room affair with no more than twenty tables in a space that had been designed to look like a country farmhouse. The floors were wide pine planks. Baskets hung from the ceiling. A gas fire burned in a tiny fireplace, producing further atmosphere without additional heat.

"So, let me look at you, Janie," said Elinore after they had taken their seats. "You're all grown-up, and you've dyed your hair red, isn't that fun? Now I want to hear everything. What's been going on with your . . . you know . . . that fighting stuff you do and all that? And your dad, how's he?"

"He's fine," said Jane meaninglessly, still trying to locate Elinore's old face within all the extra flesh, unable to get over how much she had changed.

"We used to have marvelous conversations in the old days, your father and I," said Gregory King, his face suddenly serious. "Very nice man. Really a shame about what happened."

Their waitress, a slender and crisply efficient young blonde with the poise of an actress (which she probably was), placed menus in front of them and departed.

"It's such a pleasure to finally meet you, Janie, after all these years," Gregory King went on.

"Oh, you've met her before, Greg," said Elinore. "What's the matter with you?"

"No, he's right," said Jane. "We've never met."

"Well, that's amazing," said Elinore, picking something out

of her ear. "I thought everyone knew Greg. He's a doctor, you know. An endocrinologist, whatever the hell that is. Why couldn't you be a plastic surgeon, that's what I want to know? That's where all the money is."

"That's right," said Greg with a big laugh. "That's where the real money is. But actually the secretions of the thyroid, the adrenals and the pituitary glands are very . . ."

"Everything here is so wonderful," said Elinore, cutting him off. "We'll have to have appetizers and everything. And save room for dessert. This dinner is going to cost us an absolute fortune, but you're worth it, Janie. You're the daughter of a great painter, you know."

Elinore opened her fancy menu and started reading off the dishes and rattling on about how wonderful and fantastic everything was. Jane finally settled on Copper River salmon and wild mushrooms. The Kings opted for the veal. Dr. King ordered a pair of two-hundred-dollar California cabernets against Jane's protests. Elinore made sure that everyone within earshot understood how much it would cost.

"So you practice on the East Side?" Jane asked Dr. King when the waitress departed with their orders.

"He has an office on Park Avenue," answered Elinore. "For all those people with endocrine problems."

Elinore laughed uproariously at her little joke. So did Dr. King. Jane tried to smile.

"I'm also affiliated with Yorkville East End," he said proudly.

"They just brought my father there for tests," said Jane without thinking. "It's a very good hospital, I understand."

"What kind of tests?" demanded Elinore.

"Oh, just some tests," said Jane, mentally kicking herself for bringing it up.

"I thought he was . . . that your father was . . . you know," said Elinore, waving her hand at the side of her head. Suddenly, her expression changed. "Is there something new? Is he taking a turn for the worse? Oh, my God! Is it, you know? Like . . . the end?"

"He just took a fall and has been mumbling things, that's all," said Jane.

"What a relief," said Elinore, placing one hand over her titanic bosom and fanning herself with the other. "I was worried there for a minute. I thought he was . . . you know. But is he waking up? Do they think he's going to wake up?"

Jane shook her head.

"My God," shrieked Elinore, "it must be costing you a mint! That hospital is the most expensive place in town."

Jane shrugged.

"I promise to look in on him this week, Janie," said Gregory soberly. "See how things are going."

"Janie, Jane honey, Jane," said Elinore, patting Jane's hand, her piggy eyes sparkling. "I know we've maybe had our little differences, but you know I'm your friend, don't you? We go back . . . since you were . . . you know, like a teenager and all. I care about you. I really do. If you want to talk, I'm always there for you. And if you need help with the money, I'm sure we can think of something. I know you don't have a pot to pee in."

"Actually, Perry Mannerback is paying," said Jane in her sweetest voice. Now that the cat was out of the bag she might as well see where it would run.

"Perry Mannerback!" exclaimed Elinore, looking genuinely astonished. "How did you get Perry Mannerback to pay?"

"I didn't get him to pay. He volunteered. I'm working for him."

"No!" said Elinore, falling back against her chair in amazement. "When did this happen?"

"I called him up to talk about my father and he offered me a job," said Jane, happy to see Elinore so nonplussed.

"That's fantastic," said Elinore. "Simply fantastic. But I still don't understand. Why is he paying for Aaron?"

"Actually, I'm not really sure myself," said Jane. "Do you know of any reason why my father might be mumbling things about Perry, repeating his name?"

"I'm thinking," said Elinore, holding up her fork like a divining rod. "I'm trying to think. But nothing's happening."

"Isn't this a lovely room?" asked Gregory King. "It reminds me of . . ."

"Will you please shut up, Greg?" snapped Elinore. "You're so stupid. What's the matter with you?"

"I just . . ."

"He's always like that," said Elinore to Jane angrily. "He just butts in like the village idiot. It's really amazing he could get through medical school. Do you know that, Greg? Do you know how stupid you are sometimes?"

"Yes, yes," said Gregory, reddening. "That's probably true. I'm sorry, El."

Jane looked away in embarrassment. If the purpose of this evening was to win Jane's trust, Elinore certainly had a strange way of going about it. Did she really think she would make a better impression by castrating her husband before the appetizer?

"You know what I think?" declared Elinore, buttering a roll and stuffing it into her mouth.

"About what?" asked Jane, wondering how she was going to get through an entire evening of this.

"I think Perry Mannerback is trying to hook up with you so he can get an inside line on more of Aaron's paintings."

Jane couldn't keep from rolling her eyes, the idea was so ridiculous.

"No, I'm not kidding," pressed Elinore. "Perry owns that one painting of Aaron's and he wants another."

"I really don't think so."

"Janie," said Elinore to Jane, shaking her head. "Darling. Sweetie. You're a very smart girl. You're a brilliant girl. But you're very naïve about a lot of things. You don't know how these people operate. This Perry Mannerback is a very shrewd and sharp operator. If he's paying for all these tests for Aaron, he's not doing it for charity, believe me."

"Charity is practically his middle name," said Jane. "He spends most of his time giving away his money."

"Which is why he's probably looking for a nice painting he can give himself," said Elinore triumphantly.

The waitress arrived with their expensive wine at this point, mercifully cutting her short. The next hour was a blur of fancy food, husband-bashing, and Elinore's opinions about everything under the sun.

Jane found herself drinking more than she was used to and tuning out. It wasn't until dessert and Sauternes that Elinore finally brought the conversation to what she really wanted: Aaron Sailor's paintings.

"So, Janie, honey," she said, sticking her spoon into Jane's *crème brûlée* and helping herself to a taste. "You don't mind if I try a little of this, do you?"

"I'm not going to ask for it back," said Jane wearily.

"I think I know what's bothering you. It's the percentage, isn't it?"

"I don't know what you're talking about."

"You know," said Elinore. "The seventy percent I'm getting from Aaron. That's what a dealer gets, it's totally standard, believe me. Isn't it totally standard, Greg?"

"I . . ." Greg agreed before she cut him off.

"I'm the one who has all the expenses," said Elinore. "I'm the one who does all the work, but I understand how you feel. We can split sixty-forty if that's what you want. That's incredibly fair. I don't care about the money. It's not the money I'm doing this for, it's your father."

"I'm glad you've brought this up, Elinore," said Jane, happy that she could finally put her cards on the table. "I've tried to tell you how I feel about this before, but I haven't been able to get through to you. Please listen to me. I'm not ready to sell my father's paintings. They're all I have left of him. Maybe I'll want to do something in the future, but not now. I'm just not going to do anything right now. Okay?"

"You're right to take your time," said Elinore. "You're very smart. I mean, I don't want to say this, Janie, this is the last thing I would ever say in a million years, but if Aaron dies, everything is going to be even more valuable, that's all I'm saying. Just think about it, that's all I ask. I know you need the money. You can't imagine the work I've had to do to get everything to this point. Remember, you owe me."

"Look, Elinore," said Jane evenly, "I'm trying to be nice about this, but I don't owe you anything. The Fyfe decided to include my father in their show on their own, not because of anything you've done. I haven't heard from you for eight years. Now all of a sudden it's like you're all over me, and it isn't because you like me so much or respect my father's work, it's just about money. Let's be honest."

Elinore brought her hand to her bosom.

"Janie, Janie. You're really hurting me, you know that? Here we're having this beautiful dinner, and you're making me sound like I'm some kind of monster. I mean, if I were this big monster, why would so many artists come to me? They love me, they owe their careers to me, their entire careers. Don't they, Greg? I'm not such a monster, Greg? Am I?"

"No, no," said Greg, "of course not."

"Of course not," agreed Elinore, whacking the table with her spoon for emphasis. "You know, Janie, just because I'm a successful art dealer doesn't mean that I'm not still a woman with a heart and feelings and all that."

Jane didn't say anything, damned if she was going to let Elinore manipulate her into feeling guilty.

"Just think about it, don't say yes or no, just think about it, that's all I ask," said Elinore. "That article is going to be in the what-do-you-call-it magazine tomorrow. The *Times*. There's going to be big new interest in Aaron's paintings and we've got to take advantage of it. That's why Perry Mannerback is doing all of this for your father, you'll see. It's just like I said—he has that one painting and he wants another. That's what this is all about."

"Fine, let's talk about Perry's painting," said Jane. The evening wouldn't be a total waste if Elinore could just answer a few questions. "Do you know who the model for it was?"

"The naked girl, you mean? I met her at some party your father brought her to. Creepy-looking, if you ask me. And she didn't have a good body at all, not at all."

"Do you know her name?"

"Don't have a clue," said Elinore dismissively, trying to scrape a last bit of chocolate from her empty dessert plate. "She wasn't even pretty. She was nothing."

"Did Perry Mannerback know her?" asked Jane.

Elinore shrugged.

"I have no idea," she said. "I suppose Aaron could have introduced them. Why? Don't tell me Perry wants another painting with that same girl in it? What an idiot! Aaron only used her in that one painting."

The table fell silent. Jane tried not to feel disappointed. Elinore looked over to her husband, who hadn't touched the kiwi tart in front of him and was staring into his Sauternes.

"Why are you so quiet all of a sudden?" she demanded.

"Oh, I'm just thinking about poor Aaron," he said with a sigh.

"Hey," said Elinore, brightening. "I got an idea. Janie, why don't you bring Perry over to the gallery this week? Then we can find out for sure what he's looking for."

"I told you, Elinore. He's not interested in art."

"Just take five minutes. Five minutes won't hurt you. Can't you do that much for me after all I've done for you?"

Jane couldn't stand it any longer. She had controlled herself the entire evening, but now she could actually see herself in choreographic detail grabbing Elinore by the hair, banging her head a dozen times on the table, and then stuffing a napkin down her throat. It was time to bail out.

"This really has been fun," Jane said, standing up, looking at her watch. "But look at the time. I'm afraid I have to be going. Thank you for a lovely dinner."

"But it's still early," screeched Elinore. "I thought we'd go out for an after-dinner drink. You're not going to desert us so soon, are you? We're having such a good time."

"I'm sorry, but I have to go."

"So nice to have met you, Janie," said Greg with a big smile, reaching over and shaking Jane's hand. He had stood up the moment she had risen from the table. "Don't worry about a thing. I'll look in on Aaron. I'm sure they'll take good care of him."

"Wait a second, Janie, here's another thought," said Elinore, waving her napkin for attention. "If you don't want to come by the gallery, why don't I stop by Perry's office next week? That way you can reintroduce us in an informal kind of way. We could talk about art."

"I'm afraid that won't be possible," said Jane curtly. "We're going to be out of town. We're leaving Monday morning for Seattle."

"That's fantastic," said Elinore, grabbing Jane's sleeve. "My daughter lives in Seattle. She's a fantastic girl. Isn't she, Greg?"

"Great girl. Fabulous."

"Everybody is crazy about her," Elinore rattled on, "works for this nonprofit, with the environment and all. What time's your flight?"

"Ten-thirty," said Jane, removing Elinore's hand from her sleeve and resisting the urge to break the woman's wrist in the process. Other diners were looking up from their food in annoyance with looks that said, "Go, already."

"You're going to think about what I said, aren't you?" said Elinore as Jane began walking away. "Aren't you?"

Jane shot a frozen smile over her shoulder and practically knocked over a table as she made her way to the door.

"Call me when you get back," shouted Elinore across the room as Jane escaped into the night.

She promised herself that it would be a long, long time before she saw Elinore King again.

ecccccccccccccccccccccc — Seven

"The captain has turned off the 'fasten your seat belt' sign,'"
said the soft voice of the stewardess over the loudspeaker. "You are
now free to move around the cabin if you like."

"It's what's called a lighthouse clock," said Perry Mannerback
happily. "The dial is rather like that of an old-fashioned alarm
clock, but it sits under this high glass dome atop a cylindrical
mahogany base. The whole affair is a few feet tall and looks like a
lighthouse, hence the name."

Jane smiled. Perry had been talking nonstop about the clock
they were flying out to see since he had picked her up this morning.
This was the third time he had described it for her, but it was
impossible not to get drawn into his excitement. Judging from the
beatific look in his eyes right now, Jane was willing to bet that he
was getting ready to tell her again about the clock's maker, Simon
Willard, who had belonged to a family of clockmakers in early
nineteenth-century Massachusetts.

Jane was dressed in comfortable clothes for the long flight,
jeans and a long-sleeve cotton rugby shirt. Perry had on his usual

dapper outfit: black blazer, gray slacks, robin's egg blue vest. His only concession to comfort was the ascot he wore in lieu of a tie. Jane had never seen anyone in real life wear an ascot. On Perry it somehow looked natural.

They were seated at the front of the first-class cabin. Perry had taken the window seat and made "vroom-vroom" noises during takeoff. Jane had sipped her complimentary orange juice and enjoyed the wide reclining seat, about as far from the cramped contraptions in coach as a La-Z-Boy was from a bicycle seat. Two paperback Shaw plays were stashed in a carry-on bag under the seat in front of her, but Jane had the feeling that between Perry Mannerback's clock lectures and the in-flight movie, she wasn't going to have much chance to read. Maybe she'd try after the layover that the plane was scheduled to make in St. Louis.

"The lighthouse clock was Simon Willard's last invention and is quite rare," said Perry excitedly. "It was a terrible flop actually, the Edsel of clocks, but now everyone wants one. There's even one in the White House. Did I tell you about the Willards? There were plenty of great British clockmakers running around during Georgian times, you see, but in America such artisans were rare and the Willards were the absolute tops. They were a whole family of clockmakers. There was Simon—who also invented the banjo clock, of course—Benjamin, Ephraim . . ."

"Well, hello there, what a coincidence, what a surprise," shrieked a voice like fingernails on a blackboard.

Jane looked up in amazement to see the bloated form of Elinore King standing in the aisle beside her, smiling like a hyena.

"What are you doing here, Elinore?" Jane demanded, unable to believe her eyes.

"Perry Mannerback, isn't it?" said Elinore, ignoring Jane, reaching her hand over to Perry, who had stood up politely. He might be an eccentric screwball, but his manners were impeccable.

"Remember me, Elinore King? I was Janie's dad's art dealer.

I sold you that painting, remember? The big one with the naked girl and the clock?"

"Oh yes, indeed," said Perry, shaking her hand. "I remember very well. We talked about the fleeting nature of existence. Most interesting. And then you gave me that special thingamajig. What was it called? Oh, yes. The discount."

"What are you doing here, Elinore?" asked Jane again, through clenched teeth.

"Well, Janie, after we talked about my daughter in Seattle the other night, I got so lonesome I decided to fly out and see her," said Elinore breezily. "It's been ages since we've had a visit, and I just love her to pieces. This was the only flight I could get at the last minute. All the direct flights were sold out weeks ago. Of course, I always fly first class, it's the only way to go. But I want to talk to Perry. Perry, it's so amazing to run into you like this. I was just thinking about you. You saw this, didn't you?"

Elinore passed over a copy of Sunday's *New York Times Magazine*, which she had been holding behind her back. It was opened to a half-page reproduction of his painting, the seated nude on the staircase with Grandmother Sylvie's handless clock between her legs.

"No, I didn't," Perry said, taking the magazine, and pulling out a pair of half-moon reading glasses from his inside pocket with which to study it better. "Why, that's my painting. This is fabulous!"

"It's a story all about Aaron and his art, and the big show they're having at the what-do-you-call-it museum in San Francisco," screeched Elinore cheerfully. "And about me, of course."

Jane rolled her eyes. This was too much, even for Elinore.

"You see? Here's a picture of me, standing right next to Aaron during my show," said Elinore, turning the page to a large black-and-white photo of Jane's father and the Elinore of eight years ago, with a dazed-looking Gregory King in the background (in the caption he was identified only as Mrs. King's husband). "Of course, this is when I was young and beautiful, but I hope I'm not completely so terrible now."

"No, not at all," said Perry, leafing through the rest of the article with evident delight. "I didn't realize that your father was such an important artist, Jane. Did you read this?"

"I read it," said Jane evenly. The way Elinore had managed to get herself quoted throughout the piece, it sounded as if she had found Aaron Sailor one morning in a melon patch and then taught him how to paint.

"It's an incredible story, isn't it, Janie?" said Elinore. "The same critics who were spitting on Aaron's work when I had my show are now going crazy. I'd love to tell you all about it, Perry, about why your painting was such a great investment. That is, if you don't mind, Janie."

"I really don't think Perry is very interested in art," said Jane.

"No, no, that's all right, Jane," said Perry. "I wouldn't mind hearing."

"Hey, here's an idea," said Elinore. "Janie, why don't you and I trade seats for a little while, so Perry and I can talk? That way I can tell him the whole story."

"Elinore . . ."

"Oh, look how protective she is of you, Perry. You know, you're so smart to hire Janie. She's a great girl, a fantastic girl. So can I sit down? I don't want to impose or anything."

"Not at all," said Perry Mannerback. "That is, course, if it's all right with you, Jane?"

"That's right, Janie," said Elinore. "If you don't want to move, if it's too much trouble or something, you just say the word. I'll just go right back to my seat. No problem. I'll be okay, really I will."

Jane opened her mouth to protest, but realized instantly how petty and childish it would seem. Elinore had completely outmaneuvered her.

"Fine," said Jane in a quiet voice, standing up. There was no shame in walking away from a fight that you could not win. She would gain nothing by throwing a temper tantrum in front of Perry.

"I'm just back over there," said Elinore, pointing at an empty seat several rows behind them in the spacious first-class cabin. "Next to that handsome young man with this divine British accent. He's very nice, some kind of stockbroker or something. Maybe I can get him to ask you out on a date when you're in Seattle."

"Isn't Janie such a doll?" Elinore was saying as Jane grabbed the bag from under her seat and stomped away. "You should have seen her when she used to come home from college on the holidays. She was so cute with the stories of her little boyfriends and her drama club stuff . . ."

Jane plopped down into Elinore's seat several rows back. She reached into her bag for the paperback copy of *Candida*. She opened the book, closed it just as quickly, and stuffed it back into the bag. Then she sat with her arms crossed in front of her, seething.

"I could simply kiss you," said a bright British voice at her side.

"What?" snapped Jane, looking over angrily into a pair of large blue eyes. The man in the seat next to her was a gangly, slightly goofy-looking fellow in his mid-thirties. He had a thick mop of reddish hair that was long overdue for a trim, about a million freckles, and a twinkle in his eye.

"I said, I could simply kiss you," he repeated. "Or kiss you in a more complicated fashion if you prefer. I certainly owe you something for rescuing me from that horrible woman. She's been talking at me since I sat down, and I have no idea what she was saying. I think she wanted to sell me a subscription to the *New York Times*."

Jane's new seat companion pointed to the floor between them. In a Bergdorf Goodman shopping bag were at least twenty copies of the same *New York Times Sunday Magazine* that Elinore had brought over to show Perry. Jane felt some of the venom run out of her.

"I hope you didn't buy anything," she said.

"Certainly not," he replied with a lopsided grin. "I have pretty good instincts about people. My instincts in this case wanted to give her a whack with a cricket bat on the old brainpan. Is she a friend of yours?"

"I know Elinore, but she's no friend."

"I'm Valentine Treves. It's nice to meet a fellow redhead."

"Jane Sailor," Jane said, looking around, then blushing crimson when she realized he was talking about her. He was dressed in gray slacks and a sweater. An expensive leather briefcase was on the floor in front of him.

"How did you happen to get tangled up with such a character?" he asked with an easy laugh.

"She's something I inherited from my father."

"I understand perfectly. I got a hammertoe from mine."

Jane glanced at his big blue eyes, his unruly hair, his goofy smile. He was not her type at all. But pretty adorable. It was a good thing she had sworn off men.

"Elinore said you were a stockbroker?"

"Not really," he said. "I'm with a financial services company. My actual title is Vice President of Special Acquisitions, but I do a bit of everything. Strategic planning. Finance. Poetry."

"Poetry?"

He wasn't going to recite, was he? Was he an actor, too?

"Tell me three words. Any words you like."

"Ambushed," said Jane, craning her neck and trying to see what was happening between Perry and Elinore. "Witch. Murder."

"Give me just a minute," said Valentine, taking a small notebook out of his pocket and a silver pen. He began scribbling furiously, then tore out the page and gave it to Jane. She had to read it three times before she could believe it.

*Ambushed* by the puzzle of her face
I waited underneath my fears
And paused a moment in the chase
Of worldly men and flight and years.
Emerging from behind a rich
Unruliness and purity
She threw enchantments like a *witch*
and purged my insecurity.
Yet when I offered her my kiss
She fled in laughter, teasing me
With truths that I cannot dismiss
And eyes that I forever see.
I would have fit her like a glove.
*Murder* is the loss of love.

"How did you do this?" Jane finally asked, astonished. "You just sit down and it comes out in rhyme and everything?"

"It's just a peculiar little talent I have. Not very practical. I hope you don't think what I wrote was too personal. I had to go where the words you chose took me."

"I'm very impressed," she said, trying to hand it back to him.

"No, it's yours," said Valentine, shaking his head, smiling at her. "My gift."

"But I couldn't."

"You'll have to. Unless you'll take a kiss instead."

"Don't you want to keep a copy?"

"No. I wrote it for you."

Jane finally had to smile back.

"Thank you," she said, folding the sonnet carefully and putting it into her pocket. "I'm flattered. I suppose you write a lot of these. Impress lots of women."

"Not so many," said Valentine. "Women these days are more impressed that I'm in financial services. Poetry isn't very romantic any more, I'm afraid, except to us diehards. What about you? What do you do?"

"I'm a bodyguard-assistant."

"Indeed? Are you guarding and assisting some specific body, or can anyone apply?"

Jane ran a hand over her Raphael Renaissance Red locks.

"Elinore's probably boring my employer to death even as we speak."

"Who is he, I wonder?" said Valentine, scrunching together his eyebrows in exaggerated thought. "Gangster? Politician, perhaps? Famous movie star?"

"Just a businessman. His name is Perry Mannerback."

Valentine Treves sat forward with a start.

"Did you say Perry Mannerback? *The* Perry Mannerback?"

"Yes," said Jane. "Why? Do you know him?"

"Well, not personally," sputtered Valentine. "I know *of* him of course. He's a very prominent individual. Captain of industry and all that. You're really his bodyguard?"

"Bodyguard-assistant," said Jane, surprised at how impressed he was. It was easy to forget Perry's importance in the world after you had eaten a few dozen gummy bears with him.

"However did you get into that, I wonder?"

Jane sat back and began to tell him. She told him about her own peculiar little talent and about her work in the theatre. She told him that she had taken the job with Perry as a summer lark, not wanting to get into the complicated story of her father. Valentine listened, asking questions, making wry comments and funny observations. After a while Jane grew less self-conscious and found herself laughing.

Half an hour later, they were happily arguing about whether Richard Rodgers wrote better music with Oscar Hammerstein 2ᵈ or Lorenz Hart (Jane voted for Hart), when Elinore King appeared in the aisle, smiling like a socialite who's just had sex with her worst enemy's husband.

"So I see you two kids are hitting it off," said Elinore. "Didn't I tell you he was cute, Janie? I have such a knack about people, don't I?"

"I really resent your being here, Elinore," said Jane, rising stiffly, all her anger returning. Meeting Valentine had been so unexpected and pleasant that she had almost forgotten what Elinore had just done. It came back now in a red-hot flash.

"Oh, come on," said Elinore, brushing her off with a laugh. "I'm just coming out to see my daughter. What's so terrible about that?"

"You know what I'm talking about."

"No, I don't. I really don't. You know, sweetie, I think you've been under a lot of stress, what with your father and all."

Jane grabbed her bag from under the seat.

"It was nice meeting you, Valentine," she said.

"A pleasure. Maybe we can talk again later."

"Perry wants to buy another painting, Janie," said Elinore smugly. "I said it would cost him at least sixty thousand dollars and he didn't bat an eye. Isn't it wonderful? Janie? Did you hear me? Did you hear what I said?"

Jane was already stalking up the aisle back to her seat. When she sat down, Perry Mannerback was staring out the window. His face was pale. The damage apparently was even worse than Jane had feared.

"Sorry to subject you to Elinore's sales pitch," Jane said contritely. "I had no idea she was going to pull something like this."

"No, no," said Perry. "No bother."

"You don't really have to buy another of my father's paintings. They aren't even available. Elinore was wrong to lead you on like that."

"She said he was talking about me," said Perry, his voice dreamy and detached. "Your father. In his coma. Repeating my name."

"She had no right to tell you," said Jane angrily.

"It's true, then?"

"He's not conscious. He's raving."

"But he's said my name?"

Jane hadn't wanted to confront Perry with her father's ramblings. Not yet. Not like this. The choice had been taken away from her, however. Jane was furious at Elinore for spilling the beans but knew she had to take advantage of it while she could.

"Yes, my father has spoken your name," she said softly.

"What else has he said? What are his words?"

"He's saying, 'No, Perry, no. Don't do it, Perry,' " said Jane, watching him carefully. "He's saying, 'You're a liar, Perry; I know the truth.' "

"I see."

Perry turned and stared out the window again.

"Why would my father say things like that, Perry? What didn't he want you to do?"

"I have no idea," said Perry in a very small voice.

"Did you lie to him about something?"

"No."

"Perry, please look at me," said Jane. "What did you lie to him about? What were you going to do?"

"I don't know," said Perry, playing with his fingers, unable to meet her eyes. "Did I tell you about the Willards? The family of clockmakers?"

"Yes, you've already told me. Why do you think my father is saying these things?"

"The movie looks interesting," announced Perry, reaching over for his earphones and placing them on his head. "I'm going to watch the movie."

When the plane landed in St. Louis two hours later, Perry

was still dodging her questions. He seemed off in another world somewhere.

"I'm going to go out into the airport," he said, rising. "I've got to stretch my legs."

"I'll come with you," said Jane, stepping into the aisle and letting him pass in front of her to lead the way.

"No, no. You stay here. I'll be right back."

"Are you all right?"

"Fine, fine," he said, waving a manicured hand.

"I want to talk to you about my father."

"Soon, soon. When I get back. We'll be in Seattle in no time."

There was no way to argue with him. Perry Mannerback was still her employer, and he had made his wishes known in no uncertain terms. He darted up the aisle and out the open portal.

Jane sat down and tried to read a few pages of George Bernard Shaw. It was impossible, however, to concentrate on anything but what had happened with Perry Mannerback. This was not the way she had wanted to handle him at all. How could she get him to open up now that Elinore had put him on his guard?

Fifteen minutes passed and Perry didn't return. Half an hour. Jane's concern grew into alarm. She was about to leave the plane and go out to look for him when a blue-jacketed airline employee entered the cabin and made his way to her.

"Are you Miss Sailor?" he inquired, checking the seat number.

"Yes," said Jane. What now?

"Mr. Mannerback has been unexpectedly detained," he said, reaching into his inside coat pocket and handing her a flight envelope. "He asked me to give you your ticket. You're to go on to Seattle without him and check into the Regency Hotel where he's made reservations. He'll take a later flight. You're to wait in the room; he'll call when he gets in."

"But I should be with him," Jane said, starting to rise.

"He wants you to do as he says," said the man. "He says not to worry. He says he's sorry."

The man departed. Jane sat back, unable to think of anything else to do. The plane eventually took off. A minute after the seat belt sign had been turned off, Elinore appeared in the aisle at her side.

"What happened to Perry?" she demanded. "Why didn't he get back on the plane? I wanted to finalize things with him."

"You really have a lot of nerve, Elinore," said Jane, livid. With Perry gone, there was no longer a governor on her temper. Usually when her anger came out, it came out red-hot. This time, however, it was as cold as ice. "I can't believe you ambushed us like this."

Elinore waved her pudgy hand dismissively.

"Ambush, shmam-bush. I have legitimate business in Seattle. I'm going out to see my daughter. Is there a law against that?"

"You've gone too far this time, Elinore. You really have."

"Oh, come on, Janie, drop this self-righteous shit, okay? Didn't you hear what I said before? Perry wants to buy another of your father's paintings. Sight unseen. Sixty thousand dollars. I'm so stupid, I should have asked for more. He wouldn't know the difference."

"No," said Jane.

"Oh, you don't know this man the way I do," said Elinore happily. "He'll pay, I'm sure of it. We'll let him pick out whichever one he wants, and if it's one of the big ones, we can tell him it's a hundred thousand and he'll go for it. That kind of money is nothing to a man like Perry."

"You're not selling any of my father's paintings, Elinore. None. Not to Perry, not to anyone. Not now, not ever."

"Now, Janie, don't be like that, don't be a baby. We have an agreement. I have a contract. No matter how you sell those paintings, I'm going to get paid, so just relax and let me do my job, okay?"

"No, not okay," said Jane.

"Well, you have no choice."

"Yes, I do. I've decided that I'm not going to sell my father's paintings at all. I'm going to donate them to museums. The Fyfe will want some. I'm sure there are other museums that will be delighted to have the rest."

"Don't be ridiculous," said Elinore with a nervous little laugh, her beady eyes widening. "Don't you understand? We can finally make some money off of this. Maybe not a fortune, but sixty thousand isn't exactly chopped liver either. At least it's something after all these years, after all this has cost me with Aaron. Don't tell me that you don't need money."

"I don't want it."

"All right," Elinore snarled. "We'll split everything fifty-fifty. That's obviously what you're after, but I really resent the way you're doing this, Janie, cramming it down my throat like this. There are better ways to negotiate. I thought we were friends."

"We're not friends, Elinore," said Jane. "And I am not kidding. I'm donating the paintings to museums. I'm not going to take a nickel for them. Ever. And neither are you."

"You'll calm down," said Elinore. "You'll think about this and see I'm just doing what's in your interest. What's in Aaron's interest."

"Get away from me, Elinore," said Jane.

"Now, Janie . . ."

"Get away!" shouted Jane.

Heads turned throughout the cabin. Elinore looked around, reddening.

"We'll talk when you get control of yourself, young lady," she said stiffly, then turned and walked back to her own seat.

"I'm not a young lady," Jane hollered after her. "I'm more than old enough to hire a lawyer and sue your fat ass off if I decide to!"

Jane could feel the eyes of everyone in the first-class cabin on her, but she felt better nevertheless. She felt better than she had felt for a long time. No amount of money was worth being stuck to someone like Elinore. Just look at what she had done to her husband.

Jane hadn't realized what a burden her father's paintings had been. Much better that they would be in museums for everyone to enjoy, rather than on the walls of a few privileged rooms. Yes, she could have used the money, but never having had it, she wouldn't miss it either. Aaron Sailor would have preferred public recognition to money anyhow. The only reason Jane hadn't thought of this before was that the art establishment hadn't wanted anything to do with him for so many years.

Two hours later, the plane broke through the gray clouds and landed at Sea-Tac Airport.

As the first-class cabin emptied, Elinore made a great show of sticking her nose in the air and letting Jane pass in the aisle. A pale, stoop-shouldered woman met Elinore at the gate.

This must be the daughter, Jane understood, feeling nothing but sympathy for her. The poor thing flinched at Elinore's every gesture, like a dog that has been beaten regularly. Elinore's screech owl voice, determinedly cheerful, harangued her daughter all the way down to the baggage carousels. Jane took up a position as far away from the two women as was physically possible, though Elinore was pointedly ignoring her.

"Hello, again," said a voice at Jane's side.

She turned and found herself looking into the big blue eyes of Elinore's seatmate on the plane, Valentine Treves.

"Hi," said Jane.

"It turns out I didn't have to buy a subscription after all," he said, holding up the *New York Times Sunday Magazine*. "Complimentary copy. All I had to do was promise to ask you out on a date. Of course, this was before you got into the fight with her. After that, she informed me that you are really the Creature from the Black Lagoon and I'd be very foolish to have anything to do with you."

"Elinore's days of looking out for my welfare are over," said Jane curtly.

"Yes, and for this I owe you another vote of thanks. The woman barely said two words to me all the way from St. Louis. She just sat there with steam coming from her ears."

"I'm glad."

"It was a sad story," said Valentine, holding up the magazine. "About your father. I'm sorry."

Jane nodded.

"I don't see Mr. Mannerback."

"He's taking a later flight."

"Ah," said Valentine, his eyebrows colliding in thought. "I'd like to show you the town, but I'm only going to be here for a few hours. I've got meetings in San Francisco tonight."

"That's okay," said Jane, disappointed somehow. "I've got to wait for Perry at the hotel."

"Are you going back to New York soon? Perhaps we could get together there. I could take you to dinner. You could show me your lagoon."

"Do you live in the city?" asked Jane.

"When I'm not in London. I have a pied-à-terre on the East Side. May I ring you up? Are you in the phone book?"

He smiled a cockeyed smile. It wasn't fair, thought Jane, remembering her last disastrous encounter with a member of the male species. Why was his dopey, hopeful expression so attractive? Jane felt vulnerable but very charmed.

"I'm listed under Jane L. Sailor," she heard her voice saying. "On West Ninetieth Street."

"What does the L. stand for?"

"Luria. Family name."

"Yes, I remember from the article. Take care of my heart, Jane L. Sailor, now that you've got it in your pocket."

With a wink, he turned on his heel and disappeared into the airport crowds.

Smiling despite herself, Jane collected her suitcase and the one Perry had checked when they had boarded the plane in New

York. Then she took a cab to the Regency, a new hotel in the center of Seattle. Its forty-story spire featured three-room suites that made her apartment back home seem like a hovel.

Once she got settled in her opulent rooms, Jane opened a can of Coke from the kitchen refrigerator, took out her Shaw plays, and waited for Perry to call. Because of the time change, it was barely three-thirty local time.

At seven, having finished both *Candida* and *Major Barbara* (and reread Valentine's sonnet more than once), she phoned down to the desk for the umpteenth time to ask if Perry had checked in yet. He hadn't. Jane ordered a salmon steak and an imported beer from room service and turned on the television.

It was eight forty-five, nearly midnight New York time, when the phone finally rang.

The noise made Jane jump. She grabbed the remote and turned off the set. It was Perry. He was calling from New York.

"I thought you were taking a later flight here," said Jane, confused and concerned.

"Yes, sorry about that," said Perry, sounding more scattered than usual. "Something came up. I needed to come back to the city. There was some business I had to attend to that couldn't wait."

"What am I supposed to do?"

"About what?" said Perry.

"About the lighthouse clock."

"Oh, yes, the clock. That's right. I forgot."

"You forgot? How could you forget? Wasn't the clock the whole point of this trip?"

"I suppose you'll have to check it out for me."

"But I don't know anything about clocks!" exclaimed Jane.

"Just go to One Thousand First Avenue tomorrow morning and see Mr. Honeychurch," said Perry as though it was an after-thought, as though he was busy threading a needle or defusing a bomb and just happened to be speaking with her at the same time. "He's expecting me, we spoke on the phone at the end of last week.

Tell him that I'm prepared to buy, but say the price is too high. Dad taught me that. They call it negotiating. Look him right in the eye and say, 'You've got to do better.' It often works."

"But I can't . . ."

"I've already seen a picture of the piece. There's an ad in the new *Antiques* magazine coming out next week. I have a contact at the printers, which is how I've gotten the jump on the competition. Let Honeychurch know the sale is null and void if I find the clock is not as described. I'll have it checked out here in New York."

"But what if he won't give me a better price? What should I do then?"

"Just buy it," said Perry. "The important thing is to buy it. The minute the magazine comes out, there are other people who will be interested. Agree to pay the full hundred and twenty-five thousand if you need to. We'll wire-transfer the funds."

"A hundred and twenty-five thousand dollars?" exclaimed Jane. "For a clock? This must be the most expensive clock that ever lived!"

"I've got to go now," said Perry. "Take the first flight you can get back to the city. I'll see you when you get in."

"About my father—" began Jane.

"I'm sorry for all this, Jane. Please believe that. Very, very sorry."

There was a click. The line went dead.

Still on New York time, Jane was up early and out of the hotel by eight o'clock the next morning.

The answering machine at Honeychurch Antiques had indicated that store hours began at ten, not giving her much time to explore Seattle. Determined at least to see the city's famous market, she made her way from the hotel to the bottom of Pike Street.

The Pike Street Market was an old sprawling structure filled with men and women selling everything that grew, flew, grazed, or swam in a five-hundred-mile radius. Wonderful things to eat stretched out in both directions. Case after case of fresh trout, salmon, orange roughie, cod. Vegetable stands of broccoli and carrots, peppers of every color, apples and grapes. Butchers displayed free-range chickens, meats of every description. Open bushels of clams and oysters were everywhere. Smells of brewing coffee and baking bread filled the air.

After half an hour Jane stopped at a little café across the street from the market for a coffee and croissant, both of which were fresh and delicious.

The sky was gray and a light rain fell over the city, off and on. It was a strange kind of rain that didn't seem to bother anyone. Unlike the driving rains in New York that soaked you to the bone, the drops here had worked out a way to fall a few inches apart so no one got very wet or had much need of an umbrella.

The time passed too quickly. At ten o'clock exactly, Jane made her way over a few streets to Honeychurch Antiques, which occupied the ground-floor corner of a small four-story brick building. In its window were a pair of Queen Anne chairs, a floral Aubusson tapestry, and a Chippendale desk upon which sat a lighthouse clock. It was exactly as Perry had described it. The cylindrical mahogany base sat on four gold-painted ball feet and supported a white-dialed clock under the shelter of a tall, tapering glass dome.

It was a bit smaller than Jane had imagined, perhaps twenty-eight inches from top to bottom. At a hundred and twenty-five thousand dollars, that worked out to something like forty-five hundred dollars per inch.

Jane opened the door and walked into the shop.

It was a long room with a high ceiling. Well-appointed furniture was spread throughout, including a few grandfather-type clocks with silvered dials and mahogany cases. Coming from New York where space was at such a premium, Jane was instantly taken with how uncrowded the place was. On Madison Avenue, probably ten times as much stuff would be crammed in, but then the rent on Madison was probably ten times what it was here.

After Jane had browsed for a few minutes, a tall, thin man in his forties walked out from the back. He was dressed casually, a sport shirt, dark pants. Again, it was quite a difference from New York, where the owner of a fancy antique shop like this would probably be in a suit.

"May I help you?" he asked. "I'm Bill Honeychurch."

"Yes," said Jane, speaking in what she hoped was a confident voice. "I believe my employer, Perry Mannerback, spoke with you. We're interested in the lighthouse clock in the window."

"I'm afraid that clock is sold," said Honeychurch, "but I've got some great mantel clocks in the back that I'm sure Mr. Mannerback would like, and if you're looking for a long case piece . . ."

"Sold?" blurted Jane. "How can it be sold? It's right there in the window."

"Gentleman came in yesterday and made me an offer I couldn't refuse," he said with a grin.

"But Mr. Mannerback spoke to you. I've come all the way from New York for the express purpose of buying it."

"Sorry," said Honeychurch. "Mannerback just told me he wanted to see it, we didn't have a deal or anything. The other fella was here first with a check. Like they say, early bird gets the worm, and all that."

"I can't believe this," said Jane.

"Neither can I," said Honeychurch happily. "I've got an expensive ad for the darn thing coming out next week. Looks like I could have saved my money."

"Do you think the man who bought it would be interested in selling?" said Jane, trying to think of what Perry might want to do in this situation.

"I know he wouldn't be," said Honeychurch.

"But maybe . . ."

"The gentleman specifically told me to tell anyone who came calling that the clock was not for sale. It was like he knew that people were going to come round and he wanted everyone to know the score. The clock is now a permanent part of the Bogen Collection, he told me to say. That's B-O-G-E-N. He wanted me to spell it out so there would be no mistake."

Jane walked back to the hotel feeling terrible, as if she had let Perry down somehow. It was foolish, she knew. There was no way she could have prevented this Mr. Bogen from finding his way to Honeychurch Antiques and buying the clock; but still it seemed like her fault.

Back at her room, the message light on her phone was blinking. Jane pressed the voice-mail button and a crisp baritone voice came on the line.

"Miss Sailor, this is Dr. Bleiweiss at Yorkville East End Hospital. I need to speak with you about your father. Please call me as soon as possible."

He gave a number, which Jane jotted down on the notepad that the hotel had provided by the phone. The hospital probably wanted permission to do more tests, she thought ruefully. Just what her father needed. Depressed, she dialed the number for OmbiCorp instead and was put through to Miss Fripp.

"Mr. Mannerback didn't come in today," said the secretary in her precise British voice, as cold and clipped as Valentine's had been engaging and soft. "He's at the apartment."

"Is he ill?"

"I couldn't say. He's not very communicative. Oh, and a Dr. Bleiweiss from Yorkville East End Hospital has called several times trying to locate you. It seems to be important. About your father."

"Yes, I've got that message. Thanks."

Jane put down the receiver. She'd call the hospital, but first it was more important to tell Perry what had happened.

Olinda was not happy about disturbing her employer, but finally she put the call through.

"Hello, Jane," Perry Mannerback said at last. His voice sounded dull, almost dazed.

"Hi," she said. "Did I wake you? I'm sorry. I understand you're not feeling well."

"No, no, no," mumbled Perry Mannerback. "Not well. Not at all. Don't have to get up if I don't want to. Stay here all day under the covers if I choose."

"About the lighthouse clock . . ."

"What?"

"The lighthouse clock," said Jane. "We were flying across the entire country to see it, remember?"

"Oh, yes. The lighthouse clock. Simon Willard. Very important. Great addition to my collection."

Jane took a deep breath.

"I'm afraid I wasn't able to buy it."

"Oh, dear," said Perry with a sigh. "That is disappointing."

"I'm sorry."

"No, no problem. It's not so important in the great scheme of things, I suppose."

"I'm glad you're not upset," said Jane, relieved.

"No, no."

"It went into the Bogen Collection."

The sound began softly, but then grew and grew—almost like a jet taking off—until it was a blood-curdling, inhuman roar.

*"WhaaaattTT? What did you say?"*

Jane had to pull the phone away from her ear.

"It went into the Bogen Collection," she repeated, not comprehending. "That's B-O-G . . ."

"I know how to spell it, damn it," yelled Perry. "That fiend! That subhuman, monstrous, odious, wretched bastard! That filthy, abominable substitution for a human being! That greedy progeny of a hound!"

Jane took the phone away from her ear again, as Perry's tirade continued. She had never heard him even a little bit angry. This was practically hysteria. She was stunned.

"I take it that you know the man who bought the clock?" she ventured in a quiet voice when he stopped for a moment for air.

"Know him? He's my absolute nemesis! I revile his very existence. That miserable bastard, Willie Bogen. They call him Willie the Weasel. Willie the goddamned Weasel, and he's done it to me again. Damn him! Damn, damn, damn, damn, damn him to hell!"

"Who is he?" asked Jane in a quieter voice still, trying to calm him down. This was one of the techniques she used in teaching stage combat that transferred well to daily life. You responded to anger with increasing gentleness, setting an example. It usually worked. But not today.

"He's a monster, that's who," shouted Perry, a notch louder. "A liar and a scoundrel and a cheat! Oh God! Nothing is going right. Everything is a mess. My whole life is a mess. I can't talk. I've got to go. We'll speak when you get back to New York. Good-bye."

The phone went dead.

Jane sat mystified for a moment, still feeling somehow responsible for what happened. But it wasn't her fault, she told herself. This Bogen fellow had simply gotten there first, that's all. If Perry hadn't flown back to New York and made her wait all day in the room for his call, they could have gotten to Honeychurch Antiques yesterday and maybe beaten Bogen to the punch. If it was anyone's fault that they hadn't gotten the clock, it was Perry's.

Feeling unsettled and guilty nevertheless, Jane dialed the number for the doctor at Yorkville East End Hospital that Fripp had given her. She might as well get this over with.

"Dr. Bleiweiss," answered the same deep voice that had been on the hotel voice mail.

"This is Jane Sailor," she said. "I understand that you wanted to speak with me about my father?"

"Yes, Miss Sailor."

"What is it? More tests? I've got to tell you, Doctor, that I really don't see the point. Do you really think that any of this is going to make a difference?"

"I'm afraid I have some sad news, Miss Sailor."

There was a pause. Then Dr. Bleiweiss spoke again.

"I'm afraid your father died last night."

"What?"

"He died."

"He died? How could he die?"

"People in coma are in a precarious place between life and

death," said Dr. Bleiweiss gently. "Though their state may seem constant, they are always subject to certain negative processes. Your father's death was a peaceful one. It happened very quickly. Miss Sailor?"

"I . . . I'm out of town," Jane stammered.

"I know."

"I'll be back as soon as I can."

"We're all very sorry."

"Thank you."

Jane hung up the phone and stared out the window at the towers of Seattle and the pewter sky, waiting to feel something.

It had been so long since she had allowed herself to feel anything for her father that she didn't even know where to look for it. He had been dead so long already that she didn't think there were any feelings left. She was surprised, therefore, after a minute when she found her eyes full of tears.

"Isn't this silly, after all this time . . ." she started to say out loud. Then, like a dam that had burst, all the pain and guilt and frustration that Jane had been holding in for so many years was suddenly coming out. She cried until her sobs filled the entire world. And then she cried some more.

*e e e e*

The time change added three hours to the five-hour flight time back from Seattle. When Jane finally opened the door to her apartment in New York, it was nearly eleven o'clock at night. The light on her answering machine was blinking like a tiny lighthouse across the room. Jane pressed the message button, turned on a lamp, and caught a glimpse of herself in the mirror above the painted Norwegian chest of drawers that held her clothes. Her hair was still that ridiculous color. Her eyes were red from crying. She looked awful.

"Miss Sailor, this is Dr. Bleiweiss from Yorkville East End.

It's about eight-thirty in the morning. I need to speak with you. It's very important. I'll try you at the OmbiCorp office later."

Jane's eyes, which she thought were all cried out, filled with tears yet again. She had gotten that message already. It was still hard to believe that it was over. The tears weren't coming from sadness, she knew. Nor were they for her father. They were tears of relief and they were for herself. It was finally over. At last her father was at peace. Perhaps now she could find peace, too.

Dr. Bleiweiss's message was followed by a string of hang ups. Who could be calling her, Jane wondered. Dr. Bleiweiss trying again? People calling to express their condolences? Had word gotten out about Aaron Sailor's death already?

As she stood there, trying not to be overwhelmed by it all, the phone rang—an impossibly loud sound shattering the quiet of the little apartment. Jane picked it up.

"Miss Sailor?"

"Yes?" said Jane, glancing at the time, wondering whose condolences couldn't wait for the morning.

"Miss Sailor, my name is Octavio Folly. I'm a detective lieutenant with the New York City Police Department, nineteenth precinct. I'm sorry to be calling you so late, but I know I'm not disturbing you. I've been trying your phone for several hours. I know you were flying back tonight from Seattle."

"I just got in," said Jane, not comprehending. "You said you were from the police?"

"Yes," said Detective Folly. His voice was sibilant and mellow, almost like a loud whisper. "I'm very sorry about your father."

"Thank you," said Jane. "I'm sorry, Detective . . . ?"

"Folly."

"I'm sorry, Detective Folly, but why exactly are you calling me?"

"I know this is a very difficult time for you, Miss Sailor, but I'm afraid that I need to ask you some questions. Do you know if anyone would profit in any way by your father's death?"

"No. My father has been dead for all practical purposes for many years."

"Did he have any enemies?"

"What is this about, Detective? Before I answer anything, I want to know what this is about."

"There are certain problems with your father's death."

"Problems? Being dead isn't a problem enough?"

"Your father could have lived for decades longer in his state," said Detective Folly, "but it didn't surprise anyone that he had died. Didn't surprise anyone, that is, except for one doctor, an endocrinologist, who stopped in on his way out last night and who was familiar with your father's condition. A Dr. Gregory King. Says he knows you."

"Yes," said Jane. "His wife is my father's dealer. Was."

"Dr. King noticed some symptoms," said Folly. "Rapid heartbeat, shallow breathing, sweating. Nothing that appeared dangerous, but something to keep an eye on, he thought. Something he had seen before. When he learned that your father had died in the night, Dr. King suggested to the doctor who was doing the routine autopsy that he consider an insulin overdose as a possible cause of death."

"An insulin overdose?" repeated Jane. "I don't understand. Why would they be giving my father insulin? Isn't that for diabetics?"

"They weren't giving your father insulin, Miss Sailor. But an insulin overdose can result in rapid heartbeat, shallow breathing, sweating. Later, the patient goes into shock and coma, resulting in death."

"My father was already in a coma."

"Which is why his death probably would have been put down to natural causes were it not for Dr. King," said Detective Folly. "When a healthy person loses consciousness and falls into a coma, it is a very alarming event. But as you say, your father was already in a coma, so there was no dramatic change in his condition that would alert anyone that something was wrong. Also, insulin metabolizes very quickly. If the autopsy hadn't checked for elevated levels right away, it would never have been found. No one would have ever known."

"Are you saying that you believe that someone did this to my father deliberately?"

"Because insulin is an enzyme that is naturally present in the body, there is a certain amount of uncertainty," said the soft voice. "The medical examiner, however, now believes that insulin overdose is the most probable cause of your father's death. And this insulin would have had to be administered to him intentionally by someone. Do you understand, Miss Sailor? Do you see what this means?"

"Yes, I do," said Jane, her voice suddenly very calm, the tears entirely gone from her eyes.

Aaron Sailor had been murdered. Again.

The funeral was Friday morning.

"*Murder* is the loss of love," Valentine Treves had written in his sonnet. Jane already knew all about the impact of death, but its logistics were something else entirely. Again Perry Mannerback came to her assistance with another display of spontaneous generosity. Not only did he put the formidable Miss Fripp at her disposal to assist with the details of the funeral, he insisted on paying for it.

Jane was too dazed by events to mount an effective protest. The service was held at Frank E. Campbell, the toniest funeral parlor on the Upper East Side, a fitting nonsectarian arrangement for a half-Jewish, half-Catholic artist who had pretty much rejected all religion.

Thanks to the previous week's article about Aaron Sailor and the follow-up coverage in the wake of his death, a surprisingly large crowd showed up. There was no mention of murder in any of the news stories—though Jane wasn't sure whether the police had arranged this out of consideration or cunning.

The obituaries all took a respectful tone, repeating personal information that had been included in the *Sunday Times Magazine* just a few days before: how Aaron Sailor's mother had fled Belgium during World War II, how the artist had been raised by his father but left the family's cabinetry business to become a society portraitist, then rejected the security of that life to paint what he wanted. The failed show of a decade ago was touched on. So was the current retrospective at the Fyfe. His wife had died eighteen years ago. He was survived by a daughter, Jane L., of Manhattan.

"I'm so sorry, Jane," said Miss Fripp afterwards. She was actually a small woman, no more than five feet two, which always surprised Jane. On the phone, Barbara Fripp sounded like she was eight feet tall.

"Thanks," said Jane, wondering who all these people were. Some of the faces looked vaguely familiar, but the somber room was largely filled with strangers who now converged around her, waiting to shake her hand and murmur their condolences.

"Perry's outside," said Miss Fripp. "He'll meet you in the car."

Jane nodded, not looking forward to the drive to the cemetery in the Bronx. The crowd surged forward. Jane nodded and listened and smiled politely. It was amazing how many East Side ladies had come with stories of how Aaron Sailor had painted their portraits.

"We're so, so sorry," said Gregory King a few minutes later, rescuing Jane from yet another woman with an endless anecdote about her sitting.

"Thanks."

"Elinore was crushed," Dr. King went on, "simply devastated by the news. She's still out in Seattle and couldn't get away. She promises to call."

"That's really not necessary," said Jane unhappily. Leave it to Elinore to try to use Aaron Sailor's death as a lever to get back into business.

"How are you holding up?" asked Dr. King, looking genuinely concerned.

"Fine. I guess I owe you my thanks. For figuring out about the insulin, I mean."

Gregory King reddened. He laughed an embarrassed laugh.

"No, no. I'm sure they probably would have found it anyway. Look, I wish you wouldn't mention it to Elinore. That I got involved and all."

"Why not?" asked Jane.

"Well, Elinore has some funny ideas, you know," said Gregory King, searching nervously for a place to put his hands, finally settling on his pockets. "She doesn't like to get . . . I mean . . . for us to be involved and all. And now the police have had to talk to her out there, ask her where she was and all that. If Elinore found out that it was because of me . . . well, she'd probably be pretty peeved."

"You haven't done anything wrong," said Jane. "You shouldn't be afraid of her."

"Oh, no," said Dr. King with a chuckle and an exaggerated headshake. "I'm certainly not afraid of Elinore. No, no. No way. I just know how to handle her after all these years, that's all. Elinore has her little routines, and I can hold my own, believe me. But sometimes if you try to fight her head-on . . . Well, it's just easier . . . I mean, sometimes it's difficult to . . . It's just better not to set her off, if you know what I mean."

Jane nodded. Elinore's poor husband was so beaten down that he couldn't even see the problem.

The crowd surged around her again and Gregory King faded back. Jane listened to condolences until the words stopped making sense and the faces in the room began to coalesce into a blur—except for one man who didn't seem to fit in at all.

He was not the only African American in the room—there was also her father's former accountant and a few artists and their wives—but this man somehow felt different from everyone else. He seemed aloof, remote, as if he were indifferent to both life and death. He was very tall and very thin. He sat quietly in a pew at the back of the room, his long legs sticking out into the aisle. It was impossible to tell whether he was watching the proceedings or simply staring off into space. His face was a hard, impenetrable mask.

"Jane, darling, my poor little *draga*," said a giant of a man, stepping forward and giving her a bear hug.

"Uncle Imre!" said Jane with delighted recognition.

Aaron Sailor's old friend still worked hard to look like he imagined an artist was supposed to look. This meant that today Imre Carpathian had draped his six-foot five-inch frame in a black cape and sported a hat that might have been made for a Russian czar or perhaps a character from Gilbert and Sullivan. He had let his graying hair grow to shoulder length, which made his deeply lined face look even craggier and more forbidding. He smelled of turpentine and peanut butter.

"I should have come to see you before this," he said, holding her at arm's length. "Now Aaron is dead. I am hateful louse. You have permission to break my legs. Go ahead, break."

He stuck out a leg.

"Sorry. This isn't my leg-breaking day."

"It is I who am sorry, Janie. Verrrry sorry."

"Thanks, Uncle Imre."

The old artist's expression grew soft.

"Is good to see you wear your mother's cross," he said in a subdued voice. "Imre has not seen this cross for many years."

Jane fingered the dragonfly on its black ribbon around her neck. It had seemed fitting that she wear it today.

"My father gave it to her," she said. "It was a family heirloom."

Imre nodded solemnly.

"You have someone to be with you today?"

"Sure," lied Jane, looking around. The room had finally begun to empty. The mourners had come only to pay tribute to Aaron Sailor, not to console her. Jane barely knew anyone in New York any more and didn't have any close friends. Her acquaintances from the theatre lived in places like Minneapolis, Chicago, Denver. A few people with whom she had worked had called over the past few days. Others probably were off on tour and hadn't heard or didn't feel they knew her well enough to intrude.

"Is not good to be alone at time like this," said Uncle Imre, shaking his finger. "You need company, you call me, okay?"

"Sure."

"You call me, you hear? Now you talk to these other people. I hate funerals."

"Thanks for coming," said Jane. A group of men from the funeral home began to wheel the closed coffin out of the room. Most of the mourners had left. When she turned, the tall, thin black man who had been sitting in the back was standing right beside her. He spoke in a soft, familiar voice.

"Miss Sailor. I'm Octavio Folly."

"Oh, yes," said Jane, surprised. "Detective Folly. Nice to meet you."

She had spoken with him several times on the telephone since getting back from Seattle Tuesday night—had it only been a few days ago? It felt as if months had passed. From his soft voice, Jane had expected someone more gentle-looking. There was nothing gentle-looking about Octavio Folly, however. His chin and cheekbones looked chiseled out of rock. There was a long, shiny scar on his neck. His eyes were like two tiny coals.

"I need to ask you some more questions," he said, holding up his gold shield and identification. "I'm sorry that it has to be now, but we're looking into a few things, and time is of the essence in an investigation like this."

The remainder of the mourners filed out. They were suddenly alone.

"Who were all these people here today?" Folly asked. "Were any of them close to your father?"

"Only Uncle Imre really," said Jane, relieved the crowd was

finally gone but wary of the hard-faced, aloof detective. "He was my father's best friend. The others were mostly acquaintances of my father, too. I didn't know he had so many."

"Uncle Imre would be the tall man who hugged you?"

"Yes."

"What's his full name?"

"Imre Carpathian," said Jane. Folly had taken out a little note-book and was jotting down the name.

"Where does Mr. Imre Carpathian live?"

"In a loft on Broome Street. Do we really have to do this now?"

"I wanted to see these people with my own eyes," said Folly. "It won't take much longer. We're still trying to come up with someone with a motive to harm your father."

"What about a nurse?" said Jane, who had given the matter some thought herself over the past few days. "There are always stories in the papers about nurses who decide to play angel of mercy with hopeless patients. My father certainly qualified."

"We're looking into that, though there's no pattern of sus-picious deaths at the hospital. Let's talk about the fall down the stairs eight years ago that put your father into his coma. Did you ever consider that it might not have been an accident?"

Jane didn't answer.

"Did you ever speculate that someone might have pushed him down the stairs?" repeated Folly.

"Maybe," said Jane reluctantly. "But there's no way to be sure, no way to prove anything."

"Who might have had a motive to push your father down the stairs eight years ago, Miss Sailor? Did Mr. Carpathian benefit in any way by your father's accident?"

"Absolutely not," said Jane, indignant. "I told you. Imre was his best friend. He'd known Dad forever. He knew my mother."

"What about Dr. King's wife, the art dealer?"

"Actually, Elinore was probably the one who lost the most by my father's incapacitation," said Jane, trying not to make a face. "At least in terms of money. Nobody wanted the paintings that Dad had done for her show, but the contract had another three years to run. If Dad had gone on working, he might have come up with something more sellable. Elinore had spent a lot of money promoting him, according to her. When Dad fell down the stairs, she lost whatever chance she had to recoup—which she would have done out of his share of any sales, naturally."

Folly wrote into his book and spoke again, not looking up.

"Does she still have any financial interest in your father's work?"

"I own all the paintings," said Jane. "Contractually, Elinore would still get a big cut if we sold anything, but I intend to donate everything to museums. She won't get a nickel now. Besides, Elinore couldn't have anything to do with my father's death. She was in Seattle."

"Yes," said Folly, nodding. "I've checked that. She was out with her daughter at a restaurant in Seattle Monday night. A group from Microsoft at the next table corroborated her story. Apparently, she tried to sell them a Picasso or something. I'm just going through a process of elimination, Miss Sailor. The only name on my list that I haven't eliminated is Peregrine Mannerback, known as Perry. Was Perry Mannerback here?"

"He was at the service, yes," said Jane uncomfortably. He was outside right now, waiting for her in his limousine, only Jane didn't want to mention that.

"He was the slight man with the bow tie, right? High forehead?"

"Yes."

"Dr. King claims that Aaron Sailor was calling out this Perry Mannerback's name in his coma," said Folly.

"That's not exactly accurate," said Jane, flustered.

Folly raised an eyebrow and turned the pages of his notebook.

"King said you told him so at dinner last Saturday night."

"My father was calling out the name Perry, yes," said Jane. "I don't know that Perry Mannerback was the Perry he was referring to."

"What did your father say?"

"He was just raving."

"Perhaps," said Folly. "But I'd like to be the judge of that. Just tell me every sentence you heard him say, every phrase you can remember. Exactly as he said it."

Reluctantly, Jane told him. No, Perry, no. Don't do it, Perry, Don't do it. You're a liar, Perry. I know the truth.

"Did your father know anyone else named Perry?" asked Folly, after jotting down Jane's comments in his notebook.

"I don't know," said Jane.

"But your father knew Perry Mannerback eight years ago."

"Perry bought one of my father's paintings."

"Wouldn't that painting be more valuable now that your father is dead?"

"It's not like my father was ever going to paint anything else, even if he had lived."

"But after the article last week, his death could increase demand, couldn't it? Prices would go up. The value of Perry Mannerback's painting would go up."

"I suppose," said Jane, "but that doesn't matter. Perry already has more money than he knows what to do with."

A dark-suited man from the funeral home had come into the room. He glanced at Jane, then at his watch.

"My experience is that folks never have enough money," said Folly with a wry smile. "The more money a person has, the more he seems to want."

"Is that all, Lieutenant?" asked Jane. "I have to go to the cemetery."

"I'm sorry to have had to trouble you today, Miss Sailor. I'll be in touch. If you think of anyone else who might conceivably have wished your father ill, or profited in any way from his inca-pacitation or death, please call me."

He handed her a white business card with his phone number, then said good-bye.

Jane waited for a few minutes until she was sure he had gone, then slowly made her way outside to Perry Mannerback's waiting limousine.

"I'm so sorry about this, Jane," said Perry, patting her hand as she got in beside him. "So very sorry."

Jane nodded. No wonder Lieutenant Folly was suspicious of Perry—Perry was the obvious suspect and he wasn't exactly acting like an innocent man. Jane searched his face for some clue. Perry looked away.

Following the hearse with Aaron Sailor's casket, they drove in silence to the quiet cemetery in the Bronx where Irving Berlin, Fiorello La Guardia, and Bat Masterson were buried. Aaron Sailor was laid to rest beside Jane's mother, a few green hills away from the mortal remains of his parents.

Jane and Perry Mannerback barely exchanged ten words on the drive back into Manhattan. When Leonid pulled the limousine up in front of her brownstone, Jane didn't move to get out.

"You don't have to come back to work until you're ready," said Perry. "Take a week. Take two. I'll just have Fripp send you your check."

"Perry—"

"No, no, I insist."

Jane swallowed hard.

"You've been incredibly kind to me, Perry, which makes what I need to say very difficult. I don't think I can go on working for you."

Perry looked genuinely surprised.

"You're quitting? You can't quit. I need you."

"You don't need me at all. I'm not doing anything."

"Yes, you are. You're doing a great deal."

"Like what?" asked Jane.

"You're guarding me. And assisting. You could have bought that clock in Seattle for me if Willie the Weasel hadn't beaten us there."

"I'm sorry, Perry. It isn't right. This isn't what I want. This isn't what I do."

He didn't say anything right away, just sat there. Jane bit her lip. Taking the job with Perry had seemed like such a smart idea two weeks ago. It didn't seem so smart now.

"There's nothing I can say to convince you to stay?" he asked in an earnest voice. "I'll give you a raise."

Jane shook her head. It wasn't fair to continue working for Perry just to spy on him. Jane hadn't meant to like him, but she did. She also didn't trust him an inch.

"I don't understand why you want to give me so much for so little in return," she said. "You're acting like you feel guilty about something."

"No, that's not so," protested Perry too quickly, his voice too loud. "I don't have anything to feel guilty about, nothing at all."

"Why was my father calling out your name in his coma?"

"I don't know," said Perry, looking away.

"Why won't you tell me about the woman in the painting?"

"Never met her. Don't know who she is. Don't know her at all."

Jane opened the door and got out of the car.

"Thanks for everything, Perry."

"I'm very sorry," he said in a quiet voice, without looking up. "Truly. Very sorry."

Then the car drove away.

It was only a bit past two o'clock in the afternoon. What do you do after you bury your father? Jane wondered, as she trudged up the steps of her brownstone and opened the front door. She wasn't hungry. It would hardly do to go to a movie. Jane wished she could go back to work right now, but that was impossible, too. Fight directing wasn't something you could do by yourself. It could take months to line up a job. Until then it would be the unemployment office. Or temp work.

Wearily, Jane climbed the four flights of stairs to her apartment. When she got to the fifth-floor landing, something looked wrong. The door to her apartment was partially open. The doorframe looked like something had crashed into it.

Jane pushed open the door all the way and stared into a shambles. It took her several more seconds to make sense of the picture, to understand what had happened.

While she had been burying her father, someone had broken in and turned the place upside down. She'd been robbed!

Ten

"So, what you think?" asked Imre Carpathian, studying the eight-foot-high twisted mass of metal, rubber, and polyvinyl chloride piping.

The crazy old artist had changed out of the flamboyant outfit he had worn to the funeral. He was now dressed in his work clothes—a torn T-shirt and khaki pants that were so covered with paint they could serve as a color chart. His long gray hair was speckled with patches of blue. His bushy black eyebrows cried out for gardening.

"Very interesting," said Jane diplomatically.

"I call it *Burden of Capitalism in New York, Number Three*," said Imre, giving his creation a few miscellaneous whacks with the large hammer he was holding.

"So you sold the first two? That's great."

"There are no first two," said Imre. "I'm starting at number three."

"Are you allowed to do that?"

Imre looked over at her as if she were out of her mind.

"I am artist," he declared, indignant. "I can do anything I want."

Jane smiled and felt herself relax a bit. It had been a horrendous afternoon.

As if her father's funeral and quitting her job with Perry hadn't been enough, she'd then had to endure the shock of having her apartment violated, deal with the police about the break-in, and wait three hours for a locksmith to come and fix her door. The burglar had used a crowbar. The repaired doorframe and door now sported eighteen-inch steel anti-jimmy guards and a new deadbolt lock.

After phoning 911, Jane had called the number on the business card Detective Folly had given her. A police operator had patched her through to his cellular. Could this have something to do with her father's murder? she had asked, shaken. Why had this happened now?

Folly had been surprisingly kind. Apparently, it wasn't uncommon for burglars to go through the obituaries and hit apartments when they knew people would be off at funeral services. The detective assured her that it was just coincidence and said not to worry.

He must have spoken with the two uniformed officers who had shown up shortly thereafter because they treated her with a gentleness and tact that Jane didn't usually associate with the NYPD. They were puzzled, however, by the fact that nothing appeared to have been taken.

Probably this was because she had nothing worth stealing, Jane had said, but she began to wonder herself when the officers went through the apartment pointing out all the things that plugged into the wall. The television. The CD player. Even the answering machine. This was precisely the kind of stuff that a crackhead could sell quickly for cash. If the thief had been looking for money so desperately—her little flowered sugar bowl had been smashed and even the back of the sofa bed had been slit open—why hadn't he taken her gizmos and appliances?

"I'm glad you come for visit," declared Imre, dropping his hammer and walking over to a table piled high with what looked like junk. "You want coffee?"

"Thanks. That would be nice."

Imre pushed aside various bicycle fenders, wire spools, and sheet metal until he found a blowtorch and a battered old coffeepot. He took the pot over to a sink behind *Burden of Capitalism in New York, Number Three* and filled it with water, then lit the blowtorch and directed the flame at the pot.

"Real nice funeral today, yes?" he said.

"Yes," said Jane. She hadn't told him about the break-in, only asked if she could come down. Imre had been right about what he had said this morning. It wasn't good to be alone on a day like this.

Imre Carpathian's loft on Broome Street was a vast, industrial-looking space with grimy windows and high ceilings broken up by cast-iron pillars and unpainted drywall.

Jane had grown up in a similar space a few blocks away from here, but Aaron Sailor had finished their loft with the skill of the cabinetmaker's son that he was, and Jane's mother had filled it with beauty, music, and love—for the first years of Jane's life, at least. Imre's home looked like one of those hangars where they reassembled pieces of crashed airplanes. He had gotten the loft when SoHo was a desert of abandoned warehouses and factories, not the fashionable district it had become. Artists like Imre couldn't possibly make enough sales to afford places like this now. Looking around at his work, Jane wondered if he made any sales at all.

"So you going to take nice vacation now, yes?" asked Imre. "This is what Imre would do. Get away from city. Travel. Leave your sorrow behind."

"No," said Jane. "I couldn't."

"Why not? You got passport?"

"Yes, but . . ."

"You don't got no money?"

"That's not it," she said. Jane had been working since she'd gotten out of college and had a fair amount saved.

"So what's the big deal?" demanded Imre. "When was last time you give yourself vacation?"

"Do times when I was collecting unemployment insurance between assignments count?"

"No," barked Imre, opening the top of the coffeepot to see how the water was doing. "You have no excuses. I say, get out of town. Get out of the country, if you can. You getting hungry maybe? What time is it?"

Jane looked at her watch.

"Almost seven," she said, surprised. How had it gotten so late? Jane suddenly realized she hadn't eaten anything all day.

"Dinnertime already," declared Imre, reading her mind. "Come, hold this."

Jane walked over and took over blowtorch duty while Imre walked back to a cabinet and ruffled through paint tubes and chisels until he produced a menu from a Chinese restaurant.

An hour later, they were sitting in Imre's front living area on unmatched battered couches. Empty white cartons of chow mei fun, tai chen chicken, and shrimp with garlic sauce littered the orange-crate coffee table. They had switched from coffee to beer and Imre was telling stories about Aaron Sailor. Jane was laughing for the first time in several days.

". . . and then there was the time Aaron did portrait of this Park Avenue lady, new wife of big real estate fellow. She's born in trailer park in Tennessee but already she's worked up through two millionaire husbands. Then she steals this guy from his wife. He is the real big time, worth megabucks. Aaron, though, he is sick of portrait game, is sick of being liar with his paint, making rich ladies look like they want to look—more thin, more pretty, and like they have more brains. 'What they need is better plastic surgeon, not artist,' he would say, and I would tell him, 'When are you going to be real artist, Aaron? When are you going to tell the truth?' So this day he finally does. He paints the lady's portrait, but instead of eyeballs, he paints big dollar signs."

"You're kidding," said Jane, putting a hand over her mouth to supress a giggle.

"Honest to Pete," said Imre, solemnly holding up his right hand. "He delivers painting and woman goes crazy, and rich husband don't pay Aaron, tells him to go jump in East River. So Aaron takes painting and is walking down Park Avenue, when who should be walking up the other way but woman's first husband. He sees painting under Aaron's arm and recognizes ex-wife immediately from her dollar-sign eyeballs. Buys painting on spot for twice what first man was going to pay. This is how Aaron decides that maybe he can make living being real artist."

"That's a marvelous story, Imre," said Jane, taking another swig from her bottle of Samuel Adams. "I've never heard that. Why didn't my father ever tell it to me?"

"Maybe because I leave out part where Aaron is sleeping with lady while doing portrait."

"Oh."

"Ladies all like him a lot," said Imre, finishing his own beer. "He was lonesome for your mother. God rest her beautiful soul."

Jane's hand went instinctively to the dragonfly on the ribbon around her neck. She hadn't bothered to take it off since the funeral this morning.

"So Aaron became real artist after that, though still liar," Imre went on. "The paint is liar when things look like things, this is what I try to tell him—Aaron and me, we argue about this all the time. But at least he finally paints what he wants, not be whore for commissions. Too bad nobody wants Realism then."

"Did you see his one-man show?" asked Jane.

Imre nodded and made a face.

"Uptown gallery," he snorted, taking an angry chug from his beer. "All dealers are pigs, but uptown dealers are the worst. Greed on legs, I tell him when he wants to sign contract with that woman, but Aaron wouldn't listen. He found out."

"What did he find out?"

"She was a pig."

"Elinore King," said Jane.

Imre nodded.

"Only interested in money, like she wasn't rich already. Lived in big apartment on Central Park West with big-money art on her wall. Aaron told me all about it. Rauschenberg. Jasper Johns. Cy Twombly. You know how much this shit costs? Millions! It's obscene. But still this pig woman needs to cheat artists out of every dime, make them pay for their own shows, steals the bread out of their mouths. Anything they sell, she takes it all. What a crook."

Imre seemed to be looking around for a place to spit, but thankfully decided against it. The floor already had enough problems. It probably hadn't been refinished in a hundred years.

"Do you remember a big painting of a naked woman sitting on the stairs of Dad's loft with a handless clock between her legs?" asked Jane, her thoughts turning back to Perry Mannerback and his unconvincing denials.

"Yeah," grunted Imre. "Best painting in show, the only one they sell, I think."

"Do you have any idea who the model was?"

"Sure," said Imre. "Is Leila Peach."

Jane sat up.

"Leila Peach," she repeated. "Who was she?"

"Oh, Leila, Leila," said Imre, his face softening. "You don't remember Leila? No, I guess you were away at college then. She was subletting loft downstairs from Aaron, on second floor."

"What was she like? Tell me about her."

"Leila was pretty crazy girl," said Imre knowingly. "Or maybe not so crazy. Leila knew what she wanted. She posed for everybody."

"She was a professional model?"

"Leila did it for sport, not money, though I suppose she could use the bucks. She wanted to be part of the scene, you know? Her thing was sleeping with artists. She was *shtupping* half the artists in SoHo. Modeling was her ticket, easy way for her to get into their studios naked. She was involved with Aaron for a while, but then she dumped him for some rich guy."

Jane was totally alert now.

"What rich guy?"

"Some big rich guy, I don't know," said Imre. "Had something to do with buttons or something."

Jane's heart sank. Perry Mannerback. Of course it had been Perry Mannerback. Jane didn't know why she should be disappointed or surprised, but somehow she was both.

"Where's this Leila Peach now?" she asked. "What happened to her?"

"She left town right after Aaron had his accident," answered Imre, after draining the last of his beer and rising to get another bottle. "Moved to England."

"Do you have a phone number for her?"

"No, but I give you her address if you want. She still sends me card every Christmas. Crazy girl, but sentimental that way. Always remembers nice big Hungarian genius, and why not?" His craggy face broke into a smile. "For a while there, I was *shtupping* her, too."

ееее

It was well after ten p.m. when Jane got back to the apartment after the long subway ride up from SoHo. She turned the knob on the new deadbolt and locked herself in. At least the apartment was pretty much back together. She had straightened up while waiting for the locksmith. Yet everything seemed different somehow. Colder. The place was not the safe little haven it had always been.

Jane poured herself a glass of water—the Chinese food at Imre's had been too salty. Then she sat down next to the answering machine and listened to a series of condolence messages from acquaintances. The last message on the tape was an unexpected one.

"Hi, Jane, it's Valentine Treves," said a gentle British voice.

For a moment the name didn't register, so lost was Jane in thoughts of burglary and death and Leila Peach. She took a quick breath. Valentine from the plane to Seattle. Her goofy poet.

"I read about your father in the paper. I'm very sorry. I'm about to go out of town again, but I wanted you to know that I was thinking of you. If there's anything I can do to help, please let me know. My telephone number is . . ."

Jane got a pencil, replayed the message, and looked around for something to scribble down the number on. The only thing she could find was the back of the scrap of paper that Imre had given her with Leila Peach's most recent address in London. Apparently, Leila moved around a lot. Jane sat chewing the eraser of her pencil for a minute, then dialed.

"Hello," said Valentine Treves.

"Hi, Valentine. It's Jane Sailor. I wanted to thank you for your call. I'm not phoning too late, am I?"

"No, not at all," he said in a soft but strangely remote voice. "I'm delighted to hear from you. You may ring me up in the middle of the night if you like. I'm sorry about your father."

"Thanks," said Jane.

"I know how difficult it must have been for you. I lost my own father when I was sixteen."

"Then you do know."

"To be honest," he said, "I had wanted to ask you to dinner this week, but obviously this isn't the right time. I didn't want you to think that I had forgotten."

"Thanks," said Jane. "You said on your message that you were going out of town. Where are you going?"

"To London. On business. May I call you when I get back?"

"Yes," said Jane. "I'd like that."

"I would, too."

They were silent for a moment.

"You know, your father's work really is quite striking," said Valentine finally. "What I saw of it in the magazine article, that is."

"They're having a show of his work at the Fyfe Museum in San Francisco right now," said Jane.

"Yes, so I gathered. Is the painting that was in the magazine in the show? The nude on the staircase?"

"No," said Jane. "That was one of the few things he actually sold."

"How interesting," said Valentine. "It's a wonderful piece, very evocative. And that clock without the hands, what was the story with that? I wonder. Did your father use an actual piece he owned as a prop?"

"Why do you ask?"

"No reason. Just curiosity. Well, that's it, then. I'm very glad you called. I'll ring you up when I get back to town. Again, I'm very sorry about your father."

Jane said good-bye and put down the phone. Far from cheering her up, talking to Valentine Treves had just unsettled her more, though she was not sure why.

Wearily, Jane opened the ruined sofa bed, wondering how much it would cost to have it reupholstered. This day had been too much, but at least the leering nude in Perry's painting had a name now. Leila Peach.

Jane took off her shoes, slipped under the bedcovers fully clothed, and closed her eyes. Images of her father flooded her mind. Aaron Sailor painting in the old loft. Holding her hand after she had her tonsils removed. Babbling mindlessly in the the nursing home. After five minutes, she opened her eyes and spoke aloud to the ceiling.

"So, Daddy, if you're going to keep me up all night, why don't we talk about what happened eight years ago? Did you fall down the stairs? Or did Perry push you?"

Aaron Sailor didn't answer. Neither did the ceiling. Nevertheless, Jane felt a little better. Before, when she talked to her father, she was sure nobody was listening. Maybe now he could hear her, wherever he was.

"Were you and Perry arguing about Leila Peach?" Jane went on. "She looks like the kind of woman who might enjoy having men fight over her. And obviously she made a pretty powerful impression on Perry, considering that he won't even admit he knew her all these years later."

A siren wailed in the distance. On Broadway, horns were honking.

"Why were you saying, 'Don't do it, Perry,' in the nursing home, Daddy?" Jane asked softly. "What did Perry do? Did he do it with Leila Peach?"

There was no answer. Jane closed her eyes. The image of Grandmother Sylvie's handless clock suddenly appeared in her mind's eye and wouldn't go away. It took her a long time to fall asleep.

The next morning, Jane put the dragonfly cross around her neck again and went over to a coffeeshop on Broadway. She ordered a big breakfast but found she could eat hardly anything. She sat in the booth for the better part of an hour, drinking coffee and watching people pass by the window.

The restaurant was busy, but the waiters had seen her before and didn't hurry her out, sensing that she needed the table more than they did. Jane tried to think of theatres that she could send résumés to and directors she could call, but her thoughts kept returning to Grandmother Sylvie's clock—the exact point where the lives of Aaron Sailor, Perry Mannerback, and Leila Peach all intersected with her own.

It was a little before eleven when she got back to her apartment building. Instead of going up the stairs, she unlocked the basement door and went down to her storage cubicle. Again she took down the heavy box with Grandmother Sylvie's clock.

This time, she carefully pulled out the heavy ceramic. It looked exactly the way Aaron Sailor had painted it between Leila

Peach's legs and was no less horrible than Jane remembered. The colors were impossibly loud and the lack of hands gave it an odd, broken look somehow.

"I must be missing something," she muttered, turning the clock upside down for the first time, and nearly dropped it in surprise.

"What the hell?"

Jane stared in amazement. In the center of the clock's slightly rounded bottom was a stylized cross in deep blue glaze. It was exactly the same as Jane's mother's dragonfly cross: a flat angular head, tapering tail, crosspiece made to look like joined wings. Below the cross was an inscription, also in deep blue glaze: *Zalman Rosengolts et fils, Antwerpen.*

Jane sat down on one of the plastic milk crates, her thoughts racing. Her father had always told her that the cross he had given Ellen Sailor was a family heirloom. Naturally, Jane had assumed it was passed down from his Catholic father's side of the family. Here, however, was proof that the dragonfly cross must have originally belonged to Aaron Sailor's Jewish mother, and that it, too, had some relationship to the ceramic clock.

But the whole thing made no sense. Why would a Jewish woman have a cross? And Zalman Rosengolts sounded like a Jewish name. Why would a Jewish company choose a cross as their symbol? Why would Sylvie carry a three-dimensional version of the Rosengolts maker's mark halfway around the world when she was fleeing for her life?

Jane took the dragonfly from around her neck and examined it closely for the first time. The cross was so heavy because the joined open-ended tubes were solid inside—you couldn't look through and see light at the other end. The thicker top tube had a square opening; the opening of the bottom tapering tube was slightly striated. You could still see traces of gilding in the subtle details that were etched into the wing-shaped crosspiece. The piercing was probably just decorative, not designed to accommodate the ribbon from which the cross presently hung. There were no markings of any kind.

Jane replaced the cross around her neck and righted the clock, which stared back, its empty face revealing nothing, not even a time of day. She felt her eyes filling with tears.

The past week had been a nightmare. Her father's death, Perry Mannerback's suspicious behavior, the break-in at her apartment. And now here she was with a new mystery: a brass cross that had something to do with her grandmother's hideous clock. If only there were some family member she could ask—but of course there wasn't.

Fighting back her emotions, Jane returned the clock to its box and placed it back on the ledge. Then she locked the basement and went upstairs.

Her apartment felt impossibly small. She picked up the telephone and asked for international information. Several minutes later, an English-speaking operator in Belgium made her final pronouncement.

"No, I am sorry. There is no Rosengolts et fils, no Rosengolts at all listed in Antwerp."

"Thank you," said Jane, hanging up the receiver. If there was no Rosengolts et fils any longer, she couldn't very well ask them about crosses, could she? That was that.

But it wasn't. Jane knew she couldn't simply leave things this way, couldn't walk away from yet another unanswered question. The tiny studio suddenly seemed claustrophobic. Jane felt as if she couldn't breathe. She nearly jumped into the air when the phone rang.

"I just thought I would call, see how you were doing," said Perry Mannerback.

"Not terrific," said Jane.

"I'm sorry. Is there anything I can do?"

"Leila Peach was the name of the model in your painting," Jane blurted.

"Oh, is that so?" said Perry, his voice suddenly several notes higher.

"Yes, that's so," said Jane. "She apparently was involved with my father."

"Never met her."

His voice was ridiculously loud. He was lying.

"Please, Perry. Can't you just . . ."

"You can come back, you know," he said, cutting her off. "I'd be very happy if you would work for me again."

"The police say my father was murdered."

"Yes, I know," said Perry in a lower, more subdued voice. "They want to speak with me. My lawyer told me. They want to know why I went and saw Aaron that night."

"What night?" asked Jane.

"The night he died. They found out I was his only visitor."

A chill went down Jane's spine.

"You mean, that's why you didn't go all the way to Seattle with me? You came back to New York to see my father? That was your urgent business?"

"That's right. Wanted to see how he was doing. Poor man. Poor, poor man."

"Perry . . ."

"Must run, have important things to do. Good to talk with you."

"But . . ."

The line went dead. Jane sat staring at the receiver. What was the point of kidding herself? It had been Perry who had killed her father. It must have been Perry. He had done it not once, but twice. First eight years ago, when he had pushed him down the stairs despite Aaron Sailor's last desperate plea, then again on Monday night as her father lay helpless in his hospital bed. But why?

The walls seemed to close in again. Jane couldn't stand it. She couldn't stay in the apartment another minute. She grabbed a pair of sunglasses and charged out, down the four flights of stairs and into the brilliant afternoon.

She walked straight across Ninetieth Street until she came to Central Park. The park was beautiful in the spring, an oasis for New Yorkers any time of year. The sounds of the city suddenly vanished and the brownstones and apartment buildings were replaced with greenery and trees.

Jane made a winding course down past oaks and blooming apple trees, past the lake filled with rowboating lovers and the platoons of in-line skaters and bicyclists.

It was Saturday and the park teemed with people, most on foot like herself. As she got closer to the Zoo, the path became busier. Musicians serenaded the tourists with everything from saxophones to Chinese zithers. Jugglers juggled. Clowns clowned. Entrepreneurs on either side of the path offered services ranging from charcoal portraits to backrubs to writing your name on a grain of rice.

In the rest of the country you drove to the corner to get a newspaper. New York was one of the few places left in America where people could walk for miles and think nothing of it. Jane walked. Her mind emptied. Her spirit was calmed by the crowd and the exercise. At Fifty-ninth Street, the park opened up and disgorged its river of pedestrians into the bustling city.

Jane walked down Fifth Avenue, part of the moving sea of people, not knowing where she was going, not caring. St. Patrick's Cathedral passed by on the left. Rockefeller Center on the right. At Thirty-ninth Street, Lord & Taylor tempted her only briefly, the shoe stores and souvenir stands not at all. Suddenly the Empire State Building loomed ahead, surrounded by human walls of tourists and double-decker buses. Jane crossed over to Madison and stopped in front of the business division of the New York Public Library in the southeast corner of what had once been the B. Altman department store.

Jane hadn't consciously intended coming here, but now found herself entering the sleek new library and going down the stairs. A vast room full of computer terminals stretched ahead of her. She had been here before to do research on theatres, so she already knew how things worked. She punched in her name at a terminal and was able to get a reservation right away. She sat down before one of the dozens of computers available to the public. An Internet search engine was already on the screen.

Jane typed the words "Zalman Rosengolts et fils, Antwerp" into the inquiry box and clicked the search box with the pointer of her mouse. Within a few minutes, she had found what she was looking for.

"Rosengolts et fils have been purveyors of fine chinaware since 1921," read the description in an Internet shopping directory for London. "Originally of Antwerp, Belgium, the firm reestablished itself in England after the Second World War. It offers an outstanding array of fine wares for the discriminating purchaser."

Next to the name was a logo: a small castle within a circle, not a dragonfly cross at all.

More puzzled than ever, Jane printed the page with the phone number and address, then pushed her chair back and stood up. Now she could ask Rosengolts et fils about crosses to her heart's content. All she needed to do was call. Or she could follow Imre's advice and take a vacation, go to London, talk to them in person.

It was a crazy thought, of course, but tempting. Jane ambled back up the stairs and out of the library into the beautiful late afternoon sunshine on Madison Avenue. People didn't just drop what they were doing and go to Europe. Not people with her bank account at any rate.

But wouldn't it be nice to get away from all the pain and sadness of the past few days? Jane asked herself. And while she was there, she could look up Leila Peach. Would Leila Peach be able to tell her what had happened to Aaron Sailor eight years ago? Would she be able to supply the explanation that Perry Mannerback refused to, and perhaps his motive for murder?

Wasn't there something else that Jane wanted to do in London, somebody she wanted to see? It was a moment before she smiled, remembering who it was. Valentine Treves.

Twelve

The Royal Borough of Kensington and Chelsea was a well-kept section of London, known for its museums, embassies, handsome residential streets, and famous shops, including Harrods. Queen Victoria had been born here, at Kensington Palace, and the area had been home to such luminaries as Winston Churchill, J. M. W. Turner, and Oscar Wilde.

Jane couldn't believe that she was actually here in England. All it had taken was a credit card, plus a travel agent who was able to get her a last-minute cancellation on a six-day Royal Britannia tour package that had left Tuesday night. She was now the proud possessor of a room with semi-private bath at the Tipplebury Gardens Park Hotel in the Cromwell Road at a cost of merely an arm and a leg.

Jane was still stiff and sore from the overnight flight. Her economy seat on the plane had been significantly less comfortable than the accommodations on her recent flight to Seattle. She hadn't slept more than a few minutes, it seemed. The egg sandwich she'd gulped down at the airport after clearing Customs at eleven this morning—six a.m. New York time—had left her both bloated and hungry, and the Cromwell Road turned out to be the seedy underbelly of this desirable area rather than its tenderloin.

Still, Jane felt better than she had in days. As she left the little hotel and walked into South Kensington proper, past the Natural History Museum and the Victoria and Albert Museum over into Knightsbridge with its smart boutiques and busy storefronts, her problems felt far away.

According to the foldout map she had gotten at a newsstand near the hotel (run by Asians and complete with a large Coca-Cola sign out front), Rosengolts et fils in Mortimer Street was only a few inches away. London was far larger than Manhattan, Jane knew, but after the cramped night on the plane, she was determined to get there on foot. She had a fair sense of the city, having been here twice before—once for a week when she was in college, the second time for a few days as she passed through on her way to the Edinburgh Festival. Besides, walking was not just the best way to see a city, it was fun. You were supposed to have fun on a vacation.

It was early afternoon. The day was bright and sunny, for which the Londoners seemed surprised but pleased. The sidewalks were filled with people. Their pace was nearly as brisk as that of New Yorkers. London was a walking town.

Leaving the bustle of the city momentarily behind, Jane cut through Kensington Gardens and Hyde Park, a huge area of stately trees and strolling people. As she followed the road indicated on her map, crossing the long Serpentine Pond and heading toward Victoria Gate, Jane breathed in the strangely different air and enjoyed the sights. Men in bowler hats and unwarranted umbrellas. Teenagers with blue hair, tattoos, and rivets through their cheeks. Authentic nannies pushing authentic perambulators filled with authentic English babies (who looked pretty much like babies from anywhere else). Faces from every race and every nation on earth. London was as cosmopolitan a town as New York.

Oxford Street on the other side of the vast park was another world, a bustling commercial street of department stores and chain outlets pressed together end to end like the downtown of a city in the Midwest. The sidewalks overflowed with pedestrians and window-shoppers. The streets were jammed with buses, taxis, and a few dangerous-looking cyclists.

Past Oxford Circus, Jane turned up a street filled with offices and showrooms and quickly found herself on Mortimer, a busy but undistinguished thoroughfare filled mostly with office buildings, punctuated by a few Italian cafés and a pub or two.

When she looked at her watch, she found that more than an hour had passed since she had left the hotel. New York felt a million miles away. Imre had been right. Getting away from her troubles was just what she needed. Jane felt exhilarated and free as she approached the address she had been looking for.

It was a rather dreary little building, sandwiched between two larger gray edifices. Floral china plates and chargers filled the window. The name "Rosengolts et fils" appeared in discreet lettering on a sign above the navy blue door. Jane took a deep breath, let it out, then entered. As she did, a little bell rang.

The interior was larger than Jane had expected, a single room packed from floor to its high ceiling with chinaware, everything from demitasses to soup tureens, most of it decorated with old-fashioned floral patterns. Two different ladders were set up to reach the elevated merchandise. Wooden counters stretched the length of the shop on either side, manned by a pair of Dickensian-looking salesclerks, one male, one female, both with equally frozen expressions.

Jane approached the woman. She was a dowdy individual in her fifties, with dusty-looking hair and the eyes of a mouse. The pasty-faced male clerk stood like a statue in a cheap suit behind the opposite counter, looking on.

"Hi," said Jane. "My name is Jane Sailor."

"How may we serve you, Miss Sailor?" replied the woman.

"Is there a manager I could speak with? Or perhaps the owner?"

"That would be most irregular," said the woman, looking away. "Mr. Rosengolts does not usually see customers."

"I hope he'll make an exception for me," said Jane. "I've come all the way from America to show him something."

"And what might that be?"

"It's a personal matter," said Jane. "Won't you please ask?"

The woman stared at her fingers for another few seconds, apparently waiting to hear if there was anything more. Then, still not meeting Jane's eyes, she picked up a telephone intercom.

"A Miss Sailor from America wishes to see you, Mr. Rosengolts," she said.

Jane studied the rows of plates and shelves of serving pieces. Most of the designs were too precious or overdone for her taste, but a few simpler pieces caught her eye.

"Yes, sir," said the clerk into the phone. "Jane Sailor. She says she has brought something for you to look at. No, sir. She said it was personal. Yes, I understand. Very well, sir."

With a surprised expression, the woman put the receiver back into its cradle and turned to face Jane. "Mr. Rosengolts will see you, Miss Sailor. Follow me."

Jane followed her through a curtain at the rear of the store, down a passageway crammed with stacked crates full of china, some open, spilling their straw packing on the floor. At the end of the passage was a door. The clerk knocked once and entered, ushering Jane into a small, cluttered office.

"Miss Jane Sailor," announced the woman in a tiny voice.

An elderly man looked up from behind a battered old desk. There was an open ledger in front of him with a pencil on top of it, as if he had just stopped writing. He didn't speak, just stared.

The mousy clerk scurried away. The old man rose. He was probably in his seventies, Jane decided, tall and thin, with shrewd hard eyes, a sallow complexion, and a few gray wisps of hair. He wore a double-breasted black suit with a garish pinstripe, a blue shirt, and a wildly florid tie.

"Please, please, come in, come in," he said in an unctuous voice, waving Jane to the office's only other chair, a stiff, armless affair. His accent was a bright Cockney with a faint touch of something else, something vaguely Eastern European. "Sit down, make yourself comfortable."

"Are you Zalman Rosengolts?" asked Jane, doing her best to comply.

The man smiled as if Jane had made a very funny joke, then shook his head.

"Zalman was my grandfather. He died many years ago, as did my father. No, I am Isidore Rosengolts, the fils of the fils. And you are Miss Jane Sailor. From America."

"Yes. New York."

"Curious place, America," said Isidore Rosengolts, tapping the tips of his fingers together. "One of my grandchildren lives there. Wants to make a lot of money and thinks America is where you have to go to do that. Selling fine china is not good enough for anyone these days."

Jane looked around. There was not a photograph or a picture, nothing personal in the room. Steel shelving stood against walls stacked with the same wooden boxes as outside. The linoleum on the floor looked as if it had been there since the Blitz. There was a musty smell in the air.

"So, Miss Jane Sailor," said Isidore Rosengolts in the overly friendly voice of a salesman. "I understand you have something to show me. May I ask what it is?"

"It's a cross."

"A cross?" asked Rosengolts, raising an eyebrow.

Jane dug into the pocket of her slacks and produced the dragonfly cross, entwined with its black ribbon.

"It was my grandmother's."

She passed the cross across the desk to Rosengolts, who studied it, expressionless.

"Do you recognize it?" she asked. "I think it has something to do with your company."

"How did you come to us?" said Rosengolts, carefully ignoring her question. "How did you know the name Rosengolts?"

"It was on the bottom of the clock."

"Clock?"

"It's a rather . . . unusual . . . thing, made of ceramic, about this big," said Jane, indicating with her hands. "There are clockfaces with numerals but no hands on both sides. My grandmother brought it with her from Belgium when she came to America in the forties."

"We used to be in Antwerp before the war," said the old man slowly.

"I know," said Jane. "Rosengolts et fils, Antwerpen, is on the bottom of the clock. Along with a mark in the shape of this same dragonfly cross. But actually it's the clock that I'm more interested in. Anything you can tell me about it would be greatly appreciated."

"Do you have this clock with you? May I see it?"

"It's back in New York."

Isidore Rosengolts stared at her, his face still without expression.

"It's hard to know for sure without seeing it, but I would guess that your clock is one of my grandfather's pieces. He did all kinds of ceramic things back in the thirties. Clocks. Flowerpots. Mirror frames. They are all rather . . . well, you are being very diplomatic to use the word 'unusual.' "

"It is pretty garish," admitted Jane.

"I'm sure," said Rosengolts, nodding in a knowing manner. "I'm amazed that they've become so collectible, but then people have always been crazy. Look at Palissy ware. Look at those horrible Martin Brothers' parrots."

"Collectible?" said Jane. "You mean the clock is worth money?"

"Oh yes," said Isidore Rosengolts. "Don't sell it too cheaply is my advice to you. Collectors are constantly turning up at my doorstep offering to pay hundreds of pounds for authentic Zalman Rosengolts pieces, the more hideous the better. Bizarre, isn't it?"

Jane nodded, amazed.

"Why does my clock have the cross on the bottom?" she asked. "Isn't your company's symbol some kind of castle?"

"That's right," said Isidore Rosengolts, staring down at the cross in his hand for what seemed a long time. "But my father changed our maker's mark when we opened the store here in London after the war. He wanted to leave the past behind."

Isidore Rosengolts held up the cross and shook it gently.

"Before the war, we used a symbol much like this on our wares—but, please, it was not a cross. We are Jewish, and we would never have such a thing. No, it was a dragonfly. My grandfather adopted it as his mark after he won a competition at the 1926 Brussels International Exposition des Arts Décoratifs. The top honor was Le Grand Prix de Libellule: the dragonfly prize for fine china. The King of Belgium himself awarded my grandfather a medal that looked . . . well, it looked very like this piece you have brought today, though originally there was a yellow satin piece on top, here, with a pin in the back. When I was a little boy, I remember my grandfather would wear it on holidays sometimes and in parades. He looked very grand. If I didn't know better, I would think that this was the actual medal itself. You say it belonged to your grandmother?"

"Yes."

"May I ask your grandmother's name?"

"Luria," said Jane. "Sylvie Luria."

Rosengolts frowned, deep in thought. Suddenly, he looked up in amazement and slapped his forehead.

"My God!" he exclaimed. "I don't believe it!"

"What is it?" Jane asked, moving forward in her uncomfortable straight-backed chair.

"I think I understand," said Isidore Rosengolts, his voice growing excited, a great smile cleaving his stern old face. "These must be the people. I remember my father telling me. Yes, the Lurias. It comes back."

"What comes back?" said Jane. "Please tell me."

"This is incredible," said Isidore Rosengolts. He was a man transformed. His hands trembled with excitement. His gray eyes had come alive. Blood flowing into his face had made his cheeks rosy. "Forgive me, my dear. I was not expecting anything like this. Let me just catch my breath a moment."

Jane nodded, not knowing what to expect either. Rosengolts took a deep breath, then let it out.

"There was great confusion in Antwerp when the Nazis invaded," he said finally, his eyes far away. "I was just a boy, but as a Jew I knew what the war meant. For a time it looked as if none of my family would be able to get out of Belgium, but our neighbors the Lurias had somehow been lucky enough to arrange passage beforehand. My grandfather begged them to take the Grand Prix de Libellule out of the country to keep it safe. It had no monetary value, but it was a symbol. My grandfather saw it as the soul of our business, our future. Do you understand?"

"I think so," said Jane.

"Eventually, we did make it to Switzerland," said Rosengolts, nodding, "but we never heard from the Lurias again. We had to assume that they had not escaped after all, and had met the fate of so many. All these years we have believed that the medal was lost forever, stolen by the Nazis. Yet here you have brought it back. Le Grand Prix de Libellule, my grandfather's pride and joy. I cannot believe it."

Isidore Rosengolts held up the cross as though it was a lantern that could light the world.

"What a wonderful act of friendship for you to return this

precious medal to us," he said, his eyes suddenly moist with tears. "I am moved to the very depths of my soul by your kindness."

"I wasn't really going to . . ." began Jane, then stopped, not knowing what to say.

Isidore Rosengolts looked up in alarm.

"I haven't misunderstood, have I? You were returning it, weren't you? That's why you came here, yes?"

"Yes, of course," said Jane in a quiet voice.

"If it has a special meaning for you, then I wouldn't presume . . ."

His voice trailed off.

"No," said Jane. "You take it. I want you to have it."

Isidore Rosengolts squeezed the bridge of his nose and sniffed.

"Thank you from the bottom of my soul," he said, rising.

"I had no idea what it was," said Jane.

"No, of course not," said Rosengolts, leading her through the door and into the passageway back to the shop. "It is a fantastic thing in this cynical day and age that you would have such kindness and character to do what you have done. You are a fine young woman, and God will bless you."

"I'm glad to do it," said Jane as they entered the shop through the rear curtain. The two clerks instantly looked down, avoiding eye contact. As they made their way to the front door, Rosengolts spoke again.

"If you're looking to sell your clock, my dear, I'd be happy to help you. As I told you, I am constantly being approached by collectors. Nearly all the interest in my grandfather's wares is here in England. You'll get a much better price here than you ever could in America. You could just ship your clock over."

"Thanks, but it's not for sale."

"I could probably get you a thousand dollars," said Rosengolts.

"Really?"

"Collectors rarely go higher than a few hundred pounds, but

this sounds like a good piece. I would even guarantee you fifteen hundred, make up the difference out of my own pocket if required. You have done such a service to my family I'd like to do something for you in return."

"That's very kind of you but not necessary," said Jane.

The old man smiled a kindly smile and shrugged.

"Well, if you should ever change your mind, please give me a call. Are you staying in London long?"

"Just until Monday."

"Best of luck," said Isidore Rosengolts, pumping her hand. "And thank you again."

Jane stepped outside into the crowded street and headed back toward Oxford Street. What a strange journey the little dragonfly had had, she thought ruefully. From Antwerp to New York to London, across three generations and more than half a century, through basements and church services and now back to its rightful owners.

Jane wondered if Isidore Rosengolts would have a yellow satin pin attached and wear it on holidays and in parades. It was a funny thought, but Jane didn't laugh. She knew she should be happy that the cross had been returned, but all she felt was a tremendous sense of loss, as if she had made a terrible mistake, as if she had given away something precious that was not hers to give.

Jane walked a few blocks from the china shop, but the bad feelings only intensified. Suddenly, she stopped, turned around, and started to walk back the way she came. The dragonfly cross had always symbolized her mother, she realized, that was what this must be about. She was feeling the loss of her mother. What she needed was another symbol to take the place of the cross. Perhaps Rosengolts et fils had a sugar bowl to replace her little flowered one that had been smashed in last week's burglary. Something quiet and nice.

Jane retraced her steps back to the Mortimer Street shop, feeling a little better, wondering if she could maybe find a new butter dish, too. A hundred feet away a tall, freckle-faced man with dark red hair was at the curb in front of Rosengolts et fils, talking to the driver of the traditional black London cab that had just let him out.

Jane had to smile at herself. The man looked exactly like Valentine Treves. She must like Valentine more than she was admitting to herself if she was beginning to see him all over the place. As she got closer, however, her amusement turned to disbelief.

No, thought Jane, stepping into a doorway. It couldn't be! She had only met Valentine Treves once and there were a lot of tall men with freckles and red hair in the world. How could this possibly be the same man? But as she stood there just a few yards away, Jane knew—simply knew—that she wasn't wrong. The man standing in the street *was* Valentine Treves.

He hadn't seen her. Even if he had turned around, he probably wouldn't have picked her out of a crowd as someone he had met on an airplane to Seattle last week. It was only because he happened to be standing in front of this particular shop at this particular time that Jane was able to focus on him.

Jane wanted to call out, but found she couldn't speak. Valentine suddenly broke away from the cab, opened the navy blue door of Rosengolts et fils, and disappeared inside.

Jane stood paralyzed in the doorway, her head spinning, the dead hollow feeling of the past week returning to her stomach. What was Valentine doing here, of all places?

Before she could get her brain working straight, the navy blue door opened again and Valentine walked back to the waiting cab. He had been inside the china shop for only a few minutes.

As Valentine's cab pulled away, Jane stepped over to the curb and flagged down another taxi, this one white, with an ad for a radio station, "21 Million Britons Listen On The Road," stenciled across its sides.

"Follow that cab," she said, getting into the backseat.

"What's that, luv?"

"That cab in front of us. I want you to follow it."

"Is this a wind-up then?" said the driver, turning around and staring at her. He had a broad red English face, a long chin, and ears like tennis shoes.

"A what?"

"Are you having me on?"

"No, not at all," said Jane. "Please. It's very important."

"Bloomin' spy, she is," said the driver, shaking his head as he pulled away from the curb and regarding her suspiciously in the rearview mirror. "Let me ask you a question, luv. You don't 'ave to answer if you'd rather not."

"Don't let him get too far ahead."

" 'Eaven forbid. I'd just like to know whether all you Yanks are barmy or is it only the ones I get?"

"There's an extra five pounds in it for you if you don't lose him."

"Just like the movies, innit?"

It quickly became apparent that there really wasn't much chance of Valentine's cab getting too far ahead. The streets were clogged with traffic. Jane's cab crawled behind the black one carrying Valentine Treves, turning so often down narrow streets that she began to think they were going in circles. After ten minutes, however, the buildings themselves began to change, at first becoming massive, then growing in height and newness until several that could almost qualify as skyscrapers rose at streetside.

Finally, the cab in front of them halted at the entrance of a large modern building faced with glass. Valentine got out. Jane waited until he had walked from the curb and through the doors of the building before she paid her driver and got out, adding the promised fiver.

" 'Ope you get your man, luv," called the cabbie as she made toward the double doors through which Valentine Treves had disappeared. "And a good psychiatrist."

The lobby of the building Jane found herself in was as slick and modern as the glass exterior. The light fixtures were huge orbs of polished metal that could pass for flying saucers. The walls were unadorned white stone. The floor was gray industrial tile.

There were two banks of elevators with brushed stainless-steel doors, but Jane had no desire to make a floor-to-floor search. Instead, she walked over to a building roster in a large glass case by the door and scanned the long columns of company names and personnel. There was no Treves in the T section, but as she began again from the A's, her eye soon landed on a familiar name: "William S. H. Bogen & Co., Ltd. Pty. Room 1109." Willie Bogen. Willie the Weasel!

"May I help, miss?" said a voice.

Jane turned to find herself facing a small man wearing a uniform coat a size too big for him and an official-looking smile.

"I'm looking for Mr. Treves. Valentine Treves."

"Eleventh floor, miss," said the man, clearly proud of himself for knowing his tenants. "Works for old Mr. Bogen. Bogen & Company. Nice chap, Mr. Treves."

"I'm not so sure," said Jane, and walked out the door before the man could say another word. She felt hurt, betrayed, but most of all, confused. What the hell was going on?

The street seemed even brighter after the darkened lobby. Jane had walked several blocks before she realized she had no idea where she was, literally as well as figuratively. Her mind whirled with questions.

She pulled out her map, but it was another minute before she could orient herself. The building where Valentine Treves made his office with Willie the Weasel was in the City—the business section of London, the equivalent of Manhattan's Wall Street. Though it felt as if it was in another century, Rosengolts et fils was not too far from here.

As Jane walked in a daze back along the narrow, twisting streets, she tried to put the pieces together, to think things through logically, beginning with the question of why Valentine had been on that plane to Seattle.

The explanation was now obvious. He had been on his way to buy the lighthouse clock, of course. Perry Mannerback's arch rival, Willie Bogen, was a collector of clocks. Bogen must have somehow found out about the lighthouse clock and had dispatched his "Director of Special Acquisitions" to acquire it.

No wonder Valentine had been so startled on the plane when Jane mentioned that she worked for Perry Mannerback. Yet it was hardly a great coincidence that an agent for Willie Bogen might have ended up on the same flight as Jane and Perry. They were all going to the same place for the same reason.

But why had Valentine been coming out of Rosengolts et fils just now? It was an impossible coincidence that he had just happened to go shopping for china at this particular time at this particular store. What could Valentine and Mr. Rosengolts have in common? Could it have something to do with Grandmother Sylvie's clock?

Jane shook her head. It seemed incredible, but what other explanation could there be? Now she remembered that Valentine had even asked about the handless ceramic in Perry's painting the last time they had talked. Was it a prop, he had wondered, or an actual piece?

There were trees and wooden benches in the small grassy churchyard behind St. Paul's Cathedral, Christopher Wren's masterpiece. Gratefully, Jane made her way over to an empty bench and sat down. Her head was swirling. Her palms were damp. A woman passing on a bicycle gave her a quizzical look. Japanese tourists snapped photographs. The air smelled of taxicabs and spring.

If the clock was at the center of everything, then she had been seeing everything from the wrong point of view. Sometimes Jane worked out fight routines by pretending she was someone's fist or the tip of an actor's sword. Now she closed her eyes and pretended that she was Grandmother Sylvie's clock. What did she see?

The first thing Jane realized was that there were really two clocks—the ceramic monstrosity in her basement and its representation in the Aaron Sailor painting that Perry Mannerback had purchased. For the past eight years, the real clock had seen nothing from its box on the basement ledge. The clock in the painting had seen only what went on in Perry Mannerback's study.

Then, two Sundays ago, Perry's painting was reproduced in the *Sunday Times Magazine* where it could see—and be seen—by the entire world. After that, things began to happen quickly. Somebody had injected Aaron Sailor with insulin that very night. Jane's apartment was broken into a few days later. And now Valentine Treves was paying a call at Rosengolts et fils. How could all these things be connected to the clock's appearance in the newspaper unless . . . ?

Jane opened her eyes.

"Someone recognized it," she said out loud, stunned.

But how could anyone recognize a clock that had been relegated to top shelves and basements for decades? For someone to recognize it meant that he must have seen it in the 1930s or 1940s. He would have to be an old man now. An old man with an interest in clocks. How old was "old Mr. Bogen," the clock collector?

A chill went down Jane's spine. It wasn't unlikely that Valentine might have directed his employer's attention to the article in last Sunday's *New York Times*. Valentine would know that Bogen might be interested in a painting that featured an unusual clock.

The minute that Bogen opened the *New York Times* and saw the ceramic in Perry's painting, he would know that the real ceramic clock had once been in Aaron Sailor's possession. For the artist to paint it, he would had to have had access to it. Bogen would also know that somebody else had the clock now, since the article made it clear that Aaron Sailor had been in a coma for eight years.

And if the clock hadn't been sold or otherwise disposed of, Bogen could assume that it was now with a relative.

Who was Aaron Sailor's only living relative according to the obituary in the *Times*? Jane L. of Manhattan, who, according to the same obituary, was going to be at the Frank E. Campbell Funeral Home last Thursday morning at eleven o'clock.

In short, Willie Bogen—and his employee Valentine Treves, who just happened to have been in New York last week—had all the information they needed to break into her apartment at a time when it was certain that she wasn't going to be home. She'd even told Valentine her address was listed in the phonebook!

Jane took a deep breath. It all fit. Willie Bogen had sent Valentine to break into her apartment. And the reason that nothing was taken was because Bogen and Treves couldn't have known the clock was down in the basement.

But why did Willie the Weasel want Grandmother Sylvie's clock so badly? You hear about lunatic collectors—Jane had recently worked for one, in fact—but this was ridiculous. Bogen had just shelled out over a hundred thousand dollars for a lighthouse clock.

"A man like that isn't going to break into my house for a hideous piece of junk, no matter how collectible it is," said Jane aloud.

A woman strolling past on the sidewalk took one look at Jane talking to herself, grabbed her daughter's hand, and hastened away. More Japanese tourists took more pictures. A clock tolled ironically in the distance. Jane shook her head.

This was crazy. The *Times* had a circulation of hundreds of thousands. Someone else—a total stranger—could have seen the picture of the clock in the article, read the obituary, looked up her address in the phonebook, and broken in. Or it could have been just a random burglary, as Lieutenant Folly said. How could a man like Valentine have had anything to do with such a thing?

But then she didn't really know anything about Valentine

Treves, Jane reminded herself. She didn't know what kind of man he was or what he was capable of. Just because he could write a sonnet on cue didn't mean he couldn't also break into an apartment on orders.

Jane stood up. The sun still beamed on the ancient buildings of London. Birds still sang in the trees. Somehow, however, everything had changed.

As Jane started off again, a single thought consoled her: at least there was still nothing to suggest that Valentine might be involved in her father's murder. Royaume Israel had not been mentioned in the *Times* article and there would be no easy way for anyone to have found out that Aaron Sailor had been brought to Yorkville East End for tests.

The only person who had known about that was Perry Mannerback.

Jane awoke at a quarter after six the next morning feeling anything but refreshed after a fitful night of anxious dreams.

Yesterday she had wandered down Fleet Street and the Strand from the City, struggling without success to make connections between Willie Bogen, Perry Mannerback, Isidore Rosengolts, Valentine Treves. Eventually she had tired of walking and made her way back to her hotel aboard a red double-decker bus. Feeling jet-lagged and exhausted, she had pecked at a fish-and-chips dinner from one of the cleaner-looking Cromwell Road joints, more out of curiosity than hunger, and gone to bed at nine—four o'clock in the afternoon New York time.

This morning, things were even less clear. The bathroom was down the hall and there was no shower, only a huge tub. As Jane washed her face and brushed her teeth, she tried to laugh off yesterday's disconcerting events and the chain of logic with which she had tried to tie everything together. Was it really reasonable to believe that Willie Bogen was some kind of criminal mastermind, pursuing ceramic clocks across decades and continents? Wasn't it more likely everything that had happened over the last week had just made her paranoid?

Jane went back to her room and dressed quickly, then headed down the stairs of the fussy little hotel into a gray London morning. Maybe things would make more sense over a bagel and a cup of coffee.

Unfortunately, this part of London bore little resemblance to the Upper West Side in the eat-any-kind-of-food-you-want-at-any-hour-of-day-or-night department. There were no bagel joints anywhere, and neither the Italian restaurant across the street nor a "Workmans Café" down the block were open yet. The streets were fairly deserted.

It began to drizzle. Jane walked with her hands in her pockets, trying to figure out what to do. For a moment, she actually thought of going back to Mr. Rosengolts and asking how he knew Valentine Treves, but quickly decided against it.

Somewhere in the pit of her stomach she knew that it had been a mistake to have given her mother's dragonfly cross to Rosengolts. She felt she had betrayed herself, but she didn't know about what or with whom.

Jane had been walking for ten minutes when she found herself at the Gloucester Road entrance of the London subway, the famous Tube. Torturing herself over things she didn't understand wasn't going to help. She needed more information, and there was only one person left in London who might be able to tell her anything.

It was time to see Leila Peach.

Jane descended the station stairs and waited on an astonishingly clean platform until the train arrived. According to the address on the last Christmas card Leila Peach had sent to Imre Carpathian, she now lived in Whitechapel, which Jane's map revealed to be in London's East End, past the City on the other side of town.

Jane had successfully negotiated the New York subway system

all of her life, so the Tube didn't present many problems. Straight through on the District line, the ride took less than half an hour. At half-past seven, Jane emerged into a neighborhood far different from those she had wandered through the previous day. Threadbare ornate structures from the area's Victorian past (this was where Jack the Ripper had done his work) stood shoulder to shoulder with postwar apartment monstrosities. The streets seemed smaller here somehow, the dreary sky lower.

There were a surprising number of people on the street considering the hour, but they were much different from the shoppers and businesspeople Jane had seen swarming the busy streets of tourist London yesterday. The faces here were streetwise, with suspicious eyes and hard features. The ethnic mix varied wildly: Anglo-Saxons, Asians, Middle Easterners, and even an occasional Hasidic Jew. On some streets there were so many veiled women and men in turbans that this almost could have been a neighborhood in Bangladesh or Pakistan. Signs on buildings advertised tea and Polaroid film, solicitors and snooker, lager beer. There were even familiar signs for McDonald's and Pizza Hut, Jane shuddered to see.

It took another ten minutes to find Leila's house, a drab two-story brick building with a dry cleaner on the ground floor. Identical structures abutted it on either side, one housing a drab little clothing store, the other a place that sold "artificial jewelry." Down the street was a scaffolded derelict building which, judging from the plant life growing up the walls, must have been empty for years. For someone who had been subletting a loft on Greene Street eight years ago, Leila must have come down considerably in the world to be living in a neighborhood like this.

It was too early in the morning to pay a call on a stranger, but Jane didn't care. If Leila had a job, she'd be leaving for work soon, and Jane didn't want to miss her. She climbed the cracking concrete steps and pressed the doorbell.

After a minute, the door was opened by a tall woman with unnaturally black hair and eyebrows plucked into calligraphic thinness. She was dressed in a pink bathrobe littered with embroidered daisies. A cigarette dangled from her pale lips.

"So what are you sellin'?" said the woman, who bore no resemblance to the nude in Perry's painting. "D'you know what bleedin' time it is?"

"I'm looking for Leila Peach," said Jane.

"You're not going to find her then, are you?"

"She's left for work already?"

"She's left, flat. Cleared out Sunday, when I was at me mum's. Stuck me for two months' rent, she did. Left half her stuff. I'm going to be cleaning up the cow's garbage for a month."

Scowling, the woman went to close the door.

"Please," said Jane, stopping it with her hand. "It's very important."

"Leila owes you money, too?"

"No," said Jane, "it's nothing like that. Do you know where she went?"

The woman made a disgusted face and shrugged. The ash on her cigarette was dangerously long but miraculously didn't dislodge onto her ample chest.

"Back to New York, according to the bleedin' note she left. Leila saw a bit about some artist in the New York newspaper a week back and got very excited. Said she knew this bloke, see, and now he's famous. From the greedy look in her eyes, I should have known right then. I'm sure she's figured out a way she can cash in on him."

"She won't," said Jane, bitterly disappointed. Leila wasn't even here. She had crossed an entire ocean for nothing.

"Oh, she'll find some way to get money out of it," said the woman. "You don't know Leila."

"The man was my father," said Jane. "He's been in a coma since he fell down a flight of stairs eight years ago. He died last week."

The woman's hard face suddenly seemed to transform itself.

"You mean *he* was the one in the paper?" she exclaimed. "The same poor sod Leila left at the bottom of the stairs like that?"

Jane opened her mouth to speak, but nothing came out for a moment.

"Left at the bottom of the stairs?" she finally managed.

"You don't know about that? No, how could you? What's the matter with me?"

"I don't understand," said Jane, suddenly feeling weak in the knees.

"Are you all right, luv? Hey, I'm sorry. I didn't know, really I didn't. Please come in, won't you? I'm Suzy, by the way. Suzy McCorkle."

"Jane Sailor."

The woman ushered Jane up a rickety flight of steps and through a battered doorway, past a neat sitting room and into a small but bright kitchen. An old kettle was steaming on the stove. A little table, set for one, featured a vase of violets and the remains of a bowl of cereal.

"Maybe you should eat something," said Suzy McCorkle. "Cheerios, perhaps? Very good for one, beneficial for the digestion and all. And a pleasant name to start the morning with, that. Cheerios."

"No, thanks."

"A biscuit? Cuppa tea? No, you'd probably prefer coffee. Well, I got just the thing. Instant in a bleedin' little jar. It was Leila's and I've no use for it. I wish you'd take some. You look a bit shaky."

"All right," said Jane. "Thanks."

Suzy McCorkle flashed a pleased smile and stubbed out her cigarette into an ashtray on the table next to her Cheerios. Then she went to a cupboard, brought out a jar of coffee, spooned a teaspoon into a cup painted with flowers, and poured from the kettle. She put a tea bag into another cup and poured for herself.

"Thanks," said Jane, as Suzy returned to the table with the steaming cups.

"Feelin' a bit better? I really didn't mean to upset you like that."

"I'm not upset," said Jane. "I just don't understand what you meant about Leila leaving my father at the bottom of the stairs."

"No, of course not, you poor thing," said Suzy, pouring what looked like an unnatural amount of milk into her tea, then spooning in an equal portion of sugar. "Well, I don't know why I shouldn't tell you. I owe her nothin'. Here it is, then. Leila told me this one night a few months back. We was drinking brandy and eating ice cream, feeling sorry for ourselves, comparing sob stories. Leila told me that when she lived in the New York SoHo, there was this artist she was involved with, see? She had a loft and he lived upstairs. It was startin' to get pretty serious, I gather."

Jane nodded.

"Then they had this terrible row and a big public breakup, your father and Leila," Suzy went on, looking down into her tea. "Leila has a fierce temper and had made threats. People had heard. A few days later, she comes back to her loft from a party and she sees some bloke rushing out of the building, all upset-like."

"Who was it?"

"Leila said she didn't know, but when she opened the front door, she found her artist—your father—on the floor in the vestibule. She thought he was dead. His head was all cracked open. There was blood all over the place. Leila figured he had fallen down the stairs or something, but figured the police might not think it was an accident if she was involved. A year before this, Leila had shot another lover, see?"

"Shot him?"

"Well, just grazed him, actually, according to her. I told you, Leila has a terrible temper, and she claimed that anybody in New York City can get a gun any time they want to. Is that true?"

"I don't think so," said Jane, taking a sip of her coffee. It tasted like furniture polish with a slight hint of old shoe.

"Leila was always bragging that she knew six different places in different parts of town where a person could get a gun, day or night. 'T'isn't wholesome."

"New York has very strict gun control laws," said Jane, adding as much milk and sugar as her cup would hold. "There are mandatory jail terms just for having one."

"Yeah," said Suzy. "That's just what Leila said—you can get in more trouble for having a gun than for shooting somebody with it. That's why she got rid of hers after she shot the bloke."

Jane took another sip of her coffee, a mistake she wouldn't repeat again.

"The judge eventually threw out her case," Suzy continued, "but Leila was terrified that if the police came now and found her with another lover dead on the stairs, they'd never believe she hadn't done it—especially after the way she'd threatened him. So in a panic she went back to the party to give herself an alibi. She'd never been missed. Nobody ever came looking for her. Apparently, the authorities reckoned it was an accident."

"Why did Leila threaten my father?" asked Jane. "What did she say?"

"Oh, Leila was going to kill him if he interfered with her plans," said Suzy, making a face. "Didn't care if he was the father, said she'd kill him. Screamed this in a crowded restaurant, she did."

"Father?"

Suzy looked down.

"Leila was preggers, see? Your dad was probably the one, but she'd been seeing another man at the same time, a really rich bloke, some kind of buttonmaker. Leila had decided she was going to tell the rich chap that he was the dad, since his prospects were so much the better."

Jane took a deep breath and let it out. It was even worse than she had thought. Leila, pregnant by Aaron Sailor and about to pin the paternity on a man who still all these years later couldn't bear to admit he even knew her name.

"Perry Mannerback," Jane muttered under her breath.

"Beg pardon?"

"Perry Mannerback was the man Leila saw coming out of the loft that night."

"No," said Suzy, shaking her head. "I told you, Leila didn't know who it was that she saw that night. Figured it was just somebody who didn't want to get involved."

"It had to have been Perry," said Jane bitterly. "He was the rich guy that Leila was going to claim was the father of her child. The buttonmaker."

"No," said Suzy, taking a decisive sip of tea. "That wasn't his name."

"Yes, of course it was," said Jane. "Perry Mannerback. The greatest buttonmaker in the world."

"He may be that, but he wasn't the one Leila had been fooling around with. Believe me, I know the name of Leila's buttonmaker very well indeed. I'm reminded on a meal-to-meal basis."

As if on cue, a fat gray cat leaped into Jane's lap.

"Leila named her cat after him, you see," said Suzy. "Meet Mr. Danko."

Jane returned to her hotel feeling as though her head was about to spin off. Leila finding Aaron Sailor at the bottom of the stairs. Leila fooling around with the CEO of OmbiCorp, Ted Danko. Leila pregnant. And now, eight years later, Leila suddenly moving back to New York.

Why would Leila move back just because Aaron Sailor had gotten some good publicity? Leila already knew about the clock.

She had posed with it. Why would seeing Perry's painting in the newspaper make any difference to her now?

Cold rain slapped against the little window. There was no heat. Jane felt more alone than ever. After a few more unsuccessful minutes of trying to sort things out in her mind, she picked up the heavy black telephone next to her bed and called the airport. Her return ticket wasn't until next Monday morning, but there was no point staying in London for another four nights. All the answers were back in New York. She had to get home and find Leila, talk to Ted Danko.

"I'm sorry," said the New York ticket agent after listening to Jane's request. "I'm afraid that this is one of our busiest times. All flights are sold out until next week."

"Yes," said Jane. "But I don't need to stay in London for the whole time. Isn't there anything that can be done?"

"Perhaps you might consider making the best of things," said the woman brightly. "London is really quite an appealing place. There are museums, shops, tourist attractions. You could catch a show. Are you sure you can't use a bit of vacation?"

"I guess I'll have to," said Jane. "Thanks, anyway."

Jane hung up the phone and resumed staring at the ceiling, trying to clear her brain, trying to make room for thoughts of shopping and Covent Garden and the Tower of London. It took only a minute, however, before Leila Peach, smirking and naked on the stairs, pushed everything else out.

Why was Leila moving back to New York just because she had seen the article in the *Times*? Jane was more certain than ever that Valentine and Willie Bogen, Isidore Rosengolts and Leila Peach, were all parts of the same puzzle. A puzzle that somehow revolved around the ceramic clock. But how could she discover the connections? Obviously, no one was going to admit anything to her, unless . . .

The idea was so simple that Jane had to laugh out loud. She

reached under the end table for one of the London phonebooks, then dialed the number for Bogen & Company. When the receptionist answered, Jane asked for Valentine Treves. When asked who was calling, Jane said that her name was Leila Peach.

"Treves," he answered on the first ring. "Miss Peach, is it?"

"Leila Peach. Don't you remember me?"

"I don't think so. Should I? Your voice does sound a bit familiar. American, obviously."

Jane didn't know whether she should be happy or disappointed.

"Actually, my name isn't Leila Peach. It's Jane Sailor."

There was a pause. Jane could almost see his goofy auburn eyebrows colliding in startled confusion.

"Jane! How lovely to hear from you."

"Surprised?"

"No. I mean, yes, a little. Pleasantly, of course. Why the subterfuge, the false name?"

"I wanted to surprise you."

"I'm surprised. Funny, I don't recall giving you this number."

"Funny," said Jane, "I don't recall your mentioning that you worked for Willie Bogen."

There was another pause.

"I was going to tell you," Valentine said finally, "really I was. It just seemed so awkward. I was waiting for the right moment."

"Like the right moment in Seattle when you were buying that lighthouse clock out from under Perry Mannerback?"

"There was nothing untoward about it, Jane," said Valentine, a trifle defensive. "We simply beat you to the prize, that's all."

"What were you doing coming out of Rosengolts yesterday afternoon?" she asked angrily. Now that she was talking to him, she might as well go for broke.

"How do you know about that?"

"I saw you. I followed you back to your office."

"You're in London!"

"Brilliant deduction, Sherlock."

"But this is marvelous," said Valentine. "I wasn't able to show you Seattle, but I hope you'll let me show you London. How long are you going to be here?"

"I'm going back on Monday. You haven't answered my question."

"I'll tell you all about it over lunch, how's that? Where are you staying?"

"Please, Valentine," said Jane. "You're working for a man that Perry hates. I see you coming out of the shop of the person that I specifically came to London to see. I need to know what's going on. Just tell me what your involvement is with Mr. Rosengolts. Please."

"Well, it's certainly nothing sinister, if that's what's worrying you," said Valentine. "My employer, Mr. Bogen, happened to have been in the same Swiss detention camp as the Rosengolts family during the Second World War and he occasionally does business with them, that's all. May I ask how you happen to know Rosengolts et fils?"

"I'd rather not go into that," said Jane. "What kind of business does Mr. Bogen have with Mr. Rosengolts just now?"

"I'm afraid it would be indiscreet, professionally speaking, for me to tell you."

"Then tell me why you were so interested in the ceramic clock in my father's painting. You asked me about it when you called me last week."

There was another long silence.

"Well," said Valentine finally, "if I may be honest, this clock is the sort of thing that Mr. Bogen might be interested in. If it's in your possession, that is."

"It is, but it's not for sale."

"We'd give you a good price for it."

"How much?"

"Well, that's difficult to say offhand," said Valentine, suddenly sounding guarded and very remote. "How much would you ask?"

"How about ten thousand dollars?"

"That's certainly possible."

"Mr. Rosengolts told me that his grandfather's ceramics weren't worth more than a few hundred pounds."

"Is that what he told you?"

"Yes, that's what he told me. So why are you willing to pay so much for this particular one?"

"You know you sound very pretty this morning," said Valentine. "What are you wearing?"

"Don't change the subject. Why would you pay ten thousand dollars for my clock?"

"Mr. Bogen is a collector. It would be worth that much to him."

"Would you pay twenty thousand?"

"Perhaps."

"How about fifty thousand?"

"Jane, I know that you're angry with me. I apologize for not being more forthcoming with you. I care about you, really I do."

"Then how come you're playing games with me about the value of my clock?"

"This is business, Jane. In a negotiation, my first responsibility has to be with my employer."

"I see," Jane replied icily.

"I must tell you that you've become involved in a very complex situation," said Valentine, his voice soft and sincere. "Isidore Rosengolts is a very difficult person. He is not what he appears to be."

"And you are?"

"Please, Jane. If you'll just tell me where you're staying . . ."

Jane hung up the phone, then sat staring out the window for a long time, trying to add it all up.

Valentine Treves and Willie Bogen were after her clock. Unless Valentine was a great actor, he didn't know Leila Peach. Isidore Rosengolts now had a cross that was somehow related to the clock. Ted Danko, not Perry Mannerback, had been involved with Leila Peach.

But why would any of these facts impel someone to push Aaron Sailor down the stairs eight years ago? Why did someone give him a fatal injection of insulin last week?

And when, Jane wondered, would she ever feel safe again?

The time difference ran in the other direction for the eight o'clock flight back to New York on Monday morning. Jane arrived at Kennedy International airport a little after 10 a.m. local time.

After clearing Customs with nothing to declare but a blouse from Harrods, several cans of tea from Fortnum & Mason, and a pounding headache, she took a cab directly to the offices of Ombi-Corp International on Sixth Avenue. Having had a long weekend of cooling her heels playing American tourist in London, she didn't intend to wait another minute to confront Mr. Theodore B. Danko.

Jane finessed the young woman at reception whom she had previously befriended, then made her way to Danko's offices. She hadn't been in this part of the building before, and it took another ten minutes to make her way through three dressed-for-success secretarial gatekeepers. All of them were less than impressed with Jane's black travel blazer that now had thirty-five hundred miles worth of wrinkles in it. After satisfying each of them that she didn't intend to leave until he saw her, however, Jane was finally admitted to Danko's private office, a light-filled suite twice the size of Perry Mannerback's.

The CEO of the OmbiCorp empire was seated behind the enormous Biedermeier table that served as his desk. He was dressed in an elegantly cut black suit, a crisp white shirt with the initials TBD on its french cuffs, gold cufflinks, and a Hermès tie. Behind him was a fieldstone wall with a fireplace in the center. In front of him was a telephone, a crystal decanter of ice water, and a glass. The tabletop was otherwise bare. Danko was studying an annual report through half-moon reading glasses. Jane entered and made the long cross to one of the blond-wood armchairs opposite him. He didn't look up.

"I'd like to talk to you about Leila Peach, Mr. Danko," said Jane, sitting down. "I'm Jane Sailor. Remember me?"

Danko didn't answer, just continued to stare at the report as if there were no one in the room but himself.

"I know that you were involved with Leila eight years ago, Mr. Danko."

Still no answer.

"I know that she was pregnant."

Danko let out a weary sigh.

"I don't see why this would be any of your business, Ms. Sailor," he said in a quiet voice, peering owl-like at her over the tortoiseshell rims of his glasses.

"It's my business because my dad may have been the father of that child."

"I see," said Danko, putting his report aside, taking off his glasses, and fixing her in his cold gray eyes. "And what child would that be?"

Jane met his gaze and didn't answer for a moment. She had asked Suzy McCorkle what had become of the child Leila was pregnant with. Suzy didn't know. Leila hadn't wanted to talk about it.

"A man was seen rushing out of my father's loft building the night he fell down the stairs eight years ago," said Jane. "Was that you?"

"I'm a busy man, Ms. Sailor. I have said all I intend to say about this matter to the police. Good day."

"What do the police have to do with this?" asked Jane, surprised.

Danko studied her for a moment.

"Don't you know?" he asked, arching an eyebrow. "Isn't that why you've been giving me your rendition of the third degree?"

"Know what? What are you talking about?"

"I'm talking about Leila Peach. She's dead."

"No," said Jane, feeling herself deflate into the chair. "I don't believe it."

"They found her body Saturday morning in a midtown hotel room," said Danko with what appeared to be some satisfaction. "She'd been shot with a small-caliber handgun. Unfortunately, my name appeared in her address book, as did Perry's. I've already had a rather unpleasant conversation about Miss Peach with the police, and I do not care to have another with you. Now, if you will excuse me, I have a corporation to run."

Finding herself speechless, Jane stood up and left the room. She collected her suitcase and carry-on bag from Danko's secretary, then made her way to Barbara Fripp's office at the other side of the building.

Miss Fripp was sitting behind her old-fashioned mahogany desk in the small, philodendron-filled office between the bustle of OmbiCorp International and Perry Mannerback's quiet suite.

"Is Perry here?" asked Jane.

"He's nowhere to be found as usual," said Miss Fripp a little too breezily. Her brown hair, usually solidly sprayed together, evidenced several renegade strands. The wrinkles at the corners of her mouth and along her lips were deeper than usual. She looked harried and concerned.

"Have the police spoken with him?"

"Why would the police want to speak with Perry?" asked Miss Fripp with an uncharacteristic laugh, still poker-faced and professionally discreet.

"I know about the woman who died," said Jane. "Danko told me."

Barbara Fripp's manufactured smile disappeared.

"I don't know where Perry is," she confessed, looking relieved to be able to admit it. "The police have been trying to question him since the day of your father's funeral, but Perry hasn't wanted to speak with them. Mr. Ruiz and Mr. Apoustocle—they're Perry's attorneys—have been putting them off with written statements, but things have gotten quite impossible since that Peach woman was killed. Perry finally had to agree to a detective's ringing him up this morning at home where Mr. Ruiz and Mr. Apoustocle could listen in on the extension. I telephoned to see how it went when I got in, but Perry had already left."

"Where did he go?"

"I don't know," said Miss Fripp, shaking her head, staring out the glass walls of the office at the skyscraper across the street. "Olinda is very emotional. All I could get was that Perry had had a long telephone conversation with a police lieutenant and was very upset. Apparently, he dashed off somewhere without his coat."

"Would you mind if I called Olinda?"

"No, not at all," said Miss Fripp, turning her phone around to face Jane. "It's outrageous that the authorities would harass Perry like this. He couldn't have had anything to do with that woman who was killed, and I can't imagine why they were pestering him about your father. Perry's just a little boy. He's very sensitive. I'm terribly concerned."

Jane dialed the number for Perry's apartment. Olinda answered, but as Barbara Fripp had said, her answers weren't very comprehensible.

"Why policemen make this trouble?" demanded Olinda after

a blur of Spanish. "Perry all unhappy, very unhappy. He try to talk to them nice on the phone, but they say bad things, make him all angry. 'I no have to take this,' say Perry. 'I have big company. They write about me all the time in newspapers and on TV. I no have to take this.' "

"Where did he go, Olinda?" Jane asked again.

"Mr. Ruiz and Mr. Apoustocle, they think they're so smart. They make Perry to talk to police, and now look. He cry. Tears come onto his face. He very sad. Why they do this?"

"Did Perry say anything before he left?"

"He say he sick of questions, he want be with only true honest people in New York. He say for everybody to leave him alone. Just leave him alone."

"Only true honest people in New York?" repeated Jane. "What did he mean by that? Who was he going to see?"

"How Olinda know? Perry crazy. He run out. Not take his coat or nothing. Perry always crazy but not like this. Very bad."

Jane said good-bye, then turned to face a concerned Barbara Fripp.

"Where is Perry going to find any true honest people in New York?" asked Jane.

"Not here, that's for certain," answered Fripp, frowning. "He couldn't mean his relatives, either. Or his attorneys." She shook her head. "I have no idea."

"I'm going home and standing in a hot shower for an hour," said Jane with a sigh. "Please call me if you hear anything. It's really important that I speak with Perry."

Fripp nodded. Jane took the long elevator ride down to the real world, then caught a cab on Sixth.

Ten minutes later, the taxi pulled up in front of her brownstone. In the lobby, Jane briefly put down her bags to collect a wedge of junk mail from her box, then wearily climbed the four flights of stairs. At the top landing she dug into her pocket for her keys, but when she touched the handle of the door to her apartment, she found it was open. Only then did she see the fresh jimmy marks on the side of the repaired doorframe.

"Oh, for God's sake," she exclaimed in dismay, entering the darkened room and depositing her bags inside. The door closed behind her as she turned on a light. There was a strange woman sitting on her couch.

Even seated, the intruder looked large. She was a flat-chested, bleached blonde, with the shoulders of a linebacker. Probably twice Jane's weight, she was dressed against type in designer jeans, a loose-fitting pink cashmere sweater, and diamond stud earrings. She wore an ugly expression on her flat broad face.

"Who are you?" demanded Jane, astonished. "What are you doing in my apartment?"

"Where is it?" replied the woman, standing up slowly from her relaxed position on the couch, not bothering to reach for the little leather purse at her side. Her voice was surprisingly high and childish for someone so big—the woman was at least six feet tall, Jane estimated. She spoke with a British accent.

"Where is what?" said Jane, feeling her hands get cold and her stomach rise toward her heart. "What do you want?"

"You know."

"I don't have much money, but you can have it all," said Jane, reaching into the side pocket of her blazer for her wallet. This was no time to be a heroine.

"Where is it?" repeated the woman.

"Where's what?"

"The clock, you stupid git. I know you've got it. I didn't find it before, but you've got it, by Christ."

Finally, Jane understood. The clock. Of course, it had to be about Grandmother Sylvie's clock, safe in the basement.

"I don't know what you're talking about," she lied.

The woman reached down and pressed the "play" button on Jane's answering machine.

"Jane, it's Valentine. It's Friday afternoon. I'm in New York, at the Carlyle Hotel. I know you're getting back on Monday, and I would very much like to speak to you about your ceramic clock with no hands. Please ring me when you get in."

"Look, who are you?" demanded Jane. "Get out of my apartment. You have no right . . ."

The woman didn't wait for the rest of Jane's attempted indignation. Instead, she tore the answering machine by its cords out of the wall and hurled it at Jane's head. Jane ducked in disbelief. By the time the machine smashed against the door, the intruder had charged across the room and was upon her, giving Jane a slap that sent her flying.

"You're going to give me that clock," said the woman, showing a smile of perfectly capped teeth. "You're going to beg to give it to me."

Jane picked herself off the floor, holding her head in her hands, pretending to be dazed (which wasn't difficult, considering the stars that presently were dancing around in front of her).

Her opponent was clearly not expecting any kind of credible resistance. Smiling, she walked slowly over and drew Jane to her by the lapels of her jacket. Jane was close enough to smell the woman's expensive perfume before she suddenly stamped her foot down on her attacker's instep, then swung her clasped hands at the woman's jaw.

It was a series of movements that Jane had often used in fight routines, and it looked positively lethal.

The trouble was that, while she understood perfectly how to mimic the appearance of a kick or a punch, Jane had no idea how to actually hurt someone. Stage combat was about diffusing and deflecting energy, not directing it to do damage. When you kicked someone, you kicked from the knee and put most of your energy into your foot's return trip from its target. When you pretended to strangle, you were really pulling your hands away from the victim's neck with all your strength, while he frantically tried to hold them there. Everything was designed so that the audience would see the energy of the fight, not where it was going.

It was not surprising, therefore, that Jane hadn't stomped on her assailant's instep hard enough or landed her blow squarely enough to incapacitate. The woman had released her grip merely out of surprise. Jane's attack had hurt her only enough to infuriate.

With a roar, the woman now struck back with a fist at Jane's face. Jane dodged backwards just in time to save her teeth. The next minute was a nightmare. There was no choreography, no neat series of holds and punches, just wild swings, grasped limbs, and frantic scrambles as the intruder tried to batter Jane and Jane did her best to get away from her larger opponent.

At one point, the woman had gotten hold of her from behind. Jane was sure it was all over until she had the wits to use her teeth. At another point, she squirmed free from a bear hug by frantically jabbing her thumb into a pressure point on the woman's neck the way she had learned in a junior lifesaver's swimming class.

Suddenly they were on opposite sides of the tiny apartment and the woman again had enough room to charge. Jane was pinned into the corner that served as her kitchen, but this time she didn't try to get away.

She didn't consciously remember the jujitsu principle of using an attacker's inertia against him. In fact, there was nothing in her mind at all. She simply waited to meet the massive figure hurtling toward her, then stepped aside and helped the woman go exactly where she seemed to want to go—right through the spot where Jane had just been standing—giving a little push to help speed her along her way. The result was that the woman collided headfirst with the half-height refrigerator that Jane had been standing in front of.

Jane wasn't sure whether the resultant *thunk* was the product of head meeting metal or of the same head meeting oak floor a second later. In either case, it was a sickening sound. The fight was over just as suddenly as it had begun.

Jane stood for a second, dazed, considering the real possibility that her intruder was dead. You could easily break your neck colliding with a refrigerator, even if your neck happened to be as thick as this woman's was. Then, on the other hand, she might just be stunned, ready to get up any second, *really* angry this time.

Jane bent down and got close enough to ascertain that her attacker was still breathing. Then, very quietly—was it possible to wake someone who had collided with a refrigerator?—she walked over to the couch and opened the woman's little Coach leather purse. Inside was the usual girl equipment. Jane riffled past a lipstick, some keys, and a comb until she found the woman's wallet and unsnapped it. The name on the platinum American Express card inside was Melissa Rosengolts.

"Oh, my God," gasped Jane, suddenly understanding. In the London china shop, Jane had told Isidore Rosengolts that the clock was in her possession and that she was going back to New York on Monday. He had told her that he had a grandchild in America.

The unconscious whale on the floor had said that she hadn't found the clock "before." It had been Melissa Rosengolts who had broken into Jane's apartment during Aaron Sailor's funeral, not Willie Bogen and Valentine Treves. Melissa Rosengolts must have seen the article with Perry's painting in the *Sunday Times* and gotten Jane's address from the phonebook. Or perhaps it had been Isidore Rosengolts who had first read the newspaper in London and who had then called his granddaughter with instructions.

In either case, Jane had been no stranger to Isidore Rosengolts when she had walked into his shop last week. He must have been astounded, but he played a frighteningly good hand of poker—Jane certainly gave him that. Here, the owner of the very clock he had just conspired unsuccessfully to steal had crossed an ocean to let him know that she still had it in her possession and to present him with a nice little gift for all his trouble.

Melissa Rosengolts moaned softly.

It was time to call the police. The telephone on the table seemed no worse for having its answering machine forcibly amputated, but Jane wasn't going to hang around and wait for Isidore Rosengolts's granddaughter to wake up. Instead, she dashed out the door and down the stairs, not slowing down until she had reached the east side of Broadway, several blocks away. There she found a pay phone and dialed 911.

After calmly relating the details of what had happened—including the fact that her attacker might need an ambulance—she asked to be connected to Lieutenant Octavio Folly.

"You'll have to dial that number yourself directly," said the emergency operator.

"I don't have his number with me," said Jane.

"Try information," said the operator.

"I can't start calling all over town. Please, can't you patch me through to him?"

"I'm sorry, ma'am. I'm an emergency operator. I can't make personal calls for you."

"This isn't a personal call. It's a call to the police."

"I'll be sending the police, ma'am, just as soon as we get off the phone."

"You get me Lieutenant Folly!" Jane suddenly found herself screaming. "Octavio Folly! Nineteenth precinct! Get me Folly or I swear to God I'll have your picture on page one of the *Daily News* tomorrow!"

"All right, all right," said the voice. "Calm down, ma'am. You're not really hysterical or you wouldn't be able to make such a good threat. Give me the number of the phone where you're at."

Jane read it off the battered face of the brushed steel telephone. The 911 operator instructed her to wait by the phone. Jane hung up. She couldn't believe she had lost control like that. She had been remarkably calm in her confrontation with Melissa Rosengolts. Why was she going to pieces now that the crisis was over?

She looked down and found that her hands were shaking. Her knuckles were scraped raw and there were several places on her body that were probably turning black and blue, judging from the way they were throbbing. Jane stood there for what seemed like an hour, shooing away old ladies and bicycle messengers who wanted to use the phone. In reality, probably no more than five minutes passed. Finally, the pay phone rang. It was Folly.

"Where have you been, Miss Sailor?" demanded the detective. "I've been trying to reach you for a week."

"I had to go out of town, to England," said Jane, afraid to laugh with relief at the sound of his voice, afraid she wouldn't be able to stop.

"Funny time to up and go on vacation," said Folly, oblivious. "It would have been nice to let me know that you were leaving the country."

"It wasn't just a vacation. I wanted to talk to the woman who modeled for a painting of my father's that Perry Mannerback owns. She was living in the loft downstairs from Dad's when he had his accident eight years ago. Her name was Leila Peach."

"Leila . . . did you say Leila Peach?"

"Yes."

"Leila Peach was the model in a painting that Mannerback owns? Was that the painting that was reproduced in the *Times*? The nude?"

"Yes," said Jane. "I know that Leila's dead. Mr. Danko told me."

"Marvelous," muttered Folly. "Just marvelous. It would have been nice to have been aware of this little tidbit when I spoke to Mr. Mannerback this morning. And what the hell is going on with you now? Why are you threatening emergency operators?"

"When I came back to my apartment, there was a woman there. We had a fight."

"So I hear. Who was she? What did she want?"

"I don't know," Jane found herself saying. Suddenly it seemed important not to talk about the clock until she understood why everyone seemed to want it so badly.

"Second break-in in a month, and you don't have any idea?"

"Why don't you ask her?"

"We will," said Folly. "Units should be there by now. You're okay?"

"I'm fine," said Jane, somehow doubting that Melissa Rosengolts would say anything either.

"Maybe the paramedics should look you over. You actually knocked this woman out?"

"Just a lucky punch with a refrigerator. I'd rather not think about it. I'm worried about Perry."

"You should be," growled Folly. "Mr. Mannerback is in deep, deep shit."

The traffic on Broadway had thickened and come to a standstill. A taxicab blared its horn. Jane put a finger in her ear and huddled against the steel shell of the pay phone, trying to hear what Folly was saying.

"What did Perry say this morning when you spoke with him?" she asked urgently.

"Let's not get into that."

"Please, Lieutenant," said Jane. "Perry ran out right after you talked. Nobody knows where he is."

"We'll find him soon enough. He's got to come in for formal questioning. I told him so this morning. No more of this hiding-behind-attorneys runaround. If he doesn't come in voluntarily, we'll have him arrested."

"Won't there be some pretty gruesome publicity if you do that?" asked Jane. "Perry Mannerback is a very well known individual. The newspapers love him."

Folly didn't answer.

"If you tell me what happened this morning on the phone," said Jane, "maybe I can find him, convince him to come in."

"I'd rather you didn't do that."

"Why not?"

"You think this is some sort of game, Miss Sailor? You think going around playing detective is fun?"

"My father was murdered," said Jane. "I just want him to have some justice."

"I do this for a living, Miss Sailor," said Folly wearily. "Some men build houses or prepare tax returns or go off to work in offices. I collect statements, facts, and evidence. The D.A. takes it all to trial and sometimes people are convicted and go to jail, sometimes the case can't be proved and killers go free. In either event it's not about justice, it's about the legal system, and the process is just beginning, believe me. It can go on for years. Maybe there will be justice one day, maybe there won't, but you're not God, and neither am I. All you're going to accomplish by interfering is to get your heart broken as well as your head. So just let me do my job, okay?"

"I still have a lot better chance of finding Perry and convincing him to come in than you do," said Jane.

There was a long silence, as if Folly were debating with himself whether to tell her anything more. Finally, he spoke.

"Mr. Mannerback went to see your father in the hospital."

"Yes, I know."

"He was your father's last visitor the night he died."

This time it was Jane who didn't say anything.

"I asked Mr. Mannerback why he went to see Aaron Sailor that night," Folly went on, "why he flew back to New York when he was halfway to Seattle with you. It seems that Dr. King's wife was on the same plane. She told Mannerback that your father had been calling out his name in his coma."

"Yes," said Jane. "I know it upset Perry."

"It upset him a lot, Miss Sailor. Contrary to your theory that it might have been some other Perry that Aaron Sailor was talking about, it seems that Perry Mannerback knew exactly why your father would be calling out his name like that, saying, 'No, Perry, no.' Mannerback told me he had done something terrible to your father eight years ago. He said that's why he had paid to bring your father into Manhattan for tests—because he felt guilty. He said that's also why he rushed back to see him at the hospital that night—to beg forgiveness, to make his peace."

Jane swallowed hard.

"What had Perry done that was so terrible?" she asked. "Did he tell you?"

"No," answered Folly. "He said that he preferred not to say. So I suggested that maybe Mr. Mannerback was feeling so guilty because he pushed your father down the stairs. And maybe, I also suggested, maybe it wasn't just guilt that was motivating all this generosity of his. Maybe he paid for Aaron Sailor to be moved to Manhattan to give himself a better opportunity to inject your father with insulin because he was afraid that Aaron Sailor was waking up and would incriminate him. Did you know that Mr. Mannerback is a diabetic?"

"No," said Jane, stunned.

"That's right. He knows all about injecting insulin. He does it to himself every day. Perry Mannerback had a motive, knew the method, and gave himself the opportunity to murder your father."

"If that's what you think," stammered Jane, "why haven't you arrested him?"

"The District Attorney's office doesn't like circumstantial cases," said Folly. "Right now, we have no physical evidence that Mannerback killed your father. If we have to go to court with circumstances, I need to understand why Perry might have pushed your father down the stairs in the first place. Now that you've told me that Leila Peach was the model in the painting that Perry owned, maybe I can figure it out. Were your father and Perry Mannerback both involved with Leila Peach eight years ago?"

"No," said Jane.

"If you're so interested in justice, Miss Sailor, then why do you want to protect a man who may have killed your father?"

"I'm telling you the truth," said Jane. "It was Danko who was involved with her. Ted Danko."

"Then how come Mr. Mannerback got so upset this morning when I told him a woman named Leila Peach had been found dead with his name in her address book? Why did he hang up on me when I told him he'd have to give us a formal statement detailing exactly what his relationship was with her? When I called back, he'd already skipped. Now I'm going to ask you again. Do you know where he is?"

"No," said Jane. A group of teenagers passed by, yelling happily. She had to put a finger in her ear again to hear.

"It will be much better for him if he turns himself in," said Folly, "but I don't want you to go looking for him. Mannerback may very well have killed your father, Miss Sailor. It's looking increasingly likely that he killed Leila Peach, too. Since no weapon was recovered at the scene, we'll have to assume he's armed."

"No, Perry couldn't . . ." said Jane. "I can't believe . . ."

"Stay away from him, Miss Sailor. If you hear from Mannerback, tell him to turn himself in, but don't get near him. He's not your friend. He's dangerous. Do you understand?"

"Yes," whispered Jane.

"Now go home. The officers will need to get a statement from you."

"Thanks, but I'd rather not be there when she wakes up."

"The lady's not going to give you any more trouble, I promise. I'll call you later, okay?"

"Okay."

Jane hung up the phone and stood in a daze, watching the endless throngs walk by on Broadway. The world had gone mad. Her life had gone mad. Even as she stood there the police were swearing out a warrant for Perry Mannerback, and the granddaughter of a man with a china shop in London was being revived and/or arrested in Jane's apartment. Jane had no desire to go back to the brownstone on Ninetieth Street now or ever for that matter. All she wanted was to find someone who could make sense of all this to her. Where could Perry have gone? she wondered. Who were the only true honest people in New York?

At that moment a professional dog walker rounded the corner on Eighty-ninth Street with a pack of at least twenty smiling, dopey, happy canines of all sizes and breeds.

Suddenly, Jane knew where to find Perry Mannerback. The question was, did she still want to?

Jane still remembered the Central Park Zoo of her childhood—
a cramped and dingy place of steel bars and pacing, anxious animals. The Zoo had undergone a renovation in the late 1980s, however. Bronze creatures still danced in the captivity of the clocktower
on an hourly basis, but the depressing cages were now nowhere to
be found. Instead, there were habitats—a moated island for the
monkeys, an indoor promenade for the penguins, an icy outdoor
pool where polar bears swam.

The children's petting zoo had recently been expanded in the
enlightened design, and environments for birds and for butterflies
had been added. A million people passed through each year and
emerged back out into the city streets calmer and happier for the
experience.

Jane found Perry Mannerback sitting on a bench at the back-
most part of the Zoo, amidst the artificial boulders that had been
created to make homes for red pandas, ruddy shelducks, and otters.
It was a secluded and quiet spot. The lunch-hour crowds were

mostly over by the front entrance, convening around the seals' circular run, waiting for the feeding-time show.

"May I join you?" she asked, but Perry didn't look up. His chin rested on his hands, his elbows rested on his knees. He apparently hadn't noticed her approaching.

"May I sit down, Perry?" Jane asked again.

This time, her former employer did look up. There were dark circles under his reddened eyes. He wore a wrinkled white shirt, but no jacket or tie. He looked rumpled and miserable.

"Jane," he said, smiling slightly and rising automatically. "What are you doing here?"

"Sometimes I get tired of people, too," said Jane, taking a seat beside him. "At least people of the human persuasion."

"They're very decent chaps, the monkeys," Perry said with a nod, sitting back down and offering her a potato chip from a bag in his pocket. "They remind me of our board of directors, only better-looking. And the polar bears are quite something, aren't they?"

"Olinda is worried about you, the way you ran out of the apartment this morning. So is Miss Fripp."

Perry shrugged, but didn't say anything.

"I understand that you spoke with the police," said Jane.

For the first time, raw emotion flashed across Perry's eyes.

"They accused me of . . . I can't even say it, it's so preposterous."

"I know you wouldn't have harmed my father."

"No, of course not. I've felt terrible about this whole thing, simply terrible."

"And now Leila Peach is dead, too."

"Yes," said Perry, "though I shouldn't wonder that she would come to no good end. Horrible woman."

Jane stared at him. Perry must have noticed her eyes widening, for he was quick to respond.

"You can't think I had anything to do with that, can you,

Jane? I haven't seen Leila Peach for years and years. I only spoke to her a few times in my entire life."

"Do you want to tell me about it?"

"No, no, no. I couldn't possibly."

"Why not?"

"I feel so terrible. I'm so ashamed."

"You're in a lot of trouble, Perry. The police want to talk with you again."

"What should I do, Jane?" asked Perry, his eyes wide. "I don't know what to do."

"Why don't you tell me what happened eight years ago? I promise I won't be mad at you. I just need to know what happened. Maybe I can help you figure out what to do."

Perry stared at her for another moment, then nodded. The wind seemed to go out of him. He slumped down in his seat and began speaking in a very quiet voice without inflection.

"After I bought my painting, I became friendly with your father. I had him over to my place on several occasions for dinner parties—nothing fancy, just a few dozen people. He was very amusing, very nice chap. Ted Danko was at one of these gatherings, along with his wife. Your dad had brought Leila Peach. After growing accustomed to her presence in my painting, it was really quite interesting for me to meet Miss Peach in the flesh—or not in the flesh, as the case may be. She seemed nice enough. I didn't talk with her much that first time, just marveled at the transitory nature of existence and all."

He paused. Jane didn't say anything. Eventually, Perry continued.

"Ted Danko was Leila's dinner partner that night and they really hit it off together. They began to see one another secretly. Ted and his wife Jill were having some personal problems then, and—I don't know, these things happen. Of course, I didn't find out about any of this until months later, when Ted came to talk with me. He was terribly distraught. It seems that Leila had told him she was pregnant with his child. She wanted money so she could get an abortion and start a new life somewhere where nobody knew her. Unless Ted paid her, she had threatened to tell his wife about their liaison."

"It sounds to me like they deserved one another," said Jane. "Why did Danko come to you? Why didn't he just pay her off?"

"He couldn't, or most certainly he would have," said Mannerback with a sigh. "As it happened, Ted had made some disastrous personal investments right before this and was dangerously overextended, financially speaking. He had no liquidity at all. He'd gone through everything to raise money to cover his losses, even invaded a trust fund for one of their children. Ted was sure he'd be able to replace the money in a matter of weeks, but if his wife found out about Leila now, he'd be ruined. Jill would divorce him for certain, he said. Her lawyers would have had enough evidence to crucify him—she'd already caught him having other affairs. He could even go to jail. Jill would take back the kids with her to her family in California, and Ted probably would never be allowed to see them again. He couldn't bear it. He was practically suicidal."

"Big tough Mr. Danko?" said Jane sarcastically.

"Oh, you don't know Ted. He's really a very emotional fellow. He may be ambivalent about Jill, but he absolutely adores his kids and was at the end of his rope. He was literally in tears when he told me about this and asked my help. Ted's an immensely proud fellow. For him to have come to me for help like this was remarkable—even now, years later, he's still embarrassed about it and compensates by treating me in a very brusque manner. But I understand. At the time, I was very touched that he would turn to me. I'm ashamed to admit, however, that all I could think of was myself, my own interests."

"What do you mean?" asked Jane, as a young mother pushed a sleeping infant by and seals barked in the distance.

"Ted has been running the company for me since Dad died," said Perry. "He's a wonderful manager. He understands what's called for and takes care of everything. When he came to me so upset, I was terrified of what might happen if his affair and financial manipulations were exposed. The stockholders would certainly demand his termination. Who would run the company then? I certainly couldn't. The day-to-day business is a terrible bore, and you have to really know what you're doing. Someone new might come in who'd wreck things, or make me spend lots of time doing all kinds of stuff I didn't want. I was frightened. I didn't want anything to change."

"So you helped him."

"Yes," said Perry, nodding, looking miserable. "I helped Ted. I told him not to worry, that I would take care of everything. I met with Leila Peach. I arranged to give her some money—a few hundred thousand was all she wanted. She promised to get an abortion and leave New York."

"And you believed her?" asked Jane. "Why couldn't she have just come back for more blackmail when she ran out of money?"

"Yes, precisely," said Perry. "Which was why I took the precaution of hiring a private investigator who procured affidavits detailing purchases of various controlled substances by Miss Peach. She had a drug problem and was involved with some rather unsavory people. At our meeting, I produced these affidavits, and I told her in no uncertain terms that if she attempted to make trouble for me or Mr. Danko in the future, I could and would have her sent to prison."

Jane stared at Perry with surprise. Apparently, he was more cunning than he let on.

"I thought that I was being so smart," he continued in a quiet voice. "I thought that I had handled everything so perfectly, but the next thing I knew your father appeared at my apartment, furious. It seems that he had just run into Leila at a restaurant and she had told him about her pregnancy, told him that the child was his and that she planned to have an abortion, which I was going to help her pay for."

"An abortion, of course," said Jane, finally understanding. Those were Leila's plans that Aaron Sailor had wanted to interfere with. It wasn't surprising that Leila hadn't told Suzy McCorkle that part of the story.

"Aaron had tried to talk her out of it," said Perry, "but she was furious at him for having ended their relationship shortly before this. That was just like Leila, apparently. She had had no problem cheating on Aaron with Ted Danko, but she absolutely couldn't tolerate that he had broken it off with her and was seeing other women. This was how she was going to get back at him, by aborting this child—and doing it with my money."

"What a horrible woman," said Jane.

" 'Don't do it, Perry,' your father demanded. 'Please don't do it.' He had been raised a Catholic, I gather, and the prospect of being party to an abortion absolutely horrified him. It was a mortal sin."

"But Dad wasn't religious at all," said Jane.

"Maybe not, but certain beliefs have deep roots. So deep they defy what's rational sometimes."

Perry shook his head and wrung his hands.

"I tried to deny my involvement," he went on in a cracking voice, "but Aaron wouldn't listen, wouldn't believe me. 'I know the truth,' he yelled, and called me a liar when I tried to contradict him. I told him that child was probably Danko's, but he didn't believe this, either. Of course, it didn't matter to me who had been the father. Leila probably didn't know herself. The bottom line was that the pregnancy was the lever she could use to destroy Ted unless I stopped her. 'Don't do it,' your father pleaded.

"But I did it. I made certain that Leila had her abortion, and I made certain that she left the country. I did it for myself, not Danko, not Leila Peach, and despite the very strong feelings that Aaron had on the subject. I wasn't interested in anyone else's problems, only my own. I didn't even know that your father had had an accident. I just wanted to put the whole thing out of my mind.

And I succeeded. I succeeded perfectly until you arrived to see me that day. Then it all came back."

"You felt guilty," said Jane.

"Yes."

"That's why you hired me. That's why you moved Dad to Manhattan for tests."

"Yes," said Perry. "I was just trying to do something decent after all this time, but somehow I've made a mess of it again. What am I going to do, Jane?"

"Why did you go to Dad's hospital room that night?" she asked. "Why did you fly back to New York?"

Tears suddenly filled Perry Mannerback's eyes and overflowed down his cheeks.

"To apologize," he whispered. "When that art dealer woman told me what Aaron had been saying, I was overwhelmed. Before that, it had all been at arm's length somehow, theoretical. But to hear how he was still repeating our last argument, that this was what had frozen in his poor broken mind . . . I just couldn't bear it. I felt so terrible. I knew I couldn't make things right, but it wasn't enough just to pay some doctors now. How was this any better than how I had behaved eight years ago? I had to tell your father I was sorry, personally, to his face."

"So you flew back."

"I sat by his bedside and talked for an hour. I know he was in a coma, but perhaps he heard me at some level. I don't know. I hope he did. I pray he did."

"You didn't talk to Leila when she came back to New York last week?"

Perry shook his head vigorously.

"No, I swear. Leila Peach wouldn't dare call me. If she had, I would have had her put in jail, she knew that. But Leila must have needed money and might have thought she could get it from Ted. Perhaps she calculated that Ted would be too proud to show weakness to me again, which is certainly right. Ted would have killed her in a minute before coming to me for help twice, and I'm afraid that's exactly what happened. You see what a rat I am, Jane? All I can think about is myself. I'm still frightened that there will be nobody to run the company if the police arrest Ted."

"What if the police arrest you?"

"It will almost be a relief," said Perry. "I know that what I did somehow led to everything. If I hadn't helped Leila procure an abortion without a care for who the father of her child was or what he might think about the matter, Aaron Sailor might be alive today."

"Did you push my father down the stairs, Perry?" Jane asked.
"No."

"Did you inject him with insulin in his hospital room?"

"Is that what they think?"

"Yes. They know you're a diabetic. Did you kill my father?"

"No. I swear, Jane. I didn't."

"Did you kill Leila Peach?"

"I'm a terrible person, Jane," said Perry. "I inherited all my wealth and never really did anything to help people but give them money. But I didn't kill anyone. You believe me, don't you?"

He stared up at her with all the earnestness of a child.

"Yes, Perry," said Jane. "I do."

"What should I do?"

"Tell the police everything."

"Oh no, I couldn't."

"It's the only way, Perry."

"They won't believe me. The man who spoke with me . . ."

"Lieutenant Folly."

". . . he said terrible things, treated me like some kind of common criminal."

"Go to them, Perry."

"I have to think."

Jane stood.

"I'm sure you'll do the right thing. You have to. I'm going home."

Jane had walked down through Central Park to get to the Zoo, but returning home the same way was out of the question. All the adrenaline that had flushed into her system was long gone. She felt like a dishrag, barely able to lift her legs. At Sixty-eighth Street she managed to catch a cab going to the West Side.

By the time the taxi pulled up in front of her brownstone, it was two-thirty. Nearly an hour had passed since she spoke with Folly. A white patrol car was double-parked in front with an impatient-looking cop at the wheel. Another impatient-looking cop was sitting on the front stoop. He stood up to meet her.

"You Miss Sailor?"

"Yes."

"Nice of you to join us. Where you been?"

"I . . . I needed to calm down. I took a walk."

"In a taxicab?"

"I walked farther than I had planned."

The cop grunted, then pulled out a notebook from his back pocket.

"We need to get a statement about the events that transpired earlier in your apartment," he said, clicking open a ballpoint pen.

"Is the woman okay?" asked Jane.

The cop made a face.

"She woke up and clouted one of the paramedics," he said with obvious distaste. "They had to give her a shot after we got her cuffed. Now she's in Bellevue, being examined by somebody. Like they say: an unexamined life ain't worth livin'."

Happy not to have killed Isidore Rosengolts's granddaughter, Jane spent the next twenty minutes telling the cop what had happened. Then, beginning to ache in places she didn't remember having, she called the locksmith.

An hour and a half later Jane's door could again be locked, though the only way the apartment would ever be secure again, the locksmith pronounced, was if she replaced the patched wooden doorframe with a new steel one.

It was now nearly half past four. Jane was still on London time, and after the day she'd had, she was quite ready for bed. She opened the bottle of Chardonnay she kept at the bottom of the refrigerator for emergencies and poured herself a glass. After taking a single sip, she went into the bathroom, took off her clothes, and turned on the shower. She had just stepped in when the phone rang.

The answering machine lay in pieces in the wastebasket, thanks to Melissa Rosengolts. Folly said he would call again. Cursing, Jane grabbed a towel and made her way to the telephone.

"So, Janie, honey, sweetheart," said Elinore King without further introduction, as if no one could possibly fail to recognize her voice. "I'm back. It's so horrible about your father. I'm sorry I couldn't make it for the funeral, but Greg gave you my regards, didn't he? I told him to give you my regards."

"What do you want, Elinore?" said Jane, dripping on the floor.

"Okay, honey. So this is the thing. I know you were, like,

upset and all when we talked on the plane, but that's okay. I want you to know that I'm not mad at you or anything. I understand, and it's okay now, because we've gotten some real offers."

Jane rolled her eyes.

"Elinore, even if we had anything to talk about—which we don't—this isn't a good time."

"It's always a good time to talk about money," Elinore announced breezily. "You're going to really love this, Janie, you really are. So you know the one with the lady's crossed hands with the cantaloupe and the squirrel? Your father's painting? Twenty-five thousand, and that's just a small one. But get this—sixty-five, that's sixty-five thousand dollars, for the couple. You know the one? With all the blue? The two women in the tree?"

"What do I have to say to you, Elinore? How can I get through? I told you, I'm not going to sell my father's paintings. I am going to donate them to museums. Period. End of story. Now I just stepped into the shower and I . . ."

"I know what you said, Janie," said Elinore with a smug little giggle, "but these are real offers. One is from a doctor who saw the show at the what-do-you-call-it museum. And I made contact with some very important collectors in Seattle; people up there have more money than God with the biotechnology and the computer stuff and all that. Now, wait, I haven't told you about the third offer, and it's really the best. A hundred and ten thousand for the diptych. A hundred and ten thousand. Net."

"No, Elinore," said Jane. "*No.* Why is that so difficult for you to . . . ?"

"I don't understand why you're being like this," said Elinore angrily. "I know you're upset about your father and all, but his death was the best thing that ever happened to him, if you know what I mean, in terms of his value and all. You can't turn this down. You can't stop the momentum or you'll never get it back, believe me, I know."

"Can't you get it through your head that I don't care?"

"Oh, come on, Janie, don't be an ass," said Elinore, her voice turning ugly. "You care plenty. You're just still angry that I talked to Perry on the plane. I don't understand why you would want to keep me away from him. He's my client, you know. I knew him a long time before you did."

"You haven't heard a word I've said, have you?" said Jane wearily. "I swear to God, Elinore, you are the most greedy, egomaniacal . . ."

"What did you say?"

"I said . . ."

"How dare you say that to me? How dare you?"

"I'll say what I please, you selfish . . ."

The receiver slammed down at the other end with such a bang that it hurt Jane's ear. She was halfway back to the bathroom when the phone rang again.

"Hello?" she answered.

"I'm sorry, Janie," said Elinore in a tearful, abashed voice. "I'm sorry for hanging up on you like that. I've been under a lot of stress lately. Sometimes, though, you just make me so mad . . ."

"I'm sorry, too, Elinore," said Jane. "But you . . ."

"No, let me finish. I know I come on a little strong, a little aggressive. But you have to be aggressive in this business. And me being a woman and all that. You can't know what it's like, you just can't."

"Elinore—"

"I'm just doing it for you, you know, honey," said Elinore, her voice brightening. "Do you know what your share is going to be if we can sell just these three paintings? A hundred thousand dollars. See? I've kept up my end of the bargain. I'm giving you fifty percent, just like I said. Now don't tell me you can't use a hundred thousand dollars. And that's just for starters."

"I don't want it, Elinore. This isn't what I want. This is what you want."

"Of course I want the money," said Elinore impatiently. "It's only fair after all the work I've done. But I'm trying to tell you that there are other things at stake here, more important things. There's a principle at stake here."

"What principle is that?" asked Jane.

"Loyalty, for one thing. I never gave up on your father and I don't intend to now."

"My father's dead."

"That's beside the point," shrieked Elinore. "If I let artists just walk away after all the work I do, even when they're dead, where would I be? You can't just decide all on your own that you don't want to do this any more, now when it's finally beginning to pay off. Aaron wouldn't have wanted you to treat me like this, believe me. Loyalty cuts both ways, you know. Look, I might as well tell you the truth. The fact is that Aaron and I were more than just friends. He was in love with me, if you want to know."

Jane shook her head in disbelief. The woman was unbelievable.

"I sweat blood for that man," Elinore ranted on. "No, let me finish. If it wasn't for me, your father would be nothing, nothing. And there wouldn't be any of this interest now in your father if I hadn't gotten that article into the *Times*. I gave them the whole story."

"That's right, Elinore," said Jane, unable to contain any longer what was really bothering her. "And because of that stupid article, because of the photos you gave them, people are dead."

"Who's dead? What do you mean?"

"You have no idea what you've set into motion with your meddling. No idea whatsoever."

"I want to know what you mean. I didn't have anything to do with what happened to your father. I was in Seattle."

"He's dead, isn't he? And a woman saw your stupid pictures and now she's dead, too. But what do you care?"

"You're crazy," sputtered Elinore. "If anybody's dead, it's because of Perry Mannerback. Perry Mannerback killed your father.

That's what the police think. They called me at my daughter's in Seattle. I know all about it."

"Perry had nothing to do with my father's death. Just leave him out of this."

Elinore pounced at the opening.

"Aha!" she shouted. "Now I understand. Now I see what this is really about. He's talked to you about more paintings, hasn't he? Perry must have killed your father because he knew it would make his own painting more valuable. And now he's convinced you not to let me sell any others so you can sell them to him directly without cutting me in! I'm sure the police will be really interested in this. It gives Perry a motive and everything. I'm going to call them. What do you think about that?"

This time it was Jane who hung up the phone with a bang. She had made it back to the bathroom and had one foot into the shower when the phone rang again. For a moment, she tried to ignore it. Then she stomped backed into the living room and grabbed the receiver.

"Now you listen to me, you miserable . . ."

"Are you still so mad at me?" said a male voice with a smooth British accent.

"Valentine!"

"I felt very bad after we spoke the last time. You know, you really have misunderstood this whole situation."

"I suppose you can explain everything," said Jane, happy to hear his voice despite herself.

"I can."

"Well, that's very nice, but I just was about to step into the shower."

"Sounds interesting," said Valentine. "Going out somewhere tonight?"

"Only to bed," said Jane, too embarrassed to resume shivering.

"More interesting still. I was hoping that I could persuade

you to come over to the Carlyle. I think we can clear everything up. There's someone here who has a very proposition for you."

"Nice try," said Jane. "But I'm not up to being propositioned tonight, thank you very much. I'm still on London time and I've had a day that you wouldn't believe."

"Oh, I'm not the one with the proposition. At least not tonight. It's my employer, Mr. Bogen."

"Willie the Weasel?"

"That's a very misleading and cruel nickname," said Valentine. "Mr. Bogen's really quite a decent chap; he just happens to be cunning in financial doings, which has engendered a certain amount of envy."

"I'm sure."

"He wants to explain to you about your ceramic clock. It will be greatly to your advantage."

"Maybe tomorrow."

"I'm afraid that it has to be now," said Valentine. "Mr. Bogen had intended to stay the entire week, but emergencies have come up in London and he has to fly back tonight in our company plane."

"Sorry, Valentine. There's nothing you could possibly say that is going to get me to come out tonight."

"Please?" said Valentine.

"I . . ."

"I'd like to see you, too, Jane. I definitely want to see more of you."

"Would you?" said Jane, reaching over and taking another sip of wine. As she did the towel around her slipped loose, leaving her naked and vulnerable in the draft.

eeee

It was a little before five-thirty when Jane stepped out of the cab in front of the Carlyle. The grand hotel took up the entire block of Madison Avenue between Seventy-sixth and Seventy-seventh streets. The tallest structure in the East Side historic district, it towered thirty-four stories above the smart shops and boutiques of the avenue. Somehow, however, the hotel was so quietly tasteful that from street level at least it seemed like nothing special. There wasn't even a grand entrance on Madison, just a small doorway with a discreet marquee on the side street.

Inside, too, the hotel stood out for what it was not rather than what it was. There was no soaring lobby, no symphony of brass and velvet like the opulent hotels downtown. The Carlyle rated its five stars simply for being perfect. The large floral bouquet in the entryway was perfect. The Gobelins tapestries, the Louis XV–style furniture, even the window treatments, all perfect. Further inside, Jane could see a perfect dining room full of perfectly behaving guests. Somewhere off to the left was the bar that Ludwig Bemelmans of *Madeline* fame had decorated with perfect fanciful zebras to settle a bill and where jazz singer Bobby Short had held court for years.

Jane glanced at herself in a rococo mirror. Her hair was still Raphael Renaissance Red, but she looked remarkably good considering that she had begun the day more than fourteen hours ago in London, had knocked out a woman with a refrigerator, and had interfered with a police investigation in the meantime. She ascended the elevator. A few minutes later, she was poised outside the room on the twenty-eighth floor that Valentine had directed her to.

Jane found herself worrying again whether this was a good idea. She still didn't know what Valentine was really up to, and Willie Bogen, according to Perry Mannerback at least, was some kind of monster. It didn't seem likely that any harm could come to her in such posh surroundings, but after recent events she wasn't sure of anything. How had she let herself be talked into this, she wondered, pressing the doorbell.

"Jane," said Valentine, opening the door. He had on a gray sweater and looked gangly, goofy, and happy to see her.

"Hi."

"So good of you to come," he said, taking her arm and leading her from the vestibule into an elegantly appointed suite, all French furniture and endless views of Central Park from picture windows. "I'd like you to meet . . ."

This was as far as he got. The answer to all Jane's questions was sitting on a tufted sofa by the baby grand piano. He was a round little man who looked as if he might make his living helping Santa.

Jane blinked, expecting the illusion to disappear and be replaced by a fire-breathing dragon. It didn't. The man's cheeks were still chubby and dimpled and red. His nose was still a cherry. The heavy black frames of his glasses magnified eyes the color of robin's eggs. A fringe of grayish hair stopped an inch above his pink little ears.

The butterball was in movement the instant they came into the room, leaping up from his perch to greet them, happily pumping Jane's hand, all the while bouncing up and down like a six-week-old puppy.

"Welcome, welcome, welcome!" said the elf, speaking as rapidly as a machine gun in an accent somewhere between British and Yiddish, his face crinkled in merriment around an enormous smile. "Valentine, dear boy, now I can see why you were so impressed. Such a beautiful creature, a goddess, an ethereal goddess. Such skin! Such a face! *Sheyna punim!* That means 'pretty face' in Yiddish, which is obviously not your native tongue, you vision of loveliness and grace. And you found her on an airplane, Valentine, you clever boy? Oy, such a doll! But here I am going on without even properly introducing myself. William S. H. Bogen, investment counselor and financial manager *extraordinaire,* at your service—but you, my tall and gorgeous darling, you may call me Willie!"

Seventeen

"The name wasn't originally Bogen, of course," said Willie the Weasel, munching a smoked salmon canapé, one of an assortment that room service had provided, along with several chilled bottles of Piper Heidseck. "It was Katzenellenbogen. Papa had to shorten it when he embarked upon his stage career in Berlin before the first war. Try fitting Katzenellenbogen on a marquee."

"Your father was an actor?" asked Jane, intrigued.

"My father was everything. You name it, he did it. Song and dance. Knife-throwing. Female impersonation. Papa was a riot. European Jewry's answer to the *Ziegfeld Follies*. In 1925, he moved to Budapest, so he could get into the movies. He ended up playing László, the Hungarian cowboy, in a whole series of silent pictures. Yippie-eye-o-kai-yay!"

Jane was trying not to fall under the little scoundrel's spell, but it was difficult. Willie Bogen was charming, funny, and ridiculously generous—at least as far as hors d'oeuvres were concerned. There was enough smoked fish and caviar in the spacious suite to feed a significant portion of New Jersey.

"I was named after the famous American silent movie cowboy, William S. Hart," Willie rattled on after taking an appreciative sip of champagne, "but the Katzenellenbogens are actually a rabbinical family of great importance. They were descended from twelve Jews who settled originally in the town of Katzenelenbogen in Germany in 1312. The family moved to Padua toward the end of the fifteenth century and then to Poland a few generations later. I'll have you know that Karl Marx was a descendant of Aaron Lvov of Trier, who was married to the daughter of Moses Cohen of Luck, who had married Nessla Katzenellenbogen and—"

"This is all very interesting, Mr. Bogen," said Jane politely, "but I don't see how it has anything to do with me."

"Ah, but it has everything to do with you, dear girl," said Willie, his eyes twinkling. "In that article about your father in the *New York Times* which Valentine so kindly brought to my attention, did I not read that the name of your paternal grandmother was Luria?"

"Yes, but . . ."

"In the sixteenth century, Isaac Katzenellenbogen married the daughter of Zeisel and Eliezer Shernzel of Lvov. Zeisel was the daughter of Jehiel Luria, whose family were descended over the previous two hundred years from none other than Mattithiah Treves of Provence."

Jane stared blankly at him.

"Don't you see?" demanded Willie. "The Treveses, the Lurias, the Katzenellenbogens. We're all related! In fact, each of our three families can trace its respective line back to Rashi, the famous Talmudic scholar, whose lineage, it is well documented, goes back through the great rabbi, Hillel, to King David, and ultimately back directly to Adam!"

"Fascinating, isn't it?" said Valentine Treves, flashing an amused smile. "Genealogy is one of Willie's hobbies."

"I know what you're thinking," said Willie, raising his hand. "But I want to reassure you, Cousin Jane—may I call you Jane?—I want to reassure you, Jane, that I cannot believe that you and Valentine will have idiot children should you choose to marry, which seems a reasonable possibility judging from the way that Valentine is admiring you at this very instant. No, the genetic connection is simply too remote."

"Mr. Bogen . . ." sputtered Jane, struggling for words.

"Willie, please call me Willie," he said, pronouncing it with more of a "V" than a "W." "Everyone calls me Willie. Don't be shy. We're *mispocheh.*"

"*Mispocheh?*"

"Family," interpreted Valentine. "The extraordinary thing is that somehow Willie manages to be related to practically everyone he's ever met. No one in my family even knew that Grandfather John had been born a Jew until Willie rooted out the birth record."

"Now, Valentine," said Willie, shaking his finger. "How many times have I told you? Connections between people are a blessing from God. We need to find the things that bring us together, not lead us apart. You have to forgive Valentine, my dear. He has an overdeveloped sense of irony because his mother named him after a song. Her funny Valentine. What kind of name is Valentine for a nice Jewish boy, I ask you?"

"What kind of name is William S. Hart?" replied Valentine in a mild voice.

"Mr. Bogen," said Jane. "Villie. Willie. I'm sure that whatever may have happened in the thirteenth century is all very interesting, but it's not what I came over here for. If you want to tell me about connections, why don't you start with how you're connected to Isidore Rosengolts?"

"I will tell you anything you'd like to hear, anything," said Willie. "Are we not *mispocheh?*"

"The truth is all I want."

"And so you shall have it, my dear, so you shall have it," said Willie, rapping the table decisively with a knuckle. "But first have some fish."

He picked up a tray of appetizers and held it out to her.

"Mr. Bogen, please," said Jane, pulling back.

"I can see why you like her, Valentine," said Willie. "She's relentless, just like you. The two of you will have wonderful fights in your old age. Come on, my dear, just a little piece so it shouldn't go to waste."

Jane reached over and begrudgingly popped a piece of salmon into her mouth.

"Okay?" she said, her mouth full.

"Good, isn't it?" said Willie. "And please try the champagne. It's very nice."

"Delicious," said Jane, taking a gulp. It was.

Willie winked at Valentine, then sat back on the couch, making himself comfortable for what apparently would be a long story.

"Okay," he began. "So here is the truth, the whole truth, and nothing but the truth. I met Isidore Rosengolts in the Swiss detention camp where I spent most of World War Two. William S. Hart notwithstanding, my father had wanted a more stable life for me than the theatre, and I had begun apprenticing as a watchmaker with a cousin of my mother's. Somehow I had managed to get a visa and was in Switzerland buying mainsprings when the war broke out. I never heard from anyone in my family again, but this is another story."

He paused, matter-of-factly took a sip of champagne, then resumed.

"The course of Isidore's life had been interrupted by events far beyond his control, too, so we had a certain amount in common. We were both young, both displaced in a strange land, and we spoke a common language: Yiddish. We became fairly friendly, as friendly as you can become with a person like Isidore."

Jane heaped a generous helping of caviar onto a little toast round and added some chopped hardboiled egg. Willie beamed and continued.

"The Swiss in their typical fashion had figured out how to

make a profit from their refugees. Rather than murdering Jews as the Germans did, the Swiss put us all to work building roads, maintaining farms, this sort of thing. It was hard work, but a considerably better fate than what would have befallen me if I had stayed in Hungary. It was with a pickax in my hand that I first heard from Isidore about a very special ceramic clock, decorated with back-to-back handless faces, that his grandfather had made for a physician in Antwerp just before the war began."

Jane stiffened.

"Mr. Rosengolts didn't seem to think it was all that special," she said.

"Mr. Rosengolts is a big fat liar," Willie replied with a smile. "Izzie was always a big fat liar. He once convinced me that butterflies had pupiks."

"Bellybuttons," said Valentine, who seemed to have absorbed a significant amount of Yiddish on the job.

"Another time," Willie went on, "he had me believing that every Catholic in Belgium had a twelve-foot-high cross in his upstairs closet that had to be shpritzed with red wine twice a week to symbolize the suffering of Christ. After a while I stopped believing anything Izzie said. I was sure he was lying when he told me about the clock for the first time, it was such an unlikely story. You can see why I was more than a little skeptical when two Sundays ago he rings me up out of the blue, after I hadn't heard a word from him in twenty years, and offers to sell me this very same clock."

"He didn't have it," said Jane flatly.

"And I didn't believe it even existed," said Willie, nodding happily. "Then the next day, Valentine rings me from Seattle, Washington, U.S.A. So we're chatting about this splendid Simon Willard lighthouse clock that I have practically stolen from underneath the *goyische* nose of Peregrine Mannerback, the famous American idiot. I tell Valentine about this make-believe clock that Rosengolts now proposes to sell me. Valentine tells me to pick up a copy of that Sunday's *New York Times*. In it, he says to my amazement, is a painting with just such a handless ceramic clock.

"So I get the article, and sure enough, there is a picture of a clock exactly like the one Isidore had described to me in Switzerland more than half a century ago. And the article says that the painter of this picture had a mother who fled Antwerp just about the time that Izzie Rosengolts's grandfather is supposed to have made his clock."

Jane glanced over at Valentine. He winked, licked his lips, and popped a canapé in his mouth. Flustered, Jane returned her attention to Willie.

"This past Thursday, I hear from Izzie again," the little elf went on cheerfully, not having missed the exchange. "We have spoken a few times on the telephone in the meanwhile, but now he actually shows up on my doorstep, demanding to know if I am going to purchase his clock. I am interested, I say, but by this point you, Jane, have come to England and have claimed to Valentine that the clock is in your possession. So I tell Izzie that I do not believe he even has this clock. He gets very insulted. He will produce something that will prove he has the clock, but there will be a price. There is always a price with Izzie. He swears that now he will never in a million years sell me the clock unless I pay him five thousand pounds that very day for this."

Willie reached into his pocket and held up a shiny object. Jane gasped. It was her mother's dragonfly cross.

"By this point, the existence of the clock seemed more believable because of a certain document that had turned up," said Willie. "I wasn't sure who had the clock, but sometimes you have to take a gamble in life. So I paid his little extortion."

"I guess Mr. Rosengolts's dragonfly medal wasn't as precious to him as he said," said Jane.

"Medal?" said Willie with a laugh, following Jane's eyes to the object in his hand.

"He said it was a medal his grandfather had won at some decorative arts fair," said Jane. "I always thought it was a cross."

"Well, then, I am pleased to enlighten you," said Willie. "It is not a medal, and it certainly is not a cross. It is a key. A clock key."

"A clock key?" exclaimed Jane. "How can it be a clock key? For what clock?"

"Why, your clock, of course," said Willie. "The small end sets the time, the large end winds the clock."

"But my clock is just a glazed piece of ceramic!"

"I'm not talking about the ceramic clock," said Willie with a chuckle. "I'm talking about the real clock. The clock inside the clock."

"Inside?"

"Yes, yes, yes," said Willie excitedly, "that's the whole point. Izzie's grandfather had created a ceramic shell to conceal a very valuable, very wonderful clock, so your family could smuggle it out of Belgium. That was the crazy story Izzie had told me in Switzerland in 1943. He said he had seen the real piece in his grandfather's workshop before it was encased. That was why I thought he was lying back then. What he described to me could only have been a portico mystery clock. What kind of fool did he take me for?"

"Portico mystery clock?" Jane repeated, staring blankly at him.

"You are not a clock person, are you?"

"I can barely tell time at this point," said Jane, dazed from the unsettling events of the day, not the least of which was what she was hearing now.

"Valentine," said Willie, looking over at Valentine, who was sitting on the couch looking very relaxed. "Why are you being so quiet? Tell your lovely cousin, Jane, about Cartier mystery clocks. Show her how brilliant you are, as well as good-looking."

"Cartier, of course, is the famous Paris jeweler," said Valentine, not missing a beat. "Its golden age was between the world wars, when under the direction of Louis Cartier, grandson of the founder, the house created some of the most spectacular and beautiful objects of the twentieth century. Among the most remarkable of these were their famous mystery clocks."

"What's the mystery?" asked Jane, wondering what wasn't a mystery at this point.

"The central dial of a mystery clock is transparent, made of quartz or rock crystal," said Valentine. "In this crystal, the clock's hands hover, seemingly unattached to anything, yet they keep time."

"But each hand is actually attached to an equally transparent crystal disk inside the crystal dial," said Willie, unable to contain himself. "That's the trick. The works are in the base of the clock and are connected to the disks by gears in the frame, so the mechanism that makes the hands turn is invisible."

"The first mystery clock," Valentine continued, "the Model A, was sold to J. P. Morgan in 1913. Cartier made about one mystery clock a year until 1930. Queen Mary and King Farouk each owned one. Hermann Goering, the swine, bought his in 1940. In 1945, Charles de Gaulle presented Stalin with a lapis lazuli mystery clock. After World War Two, they were produced again until the late 1970s."

"The later ones are not nearly as desirable," added Willie.

Numb, Jane took a sip of champagne and tried the whitefish. Not a bad way to have dinner.

"The largest, the most spectacular, and the rarest of the early clocks," Valentine went on, "were the so-called portico mystery clocks, made between 1923 and 1925. These were crafted from black onyx and rock crystal, with a splash of jade and coral for color. Each had two tall pillars with a crosspiece at the top. From this crosspiece hung suspended either a twelve-sided or a hexagonal rock crystal dial, in which open diamondwork hands kept time without visible explanation. The works for these clocks were in the crosspieces at the top, which were crowned with a Buddha or Chinese lion carved from rock crystal. In form, the whole affair resembles a freestanding Oriental archway, hence the term 'portico.' "

"Cartier made only six portico mystery clocks, or so everyone has thought," interrupted Willie again. "Izzie, however, somehow got hold of a letter from Maurice Coüet, the maker of the mystery clocks, to Charles Jacqueau, Cartier's most brilliant designer during the Art Deco period, talking about a seventh portico mystery clock. Apparently, this clock had been made for Louis Cartier himself as a prototype, but he had gifted it to a Belgian doctor who had saved his life when he had taken ill on a trip to Antwerp."

"My great-grandfather?" asked Jane.

"Willie sent me over to Rosengolts et fils for a copy of this letter last week," said Valentine, nodding. "That's why you saw me there."

"The letter clinched it for me," said Willie. "That's why I bought the key from Izzie. The key is mentioned in Coüet's letter. The dragonfly clock key, the only one of its kind Cartier ever made."

"Are you all right?" asked Valentine.

"I'm fine," said Jane, putting down her glass. "Just incredibly stupid. It's been there all along, right in front of me. I should have smashed the clock open a week ago."

"No, no, no," exclaimed Willie in horror. "I don't know how Izzie Rosengolts's grandfather was able to case the clock in ceramic, but it has to be removed with incredible care. No one but a professional should attempt it."

Jane just shook her head.

"So what do you think of my little story, dear distant Cousin Jane?" asked Willie. "Does it answer all your questions?"

Jane stared back at him. The mystery of the dragonfly cross was now cleared up. Willie's explanation had also left no doubt why Isidore Rosengolts sent his granddaughter to steal the clock and what Valentine's interest had been. But her questions were far from answered.

"I don't understand Leila Peach's part in all of this," she said.

"Yes, neither do I," said Valentine. "You used that name on me in London. Who's Leila Peach?"

"I believe that there was a Robert Peach who was Bishop of Coventry in the twelfth century," said Willie helpfully.

"Leila Peach is the model who posed with my grandmother's clock in the painting that was reproduced in the *Times*."

Valentine and Willie Bogen stared blankly back at Jane.

"She's dead," Jane added.

Still no reaction.

"Perry Mannerback owns the painting of Leila and the clock."

Willie's eyes crinkled up and his mouth dropped open. His cheeks got rosy. Jane was frightened he was having a stroke.

"No," he finally whispered in a hoarse voice.

"Are you all right?" she asked.

"Did you hear, Valentine?" said Willie, his voice coming back to its normal pitch, then rising in excitement. "Perry Mannerback owns the painting. It means he will want the clock even more when he finds out about it. It will drive him crazy unless he can buy it. He'll go insane. Isn't it wonderful?"

"Quite," agreed Valentine.

"Mr. Bogen," said Jane. "Willie . . ."

"He hasn't made you an offer, has he?" said Willie, his voice turning urgent. "Please tell me you haven't done anything foolish like selling your clock to that ridiculous man, have you?"

"I haven't sold it to anyone. It's not for sale."

"Why not?"

"Because . . . Because . . ."

"The clock is worth a lot of money, Jane," said Willie.

"How much?"

"I haven't the slightest idea."

Jane rolled her eyes.

"You don't believe me?" asked Willie in mock indignation. "You think maybe I've got a price list for one-of-a-kind portico mystery clocks in my pocket? You think values for these things are printed in the *Financial Times* or the *Wall Street Journal*? No, my darling. No one can say what such a miracle and wonderment is worth any more than they can name a price for the Eiffel Tower, which is why you must put it up for auction."

"The Eiffel Tower?"

"Your portico mystery clock," said Willie. "That's why I wanted to speak with you tonight. I have thought this through very carefully. I will not see *mispocheh* taken advantage of, no. Auction is the only way to establish the clock's true value."

"I don't understand," said Jane. "You want to bid against Perry Mannerback?"

"More than anything."

"But why? He's got all the money in the world."

"No, not all of it," said Willie, rubbing his hands together. "I have quite a bit myself, and Isidore Rosengolts still has his grandfather's first centime, he is such a cheapskate. He would buy the clock just to be able to sell it to me for a profit. Who knows who else may surface? There are other collectors. Museums. Kings. Bidding will be very spirited indeed."

"I'm not a business person," said Jane, "but I thought the object was to pay as little as possible for what you want."

"Sometimes it is," said Willie Bogen, his eyes like dancing little robin's eggs. "Sometimes it isn't. Do you know about my museum? We've taken a town house in Mayfair. The Bogen Collection will be opening to the public at the beginning of next year. What could be better publicity for the museum than for me to establish a record price for a mystery clock? And in the unlikely event that the price goes too high even for me, I will have the satisfaction of costing Mannerback the Moron a fortune. A museum can get away with paying any price for a treasure. Greedy Manner-back will just make himself more of a laughingstock than he already is."

"Why do you hate him so much?"

"Hate him?" said Willie, amused. "No, my dear. Maybe years ago I hated Perry Mannerback, but those days are long gone. I positively adore the fellow now. Driving him crazy is not merely a pleasure for me, it is a privilege."

"But why? Did he do something to you?"

"To him, it was nothing," said Willie, picking a piece of lint off his shirtsleeve. "Less than nothing. He merely destroyed my business and bankrupted me, that's all. But this was a long time ago. I'm sure you're not interested."

"Come on, Willie," said Jane, wise to this little routine. "Are you going to tell me or not?"

Willie shrugged.

"After the war I made my way to London, a penniless refugee who spoke no English," he said, his eyes far away. "I took a job with a watchmaker in the East End. For ten years I slaved away, unable to save a shilling. Then one day I received a package of chocolates from a fellow I had known from the detention camp and who had stayed in Switzerland. Chocolates were a great luxury in England after the war, and rather than eat them myself, I decided to sell them. Fifteen years later, I was the most successful chocolate importer in Great Britain.

"Then in the summer of 1971 I made a huge deal to provide chocolates for the tennis championships at Wimbledon and related events. These are held in late June, early July, and I had made arrangements to lease a refrigerated warehouse to store the chocolates I was bringing in from the Continent. There was a terrible heat wave in London that year, and to make a long story short, all of my chocolates melted because I was thrown out of the warehouse and nothing else was available at short notice. I was thrown out because the warehouse had been purchased by one Peregrine Mannerback, a young man from America who decided that he wanted to have a summer snowball fight with some of his chums and needed the warehouse's refrigeration equipment.

"Nothing that I or my lawyers said could make any difference. I was ruined; my wife left me; my employees were out on the street. Mannerback had his little snowball fight. Later, I read that he turned around and sold the warehouse to a desperate dairy company for twice what he had paid for it, such a business genius he was."

"I'm sure Perry didn't mean to hurt you," said Jane. "He's not a bad person. Just oblivious."

"Let me tell you something, my darling," said Willie in a kindly voice. "All of our actions in life have consequences. Whether we choose to take responsibility for those consequences is a matter of our own decision. I had my choice, too. Yes, I was very angry at Perry Mannerback at first, and I could have dwelt on what had happened to me forever, spent the rest of my life being bitter, feeling sorry for myself. I've seen people do this, let themselves be eaten alive by resentment and hatred or be twisted into something vile. Something bad happens to them, but rather than leave it in the past, they become obsessed with it. They carry it with them until it becomes their whole reason for being, their future, their identity. Not for me. I forgave Perry Mannerback and blessed him and went on with my life."

"Philosophy is one of Willie's hobbies, too," said Valentine.

"And so is money," said Willie with a smile. "Life is a funny old thing, is it not? I turned to the financial markets and began buying and selling shares. I am now far better off than I ever would have been if I had remained an importer of chocolate. Ten years ago, my fortune secure, I became interested in clocks again and began to collect them. To my astonishment, who turns out to be my major competition for every good piece? None other than the very same fellow who had indirectly been the cause of my present good fortune—Perry Mannerback. So why shouldn't I return the favor? For his entire life, this poor fool has been able to buy anything he's ever wanted. Every time I snatch a clock from under his nose and make him crazy, I see it as a *mitzvah,* a good deed, something that all the Mannerback millions cannot buy for him—the opportunity to learn a little wisdom."

Jane shook her head and laughed.

"So," said Willie. "I think I have answered all the questions and cleared up all the mysteries, yes?"

"Not quite," said Valentine from his position on the couch. Both Willie and Jane turned to look at him. "There's one more thing that I need to find out, and I shall be most unhappy until I do."

"And what is that, dear boy?" asked Willie.

"Does Cousin Jane plan to eat a more balanced dinner tomorrow night, and if so, will she consent to have it with me?"

The two men's eyes turned back to Jane.

"Yes," predicted Jane, popping a final canapé into her mouth. "She will."

Eighteen

Jane took the Seventy-ninth Street crosstown bus back to the West Side, thankful that she still had a Metrocard with some money on it. She had taken yet another cab across the park to her meeting at the Carlyle, and her cash was nearly gone. Tomorrow morning, she'd have to start some serious economizing while she looked for a job.

The last stop was at West End Avenue. Jane could have transferred to the M5 going up Broadway on the same fare, but instead she chose to walk the remaining distance to her apartment. It was only eleven blocks. Like many New Yorkers, the thought of waiting for a bus to go anything less than a mile always seemed crazy to her.

West End was lined with funky prewar apartments that now sold for six and seven figures. As Jane walked up the wide street, she found that the mad tangle of speculation, worry, and fear that had tied her brain into knots over the past few weeks had nearly sorted itself out. Willie Bogen had shown her the solution to the mystery of Grandmother Sylvie's clock. Perry

Mannerback had explained why Aaron Sailor had been calling out his name from his coma. Valentine Treves wasn't a villain after all, thank goodness.

Jane still didn't know what had really led to her father's fall down the stairs eight years ago or who had caused his recent death. Nor did she know who had killed Leila Peach and why. Somehow, however, these things didn't seem to matter so much any more. Folly had been right—justice wasn't her job. The police would find out what had happened to her father and to Leila. Or they wouldn't. Ultimately, the killer would have to answer to God.

Willie Bogen was right, too: Why latch on to the most horrible negative things that happen to you and make them your identity? Jane didn't want to become one of those poor souls who populated daytime television, professional victims bemoaning all the things that had happened to ruin their lives. Yes, what had happened to her father was horrible, but it had happened. Nothing that Jane could do now was going to bring him back. What she did with her life from this point forward was her own choice. She saw that it was time to move on.

It was nearing seven-thirty. The street was alive with people. Businessmen and women getting home from work. Teenagers on their way out. In front of the building at the corner of Eighty-ninth Street a gray-uniformed doorman was playing catch with a cute little kid bedecked in the standard West Side uniform for little boys and girls: baseball cap, jeans, and T-shirt from the Gap.

As Jane turned onto her block, she found herself humming "My Funny Valentine." It was a beautiful melody by Richard Rodgers, a great lyric by Lorenz Hart. Was that why Valentine Treves preferred Rodgers's music with Hammerstein? Had he once had a hard time with other little boys who didn't appreciate someone who was comic and sweet, with laughable, unphotographable looks? Weren't men dopes?

Smiling, Jane entered her brownstone, climbed the four flights, and opened her battle-scarred front door. While waiting for the locksmith that afternoon, she had straightened up the mess from her fight with Melissa Rosengolts. Except for some little dents in the walls and one big dent in the refrigerator, the little apartment looked almost cozy again.

Jane took off her jacket and began to remove her blouse. Her head was fuzzy with champagne and old melodies. She'd been awake for nearly twenty hours, been beaten up, and learned the secrets of people on two continents. In the basement was a clock that was her legacy from a family she had never known—a family that could be traced back all the way to Adam, according to Willie Bogen.

If Willie and Perry Mannerback both had been willing to pay a hundred twenty-five thousand dollars for the lighthouse clock in Seattle, how much, Jane wondered, would a portico mystery clock bring at auction? Two hundred thousand? Three? What would it be like to have real money without strings attached?

Her thoughts were interrupted by the telephone ringing. Dreamily, she picked up the receiver and said hello.

"Hello, Jane, it's Barbara Fripp," said the familiar British voice. "Sorry to bother you at home, but a policeman, a detective lieutenant named Folly, called the office several times at the end of the day looking for you. Apparently, your machine isn't working."

"Yes, I've got to get a new one," said Jane, glancing at the wastebasket where the remains of her answering machine had been consigned after its encounter with Melissa Rosengolts.

"He wanted you to meet him at a Galerie Elinore King, at seven o'clock tonight. He said that this King woman had made certain troubling accusations and that he was going over to interview her. He said it would be helpful if you could be present. I told him I'd try to reach you when I got home, but you've been out."

"Oh, for heaven's sakes," said Jane, her happiness evaporating.

"This is about Perry, isn't it?" asked Fripp.

"I don't know," lied Jane. "Do you know if Perry contacted the police this afternoon?"

"Not that I'm aware of. He never came into the office. I haven't heard from him all day. I'm terribly worried."

"There's nothing to worry about, Barbara. Believe me."

"Perry's still in trouble, isn't he?"

"I'm sure I can straighten this all out," said Jane. She said good-bye and hung up the phone, furious.

What had Elinore King done now with her stupid meddling? Just thinking about Elinore made Jane want to explode. She looked around for something to throw. A lamp, several bowls, and a flowerpot had been casualties of her afternoon. The little flowered sugar bowl had been smashed last week. There wasn't anything small left to break.

"I'll be damned if I'll let that bitch . . ." Jane said out loud, then went over to her desk, rummaged through her address book for a phone number, and dialed.

"Hello?" said a male voice. "King Gallery."

"Lieutenant Folly?"

"No, it's Greg King. Is that you, Jane? Lieutenant Folly said you might be coming over."

"Can I speak with him, please?"

"Certainly," said Gregory King. "Hold on and let me see if I can get him. He's here with a lady and gentleman from the District Attorney's office and they've been speaking with Elinore for a while. If I can just work this phone—the staff is all gone. Call me back if I disconnect you, okay?"

There was a click. Classical music played in Jane's ear. Dr. King's voice returned a moment later.

"Jane, they're sort of right in the middle of something. Mr. Folly says he'd still like you to come over, though, if you can. Is that possible? Apparently, they're going to be here for a while."

"Absolutely," said Jane. The sofa bed looked inviting, but she couldn't very well let Elinore have the last word about Perry Mannerback.

"Do you know where we are? Have you been over here before?" asked Dr. King.

"Not for years, but I remember where it is," said Jane. Elinore's gallery was on the southwest corner of Madison at Seventy-fifth, right across from the Whitney Museum—a block down the street from the Carlyle. "I'll be over as soon as I can get a cab."

"We're on the fifth floor," said Dr. King. "The building's closed at this hour, but we'll buzz you up. Just ring the bell."

Jane said good-bye, then went into the bathroom and removed two twenty-dollar bills from her emergency stash in a Band-Aid box in the bathroom. A few minutes later she was downstairs on West End Avenue again, hailing a taxi.

Twilight was descending as the cab cut through Central Park. The rush-hour traffic had thinned. Jane was still furious and weary, but she sat back in her seat, trying to center herself. The best way to counter Elinore's hysteria was to be calm, dispassionate, just tell them the truth. If the people from the District Attorney's office had any brains, Jane was bound to come across as more credible than inarticulate Elinore with her nutty conspiracy theories.

The cab pulled up in front of the address on Madison Dr. King had given her. The grand town house—once a single-family mansion like its neighbors—now housed some of the most expensive retail space in the world. At this hour, however, the security gates were down on the chocolate shop and the little boutique on either side of the entrance. The doorway to the upstairs spaces was dark.

Jane looked up at the tower of the Carlyle a block away, trying to pick out the window of the suite where she had just been. Might Valentine glance down and see her? Her funny Valentine.

She pressed the outer buzzer for Galerie King, forcing her gaze away from the hotel. A gentle buzzing came from the door. Jane opened it and entered a vestibule. To the right was a small lobby with a display case showing images of paintings in the four galleries on the floors above. Something suitably peculiar from Picasso. A nineteenth-century landscape. Galerie Elinore King featured a contemporary realist not nearly as good as Aaron Sailor.

There was another buzzer system on the wall by the elevator. Jane pressed the button for the top floor. Nothing happened for a moment. The vestibule was dark, the building obviously deserted. A strange, uncomfortable feeling swept through her, but then the intercom clicked.

"Jane?" asked a voice. It was distorted through a speaker but she still recognized it as belonging to Gregory King.

"Yes," said Jane to what seemed to be the microphone part of the system.

"Hold on. I'm going to send down the elevator. When you get in, just press five and it will bring you up."

From somewhere in the shaft there was a clank and mechanical sounds of gears began whirring. In a minute the elevator had reached the ground floor and its doors opened. Jane got into the small cab and pressed five as instructed. The doors closed. The elevator jerked, then began a slow ascent. Finally, the doors opened again and she stepped out into a large, brilliantly lit space with a cathedral ceiling and skylights that showed the darkening heavens above.

The floors in Galerie Elinore King were bare wood, polyurethaned in the fashion of SoHo lofts. The walls were painted a stark white. There were large paintings in the style of the one in the display case downstairs. They didn't come off any better in person.

Gregory King, looking pale, sat at a desk in the middle of the room about thirty feet from the entrance, dressed in bluejeans and a dark polo shirt. Standing by the outer wall of the building, across from the elevator and dressed in a hideous green sweatsuit, was Elinore. In her hand was a snub-nosed revolver.

"See, I told you she'd come," declared Elinore in the general direction of her husband. "You're so stupid. Why don't you ever trust me?"

"I don't understand," said Jane. "Where's Detective Folly?"

"He's not here, obviously," said Elinore. "I tricked you. It was Greg who called Perry's secretary, pretending to be the police. Now move over there by the window. And don't get cute and try any of your little make-believe fight stuff. I can shoot you five times before you can make it across to me. All I have to do is point and pull the trigger."

Elinore motioned with the barrel of the gun toward the wall opposite the one where she was standing—the front corner of the gallery where the two outer walls met. No paintings were hung within fifteen feet of the spot. On the ledge by the window was a piece of paper and a ballpoint pen. There was a tarp on the floor. Twenty feet away was an open can of white paint, a pan, and a roller. Nearby was a can of Spackle, a screwdriver, and a putty knife.

"You've got to be kidding," said Jane, feeling her center rise.

"Now!" shouted Elinore. "Get over there. Stand on the tarp."

Jane had never had a gun pointed at her before. It was a terrifying experience, especially since the gun was being held by someone as out of control as Elinore. The knuckles of Elinore's fat little hand were white and her finger twitched on the trigger. Jane hurried into the corner.

"There's a paper there on the windowsill," said Elinore. "Sign your name on the line at the bottom."

"Come on, Elinore, you can't be serious," said Jane, trying to laugh. "This is crazy."

"Sign that paper," said Elinore, not laughing back.

"What is it?" said Jane, picking it up. It seemed to be the last page of some kind of contract.

"Just sign or I'll shoot you," screeched Elinore. "Don't think I won't. Sign it right now or so help me God I'm going to shoot."

She raised the gun.

Jane took the pen and scribbled her name. Surely a contract couldn't be binding if signed under duress? Was the gun even loaded? The whole situation was unbelievable.

"Now put the paper down on the floor a few feet in front of you," said Elinore.

Jane did as she was told.

"Go get it, Greg," said Elinore. Dr. King stood up and walked across the room. He picked up the piece of paper and brought it over to Elinore.

"See, Janie?" cackled Elinore. "That wasn't so hard. Now I can sell your dad's paintings, all legal, fair and square. And I've settled for fifty percent, like we agreed. I always keep my word. My word is my bond. Integrity is my middle name."

"Can I go now?" said Jane.

"You really do think I'm stupid, don't you?" said Elinore, glancing down at the paper in her hand.

"Yes, I do," said Jane, taking a step forward.

There was a huge explosion. At least it sounded like a huge explosion in the enclosed space. Simultaneously, Jane felt something whiz so close to her face that it burned. Instinctively, she raised her hand to her cheek, her ear. There was no blood. The bullet had missed, but by no more than millimeters.

"Get back there," screamed Elinore, the gun raised. "Next time, I won't miss. Get back on that tarp."

Jane hastened back to where she had been.

"Get on your knees. Clasp your hands behind your neck. Now!"

Jane complied. It would take her several seconds to get up from this position. It would be impossible to try to rush Elinore again, which was obviously the point.

"I'll tell you how stupid I am," said Elinore smugly. "I'm so stupid that I knew you were going to do that. I've thought of everything. I even know this is going to make a mess, that's why you're on that tarp. And we've got paint, too. To paint over the blood that splatters on my wall. We'll dig the bullets out with that screwdriver, then Spackle before we paint. We're going to kill you."

"Come on, Elinore," said Jane in disbelief.

"No, let me finish. After it's over, we'll use the tarp to wrap your body up in. Gregory's Jeep is parked right downstairs. We'll drive to New Jersey to these woods we know. That's where we'll bury you. Nobody will ever know what happened, just like with Jimmy Hoffa. See? I've got it all planned out. I'm so smart I amaze myself sometimes, I'm such a planner."

Had anyone heard the shot? Jane wondered. No, how could they? The walls of the old building were a foot thick, the windows double-glazed, and there was no one around to hear—the building was empty. Besides, even if anything could be heard from the street, this was New York City. There were miscellaneous inexplicable explosions in the distance all the time—car backfires, trucks driving over potholes, so many that no one even paid attention.

"If you really needed the money so badly," began Jane, trying not to panic, but Elinore cut her off.

"I told you before. The money's not the point."

"Then what is?"

"After all I've been through," said Elinore, "I've got to get something out of this."

Jane looked to Dr. King, who swallowed hard and walked back to the desk.

"What have you been through?" Jane asked, turning her attention back to Elinore. As long as she could keep her talking, maybe she could think of a way out of this. Unfortunately, her brain didn't seem to be working. Most of her body had gone numb as well.

"You don't have any idea of what this whole thing has done to me, do you?" said Elinore. "You can't imagine what it's cost me, being stuck in this stupid marriage because of what happened eight years ago. The stress. The unhappiness. Why do you think I put on all this weight? We couldn't very well divorce—who knows who Dr. Moron over there might blab to, what he would say? A few hundred thousand from Aaron's paintings isn't going to make much difference, but at least I'll have some compensation for what I've had to put up with. It's only fair."

"It was you who pushed my father down the stairs," said Jane to Elinore, horrified, suddenly understanding.

"It was him," said Elinore, gesturing derisively to her husband with her chins. "The whole thing is his fault."

"You shouldn't have slept with him in the first place, El," said Gregory King.

"Oh, don't start that again, please," she snapped. "That's ancient history."

"Slept with who?" asked Jane.

"Your stupid father," said Elinore. "I told you he was crazy about me. And who could blame him? I was gorgeous. He seduced me."

Jane felt her mouth drop open, but there was no point in expressing disbelief. Or disgust. Besides, from what she had learned about her father, it was probably true.

"She threw herself at him," said Gregory King to Jane. "It was pathetic. He was depressed about his show. She was always flirting with him, always trying to get him alone with her. She had to get him drunk out of his skull that night, that was how she finally managed it."

"I wasn't the one who pushed him down the stairs."

"It was an accident, Janie," said Dr. King. "I caught them together at his loft. You have to understand. I was so angry. Elinore was lying there on the rug, naked, with that stupid smirk on her face. Aaron was putting on his pants. He came out into the hall with me, tried to calm me down. I don't even know how we started pushing one another. It was an accident, I swear."

"You are so stupid, Gregory," snapped Elinore. "He barges in like some outraged Puritan. It was pathetic. If I hadn't stopped him, Janie, he would have turned himself in right then and ruined my whole life."

"I should have."

"Oh, be a man, for Crissakes, Gregory. It's almost over."

"I believe you, Dr. King," said Jane, anxious to keep them talking. "It was just an accident about my father. The police will understand. It doesn't make any sense for you to let Elinore kill me now."

"Oh, yeah, right," said Elinore, her voice dripping with sarcasm. "Like you don't know about the woman."

"What woman?"

"That Peach woman, Aaron's stupid model. You told me yourself on the phone today that people were dead because of that article in the what-do-you-call-it magazine, the *New York Times*. Because of the photos I gave them, people were dead, that's what you said. I pretended I didn't understand, but I'm not stupid. I knew right then that you were talking about Leila Peach."

"I was talking about the clock," said Jane. "The clock was what caused all the problems."

"What clock?" demanded Elinore. "It was the picture of me that was important. The picture of me with Aaron. Leila Peach recognized Gregory in the background."

"The picture of you?" said Jane. "I don't understand."

"Oh, sure," said Elinore.

"Please, Dr. King, tell me what she's talking about."

"Leila Peach saw me that night eight years ago," said Gregory King. "I didn't know who she was at the time, and she didn't know me, either. Elinore never wants me at her art parties, so the two of us had never met. Leila had just come into the building when I pushed your father. I rushed down the stairs to see if there was anything I could do. A woman was standing there, looking amazingly calm. She got a good look at me, then turned tail and ran. I was sure she was going to go to the police. I panicked and ran, instead of calling an ambulance as I should have. I wanted to call the police when I got home and admit everything, but Elinore made me wait a few days to see what would happen, said the woman couldn't possibly have any idea who I was any more than we knew who she was. Elinore was right. No one came for me."

"Then after all these years this Leila Peach shows up last week wanting money, can you believe it?" demanded Elinore, outraged. "She had seen that stupid article about your father, and there was Gregory's picture. He was standing right behind me. She'd met me, but never him. Why did the *Times* have to identify him as my husband in the caption, that's what I want to know? That stupid woman would never have known who he was if the *Times* hadn't done that. What did Dr. Moron have to do with anything? Why couldn't they just crop him out?"

"I didn't mean to do Miss Peach any harm, Janie, you must believe me," said Gregory King in a weak voice. "Elinore made me meet with her, hear what she wanted. I went to her hotel room. It was blackmail, of course. She talked about money. I don't know what I said, but she pulled out a gun and said she wasn't afraid of me. We struggled and the gun somehow went off. I don't know how it happened."

"That's Gregory for you," said Elinore to Jane, rolling her eyes. "Doesn't know how it happened. Doesn't know how anything happens. Totally clueless. He even brought back this stupid gun— about as incriminating a piece of evidence as you can possibly get. Jesus, Greg, if it weren't for me, I don't know where you'd be."

"I wouldn't be a murderer," whined Gregory. "Everything else was an accident, but killing poor Aaron like that . . . helpless in his bed . . . I don't know how I let you talk me into that."

Jane's eyes widened.

"You killed my father in the hospital?"

"I'm sorry, Jane," said Dr. King. "I'm so very sorry."

"But why?"

"He was waking up, you stupid girl," said Elinore. "He was going to wake up, you told us so at dinner. He was saying all kinds of things. It was only a matter of time before he started blabbing about me, and about what Greg had done. It was a blessing, really. Greg was just putting Aaron out of his misery."

"But then why did he tell the police about the insulin?" Jane asked.

"He what?" demanded Elinore, turning toward her husband, but not taking her eyes—or the gun—off Jane. "What's this?"

"No one might ever have known that my father's death wasn't natural if you hadn't made them check his insulin levels, Dr. King," said Jane.

"Is this true, Gregory?" shrieked Elinore. "How could you do something like that? I can't believe you could be so stupid. Did you want to get caught?"

"No, no, of course not," said Dr. King weakly.

"Maybe he did," said Jane. "He's a doctor. He's supposed to be someone who heals people, not someone who kills them."

"Shut up, Janie," said Elinore. "Just shut up. Let's get this over with. Get over here, Greg."

"You'll never get away with it," said Jane desperately, as Gregory King stood up and walked across the room to Elinore as he'd been told. "Perry's secretary knows that I came here. She'll tell Detective Folly that someone was impersonating him."

"That's right, El," said Gregory King, alarmed. "They'll know that we were the last people to see her. They'll know we did it."

"Shut up," said Elinore.

"Why didn't you think of this, El? Oh, God, what are we going to do now?"

"Shut up," screeched Elinore. "Let me think!"

Suddenly, her face unscrewed.

"It's just lucky I'm so smart," she announced in a smug voice. "You should thank your lucky stars, Greg, that I'm such a genius."

"We should just turn ourselves in," said Dr. King. "It's the only way. We should have told the truth eight years ago."

"Don't be an idiot," said Elinore. "I've got it all figured out. All you have to do is take care of the secretary, and it will be all over. We won't have anything to worry about."

"What do you mean, 'take care' of her?" asked Dr. King.

"Shoot her, stupid. Or maybe give her an injection of something. Whatever you need to do to make it look like suicide."

"No, I couldn't possibly," said Greg, his hand coming to his mouth. "We never said anything about anyone else. Please, El, couldn't we just . . ." He reached out and touched Elinore's shoulder. She squirmed away, her piggy little eyes fixed on Jane.

"Gregory, you're not going to start again, are you? Don't start with me."

"You really are crazy, Elinore," said Jane. "Killing Barbara Fripp isn't going to solve anything for you. Detective Folly is still working on my father's death. He's investigating Leila Peach's murder. Those cases won't just go away if you kill Barbara. And he'll have to find out what happened to me, too."

"That's where you're wrong, dead wrong," declared Elinore triumphantly. "The secretary's suicide will explain everything. She's bound to be in love with Perry, secretaries are always in love with their bosses. The police already think that Perry pushed your father down the stairs because of how he was raving. So it makes perfect sense that the secretary killed your father. The woman thought that Aaron was going to wake up and incriminate her darling boss, so she removed the threat by giving Aaron a little injection. Then Leila Peach appeared out of nowhere, the naked woman from the painting come back to steal Perry away. The heartbroken poor secretary kills her, too, then ends her life.

"Greg, you'll put some insulin in her apartment where the police will find it. Plus you'll put this gun there, too, the gun that killed Leila. The police will figure it out right away. And, Janie, if your body is ever found, which it won't be, it will look like the secretary was jealous of your relationship with Perry and killed you, too. See, I've got it all figured out. I told you I was a genius."

Jane's hands had turned ice cold. Her mouth was so dry she couldn't swallow. Elinore might actually be right for a change. The people at OmbiCorp probably would tell the police that Barbara Fripp was in love with Perry. And there was a good chance that she knew all about insulin, maybe even helped Perry inject himself.

"Please, Dr. King," said Jane urgently. "You're not a killer. You can't just let her murder me like this."

"He's not going to let me," said Elinore. "He's going to do it himself. He's the one who started this whole mess and he's the one who's going to finish it. Come here, Gregory, take this gun."

"Me?"

"Are you going to argue?" she shrieked, reaching over and grabbing his hand. "I am so mad with you already, telling the stupid police about the stupid insulin. Now take it."

She practically forced the gun into his hand, then pushed him forward.

"Now shoot her."

"I . . ."

"One more isn't going to make any difference."

"Two more," said Jane, desperate. "You'll have to kill Barbara Fripp, too. And yes, it *will* make a difference. You're not a cold-blooded murderer. Are you, Dr. King?"

"No."

"Yes he is!" shouted Elinore. "He gave Aaron that insulin and he shot Leila Peach."

"That was an accident," protested Dr. King. "I can't just . . ."

"So help me God, Greg, if you don't shoot her, I am going to make your life so miserable . . . You are going to be so sorry . . ."

Greg raised the gun at Jane, who was on her knees, helpless. Panic swept through her. He was too far across the room. She could try to get to her feet, but if he didn't fire right away, Elinore would have more than enough time to take the gun from him and do it herself. Jane didn't know if her legs would work anyway. For the first time, she realized that she was going to die. Gregory King was too weak to say no to Elinore.

"It will all be over?" he asked. "We can get a divorce?"

"Are you kidding?" said Elinore, her face curling into a sneer. "Do you think I'm going to let you out of my sight for one minute so you can tell the police something else? After you've made me into a what-you-call-it—an accessory? Now do it! Pull the trigger! Let's get this over with."

Gregory King stood there with the gun raised, staring at Jane. His eyes were very small and full of fear. Like a trapped animal's.

Jane looked out the window. She could see the Carlyle. Was Valentine looking out the window, too? Thinking about her? Thinking about a dinner tomorrow that would never happen?

"Come on!" Elinore demanded. Gregory King didn't take his eyes off Jane or lower the gun. "Do I have to do everything myself? Be a man for once in your life. We don't have all night. Do you know how long it's going to take us to clean up here and drive to New Jersey?"

Jane willed herself to relax, lowered her center, calmed her thoughts. What Willie Bogen had said an hour ago flashed into her mind. You had a choice in what your life would be, you always had a choice. She didn't have to die in panic and fear. Whatever came next, whatever awaited her on the other side, she didn't want to meet it with hatred in her heart.

"I forgive you, Dr. King," she said. "I don't want you to kill me, but I forgive you. I forgive you, too, Elinore."

Something in Gregory King's eyes seemed to break. His hand holding the gun lowered.

"Oh, for God's sakes," said Elinore. "Give me that, you moron."

Elinore grabbed for the gun. Gregory King allowed her to get hold of the barrel and raise it to a point an inch to the left of her sternum before he pulled the trigger.

There was another huge explosion. Elinore seemed to leap

back a foot. On her breast was a growing red stain, on her face an expression of disbelief. Dr. King had found her heart with surgical precision. Elinore's mouth opened and closed slightly before her eyes glazed over and she toppled.

"Thank you," Gregory said in a hoarse whisper. He had made his choice, too.

Jane could swear he was smiling as he placed the revolver to his temple and pulled the trigger.

"Here we are," said N. C. Pilkington, gently wrestling the well-wrapped bundle in his arms onto the wide table of the conference room on the third floor of Sotheby's York Avenue galleries. "I think you'll be pleased with the way it's come out."

This was Jane's second meeting with Pilkington, the auction house's London-born, jumbo-sized, white-haired vice president, who specialized in oddball items.

"Anything from Fabergé whist counters to solid gold Cadillacs, if no one knows what to make of it, N. C. Pilkington is the man," he had declared at their first meeting, skeptically regarding the ceramic monstrosity that Jane claimed concealed a treasure.

After listening to Valentine's explanation, however, he had become almost like a little boy and given them what he said would be their single opportunity to guess what his initials stood for, hoping that they wouldn't throw the opportunity away with another uninspired Ned or Nick or Clark or Charles. Jane now knew officially that N.C. did not stand for North Carolina. Valentine had suggested Not Coming. This was wrong, too, though Pilkington did acknowledge that he had been a breech birth.

"Our conservators have worked their usual miracle," Pilkington declared now, whipping off the cloth with a flourish. *"Et voilà."*

Jane literally stopped breathing for a moment. Three weeks ago at their meeting in the Carlyle, Willie Bogen had described what a Cartier portico mystery clock looked like, but to see it in reality was another thing.

The clock's hands, intricately set with tiny diamonds, were curled around the central pivot in the shape of a spiky dragon. Similarly diamond-faced Roman numerals were set into a mother-of-pearl ring around the nine-sided crystal dial, its outer rim punctuated with pearls. The milky quartz pillars that supported the onyx crosspiece from which the dial was suspended by a gold chain seemed themselves to have veins of gold running through them.

Jane wasn't much one for fancy things, but somehow this clock transcended its expensive materials and projected not showiness or ostentation, but elegance, simplicity, and taste. The clock was wondrous, awe-inspiring, a work of art.

"Why, the dial is nine-sided," said Valentine. "That's unexpected."

"Yes, quite unique among the Cartier mystery clocks," agreed Pilkington. "The Greeks would have called such a shape an *enneagon,* but I prefer the Latin *nonagon.* Would that Mother had named me Nonagon. Life would have been far less complicated."

He sighed.

"It's beautiful," marveled Jane.

"Have you decided on an estimate yet?" asked Valentine, who had brought Jane here to consign the clock a few days after that horrible night with the Kings.

She had had to cancel their dinner date—there was nothing like a nice murder-suicide to spoil one's appetite. Business had then forced Valentine to return to London while she was still giving statements to the police and fending off reporters ("The Art of

Death" had been the headline in the *Daily News*). Valentine had arrived back in New York only yesterday. When she had met him downstairs fifteen minutes ago, it was the first time they had seen each other since then.

"Strictly P.O.R., dear boy," said Pilkington with a twinkle in his eye. "Price on request. Truth be known, I haven't the foggiest what the thing will fetch. In 'ninety-six, the French auctioneer Etude Tajan had Portico Mystery Clock Number Four on the block in Geneva with an estimate of six-fifty to eight hundred thousand U.S. dollars. It brought nearly one and a half million, including premium."

"One and a half million!" exclaimed Jane, sinking into a nearby chair lest she fall down.

"Of course, this one is much more desirable on its beauty alone," said Pilkington with a sniff. "To say nothing of its direct connection to Louis Cartier, and the fascinating history surrounding it. The unknown mystery clock. Smuggled from Europe. Concealed in a basement for fifty years. In the special catalogue I have been authorized to do, we will feature a picture of its ceramic camouflage: the before and after, if you will. The ugly duckling and the swan. Talk about sexy! Collectors will positively swoon. A pity the key described in Maurice Coüet's letter is missing. The dragonfly key, most unique. Cartier never made another like it."

"Actually, one of the bidders is in possession of the key," said Valentine.

"Indeed?" said Pilkington brightly, rubbing his large pink hands together. "There's an incentive for someone, certainly. It will be an interesting sale, most assuredly. Now stay right here for a moment; there are some people whom I would like you to meet— the grand Sotheby Pooh-Bahs, if you will. They're very excited about this whole thing. I'll be back in a flash."

He darted out the door, leaving Jane alone with Valentine.

"This seems to be working out quite well for you," said Valentine after an awkward moment of silence.

"Not so well for you and Willie, though. It will cost Willie a fortune if he intends to outbid everyone at the auction."

"Oh, he doesn't mind," said Valentine. "Willie's quite shrewd. This really will bring a great deal of publicity to his museum, plus he will have the additional pleasure of publicly besting Perry Mannerback in the auction rooms."

"I'm not so sure about that," said Jane. "Perry took me to lunch last week to thank me for catching the real killers, though catching is hardly the right word for what I did, which was fifty percent less than nothing, plus nearly getting myself killed. Anyway, I told Perry about the clock, and well, excited isn't the right word for his reaction, either. He literally started jumping up and down for joy."

"The other diners must have found that very amusing."

"The other diners were jumping up and down, too."

"They were clock aficionados?"

"They were monkeys. We were eating hot dogs at the Zoo."

They both laughed. There was another long silence, which Valentine again was the first to break.

"Are you all right, Jane? You seem to be very much assured on the surface, but I know that these past few weeks must have been pretty horrifying for you. I still can't believe what that pitiful woman actually planned to do."

"Let's not talk about it," said Jane. "Let's not talk about it ever again."

"Are you certain? It isn't wise to sweep one's feelings under the carpet, I'm told."

"I've had my tears and my nightmares," said Jane, "but I prefer Willie's philosophy. My life isn't going to be about what happened to me in the past. It's going to be about what happens next."

"And what will that be?"

"Don't you know?"

"You'll take me to the Zoo and buy me a hot dog?"

"Yes, but that comes later. There's something I need to do first, something I've been meaning to do for a long time."

"And what's that?" asked Valentine, raising an eyebrow.

"This," said Jane.

Then she grabbed the lapels of his suit, drew him close, and kissed him.